"Ysabeau Wilce is an original American fantasist. Unique in vision, rare in quality, Califa is one of the few truly American fantasy worlds, owing as much to the Wild West, San Francisco Bay and Mexican folklore as to Shakespeare, Dickens and Tolkien. Read and enjoy!"—Ellen Kushner, author of *Swordspoint*

"I would trade a year of my life, and things more precious still, to be transported for one hour to the sumptuous streets of Ysabeau Wilce's Califa."—Paul Witcover, author of *The Emperor of All Things*

"The Republic of Califa differs from the American West Coast in a number of small details, of course: the egregores and praterhumans, the Magick and Gramatica, the peculiar dynastic struggles of the Pontifexa Georgiana and her decadent postbears. But all these are the subtle and minuscule discrepancies of a parallel yet proximate reality, easily overlooked by the casual reader. Where Ms. Wilce shines is in her use of the larger effects— those of tone, style, and voice—which make her world so much richer than our own."—Paul Park, author of *A Princess of Roumania*

"Those who have been yearning for another voyage through Califa—and who hasn't?—will be delighted to plunge into the lives of General Hardhands and Tiny Doom, discover the mystery behind the Hand of Gory, and learn the truth of the Bouncing Boy Terror, Springheel Jack. Rich and intricate, clever and sexy, these tales never fail to deliver glorious adventure and transcendent worldbuilding. Wilce is truly a Queen among fantasists."
—Tiffany Trent, author of *The Unnaturalists*

PRAISE FOR YSABEAU S. WILCE'S FLORA SEGUNDA

"Highly original, strange and amusing."—Diana Wynne Jones

"Wilce's novel features a cast of quirky but appealing characters, a distinctive magical setting, wry humor, and some insightful comments about coming-of-age and asserting oneself over the adults

in charge. Fantasy buffs will relish the surprising plot twists, the satisfying ending, and the possibility of future escapades."
—*Booklist*

"Wilce has matters well in hand in this, her first novel. . . . The book is rich and odd. . . . The heroine is this novel's strongest suit. Like Pullman's Lyra Silvertongue or Pratchett's Tiffany Aching, Flora Fyrdraaca is a descendant of Jo March rather than a fainting beauty who needs rescuing. These wayward, determined girls do the rescuing themselves, although not wisely or always too well."
—*New York Times Book Review*

PRAISE FOR FLORA'S DARE
Winner of the Andre Norton Award

★ "This fresh and funky setting is rich with glorious costumes, innovative language and tantalizing glimpses of history."
— *Kirkus Reviews* (starred review)

"A fantastic and unique world. . . . Guaranteed thrills, chills, and amazing revelations."—*Voya*

PRAISE FOR FLORA'S FURY

"A charming conclusion to a fine fantasy series."—*Booklist*

"[A] thrilling, bizarre ride."—*The Horn Book*

PROPHECIES
LIBELS AND DREAMS

PROPHECIES
LIBELS & DREAMS

Stories of Califa

Edited and Annotated

❦ *by* ❧

Ysabeau S. Wilce

Small Beer Press
Easthampton, MA

Prophecies, Libels, and Dreams: Stories of Califa copyright © 2014 by Ysabeau S. Wilce. All rights reserved.
Page 245 functions as an extension of the copyright page.
yswilce.com

Small Beer Press
150 Pleasant Street #306
Easthampton, MA 01027
www.smallbeerpress.com
www.weightlessbooks.com
info@smallbeerpress.com

Distributed to the trade by Consortium.

Library of Congress Cataloging-in-Publication Data

Wilce, Ysabeau S.
[Short stories. Selections]
Prophecies, libels & dreams : stories / Ysabeau S. Wilce. -- First edition.
    pages cm
   Summary: "These interconnected stories are set in the Republic of Califa -- a baroque approxima-
tion of Gold Rush era-California with an overlay of Aztec ceremony. By turn whimsical and horrific
(sometime in the same paragraph), Wilce's stories have been characterized as "screwball comedies for
goths" but they could also be described as "historical fantasies" or "fanciful histories" for there are
nuggets of historical fact hidden in them there lies"-- Provided by publisher.
  ISBN 978-1-61873-089-3 (paperback) -- ISBN 978-1-61873-090-9 (ebook)
  I. Title.
  PS3623.I529A6 2014
  813'.6--dc23
                            2014022473

First edition 1 2 3 4 5 6 7 8 9

Text set in Centaur.

Printed on 30% 50 Natures Natural PCR recycled paper by the Maple Press in York, PA.
Cover illustration © 2014 by Oliver Hunter (oliverhunter.tumblr.com).

Table of Contents

Dedicated to
The House of Ono:
Nunquam Credere Piscum

Introduction

Ah, Califa! Cool white city surrounded on three sides by water, braced by fog and sea breezes. A city of mysterious barrancas, glorious vistas, towering hills, wavery sandbanks. Sitting on the rim of the continent, caught between land and sea, Califa has always been an intermittent place, a locale that has attracted dreamers, dæmons, outlaws, mavericks. Caught between the Waking World and Elsewhere, once The Current in Califa ran high, engendering danger, intrigue, excitement and power.[1]

But no more! Today Califa is decorous and subdued, and the raucous days of yore are dimly remembered. Yet, as sunlight may find its way through the tears of a curtain, illuminating the dusty furniture of a long enclosed room, so these stories cast light upon a time now dark and remote. Some are clearly fragments of a greater whole, now lost to history. Others seem to be complete as they are. Several show the singular hand of one writer, whose detailed knowledge of the events described claim an intimacy that could only come from being an eyewitness. A few are clearly fanciful, yarns for children or simpletons. Two are clearly the result of a churning propaganda machine. One is downright fantastic.

---

1   See Spiro, Joshua. *Bay of Empire: Califa Bay and the Eastward Expansion.* Arcangel: Honeycutt Press, 11-Calli-156.

But taken together, these stories offer glimpses into a world long since lost: a world we can only dream of, where human and praterhuman conspired side by side, where rule of law was subsumed by the rule of power, when the City was wide-awake to magick and intrigue. Today it is hard for us to imagine a time when the line between Elsewhere and the Waking World was so thin that humans and praterhumans mingled, where Will alone could accomplish wonders. Rough, this world was, and dangerous, but still romantic. Who among us would not have given much to have been invited to a dance at Bilskinir House, when it was under the sway of the mighty egregore Paimon? Caroused with the Redlegs' Regiment as they celebrated their birthday and their glory? Followed two daring detectives as they cut the sign of a merciless killer? Slid into the sparkly boots of a sparkly outlaw and soar into a life of crime?

We could not be there when these events happened, but through these stories, we may relive these excitements and, in doing so, gain a greater understanding of the glories and perils of days now evaporated into the mists of history.

A Lady of Quality
Pumpkinville, Ariviapa
15-Tecaptl-161

Author of *Califa in Sunshine & Shade:*
A History of Califa in Ten Volumes

The Biography of a Bouncing Boy Terror!

Part One: Crime Commences

Once upon a time, my little waffles, far across the pale eastern sands, a baby boy bounced from his mother's womb into a dark and dangerous world, into a land well full of hardship, turmoil, and empty handball courts. This boy, starting tiny and growing huge, would one day become a legend in the minds of his minions, a hero in the hearts of his hobbledehoys, the fanciest lad of them all: Springheel Jack!

And this, my dovetails, is the story of how it all started.

Now in the beginning young Jack was not a rowdy tyke, well full of the jiggamaree and the falder-a-oo. The other childer might drive their mammas mad with fancy ideas of fun, but young Jack was not made for sportive tricks. He was his mamma's muffin and he kept to her side, helping in the smelly sport of making matches, which phosphoric occupation was how the family kept fed. They were a poor household, with no extra divas for white sugar or white bread, and all ten of Jack's tiny brothers and sisters must put paws into keeping the darkness of poverty at bay. Dipping lucifers at ten glories a decade leaves little room for boisterous fun.

Well dingy was the rundown tenement in which Jack's family lived, perched atop a noisome blind tiger from which issued roust-ing and revelry all hours of the night—illegal whist games, bitter beer, and up-against-the-wall fiddling. Well dingy was the rundown room into which Jack's family squeezed, tiny oil lamp the only tiny light, tiny window opening into tiny alley, and tiny pinch-faced sib-lings with cold blue fingers dipping matchsticks into glowing blue poison. Instead of a cat, the family kept Hunger, which crouched in the corner of the tiny room, wiggling its tail and licking its prickly chops, waiting, just waiting. They had each other but they had nothing else, not even shoes to cover their frigid toes. Their days were drab and dreary.

But at night, dear doorknobs, when the dipping was done and the little pots of phosphorus illumined the shadows, Jack lay in his nest of rags, tucked up against his baby mice siblings, and he dreamed away the pallid gray world: the knobby fingers, the tightening tummies, each drab day dribbling into another drab day, endlessly endless. At night Jack dreamed of colors: glimmering, glittering, glistening, glowing colors—cyan, jade, celadon, amber, cobalt, wheat, orange, plum, lavender, and magenta. But the color that shone the most through Jacko's dreams was the brilliant tang of red: cerise, sangyn, vermilion, carmine, crimson, gules, rust, rose, cochineal. Rushing friendly warm red, delicious and hot.

Well, my nifty needles, once a week Jack's mamma would take the little boxes of matches and place them into her market basket for to redeem. The other childer stayed home, under the concern of Jack, but the baby who coughed went with mamma, wrapped in newspaper and tucked also into the basket, sleeping uneasily among the boxes of spark. At the factory of Zebulon Quarrel & Dau., Manufacturers of Lucifers, Phosphates, & Triggers, Jack's mamma would turn in the week's hundred boxes and receive into her thin hand one dull gold diva and eleven dingy glories, and on this happy day, there would be moldy cheese and squashed kale pie for supper.

But one day, Jack's mamma could carry neither basket nor baby. The sickly prickles were itching through the City, and like all Disease, they enjoyed the poorest people first, leaving the rich for a luscious fat dessert. In Jack's mamma's illness, it fell to her muffin to do her duty, else gobbling Hunger would creep from its corner and snatch the childer up, one by one. So, leaving the basket for the baby who coughed, Jack packed the boxes of matches in a crumpled cracker box and set out down the splashy wet streets to Zebulon Quarrel's crenellated factory.

Through the sloppy streets he sloshed, brave Jackling, clutching his cracker box from the splashing dillys, the clippy horsecars, and the pushing people who were eager to get home to their toasted cheese dinners and hot tea before darkfall. At the hulking behemoth gates of Quarrel's factory, wee Jack stood upon the iron shoe scraper and handed his cracker box upward to the grimacing factotum behind the window rail. Handed down he was, after a few minutes of stolid counting, the munificent sum of one dull-faced diva and eleven chipped glories. A fortune in coin.

Thus paid, Jacko slogged to the 99 Glory Tuckshop where to buy squashed pie and moldy cheese, and perhaps even a crock of spinach paste for the hungry childer's evening sup. Full darkness lingered in the wings of the sky, waiting for its cue, and the graying rain drove down like needles, stitching the evening in silvery sorrow. The streets were most empty and wet now, and only sweet Jacko, with his blue bare feet and his ragged sweater, hopped through the puddles, shivering.

Then—Jack paused.

Then—Jack poised.

Then—Jack stood staring into a glowing window front by which he had just been hurrying, and there he saw a thing that caught in his head like happy, stuck in his sight like sugar, a vision that near tore his breath away. A vision that seemed sprung from his most secret special dreams.

A pair of red sparkly boots.

And what boots—heels as high as heaven and toes as sharp as salt. Gleaming stove-pipe uppers greaving tall and slick, and on the tip of each pointy toe a snake's head leered, spitting tongue and bone-sharp teeth.

And what sparkle—glistening and glittering in the evening light like diamond rain after the shower has stopped, like snow in the sun, like a thousand stars clustered in the midnight sky.

And what red—slick wet red, sparking like sunshine, thick and rich as paint, gleaming like a pricked finger, like a stormy dawn, like first love.

Jacko opened the door and inside he went. The shop contained a vast smoky gloom from which sprang the vague hulk of cabinets and large pieces of carved wood whose shapes Jack could neither see fully nor understand. He cared not for the shadows or the smoke; he cared only for the brilliant boots in the window.

"Do you see love?" a squeaky voice inquired from the distant reaches of the room.

"Those red sparkly boots in the window—" stuttered Jack, overcome by fog and fright. A jackdaw flapped out of the shadows, perched upon a hat rack, and regarded our boy with flat button eyes.

"A most discerning young dasher," said the grammer who leapt from the back of the store with a flash of blue petticoats and took up stand beside him, gripping his arm with a grandmotherly pinch. In the gloam her teeth shone as green as grass, and her ancient monkey head was surmounted by a soufflé of a cap. "Best in the house. Chop-chop, my little darlings, and come to your bungalow baby boy."

The boots jumped out of their window, driven by their own joie-de-vie, and began to caper nimbly on the countertop, heels clacking a fandango, tongues flapping a jaunty tune. The jackdaw cawed accompaniment and even the old grammer tapped gnarled fingers as the heels clicked and spun, snapping upward, diddling downward, the snake heads gnashing their needley teeth and spitting. Jack's blue toes began to tap the splintery floor and his heart jiggled and jumped in his chest. Never before had he seen such a glorious slick shade of red, and now he was completely caught.

"The boots like your sweetness," said the grammer, and both she and the jackdaw giggled. "For a small price they shall be your daisies, and together such fun you shall have."

Jack's jiggly heart flopped. What funds did he have to purchase anything other than moldy cheese and squashed kale pie? What funds would he ever get, in his dull little room, dipping poison matches for plungers to light their cigars from? And the hungry childer and the sick mamma waiting at home for his return. His world would be forever dull; all else was a forlorn hope. Jack's wiggly heart died and he began to turn away.

"Cheap at the price, but dear in the taking," the grammer said. "And naught price that you can not pay, I warrant."

"I have no flash," Jacko said, his sad exit halted. But his fingers felt the twist of his sweater wherein he had carefully placed the coins, rubbing their rounded shapes through the thin cloth.

The jackdaw spoke up then, its voice a buzz of suggestion. "What then burns in your hand, Jackanapes?"

Jack looked down to the sudden heat in his grubby paw and there lay the coins, not so dull now. The diva gleamed like the sun, with eleven little tiny silver moons circling its golden glow.

"But—"

The boots clicked their crimson heels together, and the snake heads said in slithery tandem voices: *Darling Burning Boy, with us you shall be the Fleet-Footed Fancy Lad, the Red-Haired Child of Sunset. No obstacle you cannot leap, no hunger you cannot fill, no thirst you cannot quench. Come and let us jump for joy!*

Looking at the red sparkly boots, the color of his dreams, what could Jack think of hungry tummies in the tenement home, waiting for their crusty sup? What could he think of a sick mamma and a skull-headed baby, coughing instead of cooing? What could he think other than the glorious tap-dancing of the slaphappy boots, the rich radiant red which filled his heart with warmth, flooded his brain with fun, and made his toes tap? Oh, our Jack was a good boy and perhaps for a tiny momento he did consider the cold little faces, the grinning Hunger waiting patiently in the corner, his mamma's red swollen hands, but then the boots drummed a furious rhythm, and in that rhythm all else Jack forgot.

When all your life you have been cold, little inkwells, how can you then resist the fire?

The grammer took the diva and eleven glories and dropped them into the gaping maw of the jackdaw which flapped off into the dark shadows, still cackling. Then the knobby old lady flicked her hankie at Jacko, who jerked at the waft of hyacinth that washed over him. He coughed, and as he coughed she flicked again, speaking a strange word that crackled and snapped in the air, sparking, arcing.

Jack shut his peeps to the brilliant flicker and when he opened them full wide again, the grammer was gone, the darkness was gone, the shop was gone, and he stood, light-footed, in the center of the street. Rosy daylight suffused the air, pooling pinkly on the surface of the puddles and the wet walls of the surrounding buildings. He looked down, and the snakes hissed happily, little tongues tasting the clean morning air. Then his boots took to the sky like big red balloons, carrying him upward on their flight. The boots capered, they danced, they trotted, they gavotted, and they leapt full fifty feet in the air, tongues clacking with joy, Jack shouting with joy, as they flew.

Over the bright morning roofs they sprang, Jack and his Jack-boots, traipsing across treetops. They jumped over the milk cart, and the trash cart, and little lines of childer trailing off to school. They scattered traffic brass and barouches, flyers and flowerbeds, leaping ever higher into the sterling blue sky. Never before had Jack felt so lovely, so wise, so tall and so very very clever, and in his happiness he yodeled a little tune, full of hope and wonderment. The red sparkly boots were just the thing, and now that he had them, he could not imagine his feet, his heart, his life, without them. The world was fresh and new, and Jack with it, all dewdrop eager-eyed, truly footloose and fancy-free.

But after a time, Jack grew tired of the jumping and wanted to rest. He watched the cool green grass bounce by his springs, and yet when he tried to halt so to rest under the shade trees, the sparkly red boots kept bouncing him along. He grabbed at railings as he passed, sweaty hands sliding from the iron; he was flying so fast now that it seemed perhaps the Wide World itself was moving and he was the one standing still. Jacko shouted for help—to the brass directing traffic, to the washwoman kneeling on marble steps, to the costermonger polishing her apples, but his shouts wisped in the wind and were lost. Still he bounced on, going ever higher and higher with each leap, until his ears rang and his head spun, and he was fair ill with dizziness. He snatched at chimney pots and streetlights, at lightning vanes and flagpole finials, but still he sprang onward.

Then suddenly he stopped.

Jackie stopped and he tumbled down into the dust and lay there, thankful that the bouncing had ceased, although his head still seemed to leap and spin, spin and leap. His tum twisted and turned but was too empty to urp.

"Well, now, little leaper," a voice said, "How far can you go before you kiss the sun and burn your roly-poly red lips?"

Jack squinted up, but only a shadow could he see, bright sun burning behind a darkened head.

"I cry sorrow," said Jacko, "and offer thanks. The boots fair well skint me."

"So I see," said the friendly voice. "Perhaps you'd like me to help you take them off?"

"Ayah so," agreed Jack, whose tender tootsies, not yet used to being enfolded in leather, were now painfully raw. But no amount of pulling would remove the sparkly red boots from Jack's wee feeties, and while you, clever tulips, are probably not surprised by this turn of the ankle yourselves, it came as a huge and utter gasp to our poor little Jackomydarling.

"You have bought a bargain," said the gramper, for tugging and pulling had revealed him to be so. "And keep it you shall. The boots are tired now and need to rest, but once they have had their kip, you'll be bouncing again."

"But bouncing be done!" cried Jack. Now that the fun was resting, he was suddenly recalling the hungry siblings, the sick mamma, the coughing baby, all waiting for him to return with their chow. But now he had no money and no chow, nothing but sparkly red boots which soared and galloped but which could not keep Hunger at bay. "I must slip the boots and return for my flash, for the coins I need to buy munch for my dear loves at home."

The gramper smiled, and shook his stick. A jackdaw flapped down and perched upon his shoulder, gazing at young Jacko with flat black eyes. "The shop is closed and the shopkeeper gone. What is bought can not be returned."

"But my lovely lollies? My sweet mamma and my tiny siblings? The baby who coughs? Can they live? Must they die for my sparklies?" Tears begin to stir in Jack's eyes, and all his joy in red was gone.

"Perhaps this consideration should have come before the purchasing," the gramper said, "But such is the rashness of youth. You say you are fair well skint, of both flash and dash—maybe so."

From its perch upon the gramper's shoulder, the jackdaw spoke up then, its voice a burr of suggestion: "What then burns in your hand, Jackolantern?"

Jack looked down to the sudden coldness in his grubby paw, and there, caught in his fingers, gleamed a strand of pearls, tiny white moons strung on a golden cord. Never had he seen anything so round and pure, and yet how had it come to be in his hand? In his soaring, he must have snatched and noticed not.

"Did you not look before you leapt? Or while leaping look?" The stick was shook again, and pointed upward, towards an open window and a fluttering drape. "Doors are lock'd but who could imagine that larceny might leap on springy heels?"

The jackdaw opened his wings in a great flutter, launching upward with a hoarse cry, and when Jack lowered his shielding arm, the gramper and his fetch were gone. But the pearls remained, cool and knobby, and so too did the open window. Jack looked from one to the other, considering, and a rough red magick began to burn in his brain. He stood and tapped one red sparkly heel upon the grass. The snake head spit, and with the tamp Jack felt vigor anew course upward through his tender tootsies, his knobby knees, his empty tum, his sad heart. When he stamped again, this time with both heels, upward he soared, like an arrow, to the beckoning window.

When Jack bounced home to his family's tenement room, laden down was he with gifts bestowed upon him by his bouncing boots and many open windows. With high springy heels and unlocked doors, roofs and balconies, the whole city was his huckleberry.

The tiny siblings greeted his arrival with weak squeals of joy, for instead of squashy kale pie, Jacko brought spicy chicken galantine, savory and strong. Instead of moldy cheese, there was cherry cream custard for afters and never more that sticky gritty spinach paste. The sick mamma and the baby who coughed got a spoonful of Madam Twanky's Super Celebrated Celery Salt Med-I-Cine, which fixed them both right up. After much munching, Jack chucked the horrible match pots out of the window, and the entire family removed to the Palace Union Hotel, where they reveled in lush carpets, hot water, and toast on demand. Hunger, left behind in the empty tenement room, slunk sadly down the street, looking for a new corner to call home.

And thus, darling dishrags, did wee Jacko take to a life of snuggery and sin, poaching purses, fixing races, mashing lovers, cutting cards. Thus was Springheel Jack born, the Bounciest Boy Terror ever to be seen. The reign of the Boots had begun!

Afterword

That Springheel Jack was an actual historical personage is disputed by many. Some historians see in him an amalgamation of several legendary outlaws: Aeuthur Flashheart perhaps, with a dash of the Dainty Pirate mixed in.[2] Others, including the learned philologist Emilio Zarendeo, are convinced that the character is as fictional as The Man in Pink Bloomers, perhaps even that bogey's forerunner.[3] Though the Man in Pink Bloomers lacks springy boots, he shares other traits with Springheel Jack: a ribald sense of humor, a devilishly wicked aspect, and questionable sartorial choices. Lending credence to the Jack's fictionality is that his tales can be dated to several different historical periods, and clearly no man, not even one possessed of magickal boots, could have that longevity.[4]

Yet a person by that name is mentioned in several famous autobiographies of the Pontifexacate and the Abenfaráx Period,

---

2   See Winkle, Filonia. *Flash, Dandy & Dainty: A Ethnographic Exploration into the Epistemology of the Outlaw in Califa Myths & Legends.* Porkopolis: Widdle, Weedle & Tum, 17-Calli-156-17.

3   Zarendeo, Emilio Espejo. *The Man in Pink Bloomers is Under Your Bed & In Your Nightmares: The Reification of Prechildhood Revenants as Reflected by Hierarchical Quasi-Masculine Equipage & Post-Contextualized Narratives of Heuristic Longing & Privilege.* Cuidad Anahuatl: Villaviciosa Alba, 4-Tecaptl-156-17.

4   Gray, Penny & Robert Wise. *The Springy Boots: Stories of Springheel Jack.* Derry: Hockstetter Press, 4-Tecaptl-156-17.

notably that of the famed policeman Anibal Aguille y Wilkins (whom we shall hear more of later). These sources, including the incredibly rare Flora Fyrdraaca autobiography (only one copy of *Flora's Dare* is known to exist[5]), make it clear that while Springheel Jack was an actual historical personage, the name was claimed by several different criminals over a period of years.[6] In any event, this tale's fantastic tone, overly florid language and whimsical approach to larceny and mayhem mark it as clearly intended for children.

---

5   Kept under lock and key in the special collection of the University of Kuila and accessed with special permission only. A copy of *Flora's Fury: How A Girl of Spirit and a Red Dog Confound Their Friends, Astound Their Enemies, And Learn the Importance of Packing Light*, the third volume of the autobiography is rumoured to be in the private collection of the Keanuenue'oklani family, but this cannot be confirmed. No copy of the first volume, *Flora Segunda: Being the Magickal Mishaps of a Girl of Spirit, Her Glass-Gazing Sidekick, Two Ominous Butlers (One Blue), a House with Eleven Thousand Rooms and a Red Dog* has ever been discovered.

6   Aguille y Wilkins, Anibal. *Burnished Buttons & Mustachio Wax: Sixty Years as a Police Officer.* Califa: Hardnose & Hardy Publishing, Año Abenfaráx 75. Evengardia, Relais. *Fifty Years on the Stage.* Bexar: Shakespike Press, 2019. Wilce, Ysabeau S. ed. *Flora's Dare: How A Girl of Spirit Gambles All to Expand Her Vocabulary, Confront A Bouncing Boy Terror, And Try to Save Califa from a Shaky Doom (Despite Being Confined to Her Room).* New York: Harcourt Children's Books, 2008.

Quartermaster Returns

"... That he escaped that blow entirely is due to the consummate good luck which enabled him to steer clear of that military maelstrom ... he never had to be post quartermaster."

Trials of a Staff Officer
Captain Charles King, 3rd U.S. Cavalry

I. Wet

When Pow walks into the hog ranch, everyone turns to stare at him. At the whist table, the muleskinner gurgles and lets fall his cards. The cardsharp's teeth clatter against the rim of his glass. The cowboy squeaks. At the bar, the barkeep, who had been fishing flies out of the pickle jar, drops her pickle fork. On the bar, the cat, a fantastic mouser named Queenie, narrows her moon-silver eyes into little slits. At the pianny, Lotta, who'd been banging out *Drink Puppy Drink* on the peeling ivory keys, crashes one last chord and no more.

Even the ice elemental, in the cage suspended over the whist table, ceases his languid fanning. He's seen a lot of boring human behavior since the barkeep brought him from a junk store in Walnuts to keep the hog ranch cool; finally a human has done something interesting. Only Fort Gehenna's scout doesn't react. He wipes his nose on a greasy buckskin sleeve, slams another shot of mescal, and takes the opportunity to peek at his opponents' cards.

The barroom is dead silent but for a distant slap and a squeal—Buck and the pegboy in the back room *exercising*—and the creak of the canvas walls shifting in the ever-present Arivaipa wind.

Pow wobbles over to the bar—just a couple of boards laid across two empty whiskey barrels—leans on it—the boards creaking ominously at his weight—and croaks: "Mescal." His throat feels as though he's swallowed sixty pounds of sand. The barkeep stares at him, her mouth hanging slightly ajar. Against her garish blue lip rouge her teeth look as yellow as corn.

Pow licks his lips with a cat-coarse tongue and whispers: "Come on, Petty, give me a mescal. I'm powerfully dry."

"You're dripping wet," the barkeep answers. Pow looks down, and yes indeed he is dripping, brown water seeping from his dirty uniform, turning the ground he stands upon to mud.

"Sorry," he says. "Is it raining outside?" He looks back toward the door, which is a blazing rectangle of sunlight, bright enough to blind—it's not raining outside. Arivaipa is a goddess-forsaken wilderness of a desert, where it only rains occasionally, and then usually in the dead of night. And anyway, if it were raining outside, it would be raining inside too, for the hog ranch's roof is made of brush and is not watertight. The last good downpour was two weeks ago, and it had almost swamped the hog ranch out.

"Lotta—get the lieutenant a towel," the barkeep says, but Lotta does not spring to the order. She shrinks back behind the wall of the pianny and wishes she were invisible.

"Lotta!" the barkeep repeats, "Get Lieutenant Rucker a towel or I'll kick ya in yer hinder."

While Lotta reluctantly follows the barkeep's order, Pow wipes his face on the mustachio towel nailed to the bar; the towel, none too white to begin with, comes away black with dirt. The barkeep hands him a sloshily poured glass; he drinks it in one draught and bangs his glass down for more. The mescal is bitter and burning but it washes away the taste of mud in his mouth. He feels very clammy, and from the itch, there is sand in his drawers. The barkeep pours him another.

"Thanks, darling," Pow says and bolts his second drink. The whist game has not resumed; the players are still staring at him, and he returns their glance, saying, "Ain't you people never seen a man drink before?"

No one responds to this quip, and then the canvas curtains over the doorway to the back room part. Out staggers Buck, laughing, struggling to get her sack coat back on. She's got her right arm in the left sleeve and that's not going to work no matter how much she pulls. The pegboy follows her, grinning and snapping his galluses up over red-checkered shoulders. An air of satisfaction hovers over them both.

Buck outranks him, so Pow wafts a salute at her, and she waves at him drunkenly, collapsing in a chair at the other rickety table. The pegboy sticks a cigarillo in her mouth, another in his, and lights them both.

"Where the hell you been, Pow?" Buck says. The barkeep has already anticipated her desire and plunks a bottle of whiskey before her.

Pow licks the dirt from his lips and realizes that he has no idea.

II. Desiccated

Arivaipa Territory, where the sun is so hot that it will, after dissolving your flesh into grease, melt your bones as well. A territory of bronco natives and bunco artists, wild religiosos and wild horses, poison toads and rattling snakes. A hard dry place, an endless expanse of Nowhere. Why the Warlord wants to keep a thread of authority in such a goddess-forsaken place is a mystery, but the army doesn't question orders, just follows them. Thus Fort Gehenna, and a scattering of other army posts, sown like seeds across the prickly rocky dusty landscape of the remote territory.

The hog ranch sits on Fort Gehenna's reservation line, just beyond the reach of military authority and technically off-limits to army personnel. There are no hogs at this ranch, just cheap bugjuice, cheap food and cheap love, but these three attractions make the hog ranch a pretty attractive place to Gehenna's lonely bored hungry soldiers. So a well-worn track starts at the hog ranch's front door and wends its way through the desert scrub, up and down arroyos, by saguaro and paloverde, across the sandy expanse of the Sandy River to terminate behind Officers' Row.

Down this track, known as The Oh Be Joyful Road, Pow zig-zags. His feet kick up dust, and the sun hits his shoulders, his bare head, with hammer-like intensity. The heat has sucked the wet right out of his uniform, which now feels gritty and coarse against his skin. His sinuses tingle and burn. He feels in his sack coat pocket for his bandana, but the pockets are full of sand. So he blows his nose into his sleeve, but only a thin gust of dust comes out.

His boots are full of sand too; near the cactus priest's wikiyup he sits on a rock and pours them out. Were his toes always that black? They look like little shriveled coffee beans. His brain feels thick, as though his skull is full of mud. Pow marches on, his eyes slits of grittiness; his eyelids scrape at his eyeballs like broken glass. He can hardly see where he is going, but the urge to go is strong, and he can't help but follow it.

Pow reaches the Single Officers' Quarters and staggers up the steps into the blessed shade of the porch—a few degrees cooler and the air slightly moist from the water olla hanging from the porch eaves. He pulls down the olla, hearing his muscles crackle like dried cornstalks. The olla is fat and round, beaded with moisture, but almost empty. He licks the droplets off the clay, oh delicious wetness, and then throws the pot on the ground, where it shatters.

As a first lieutenant, Pow's only entitled to one room, and this room is now empty of his gear, its only furniture a steamer trunk and an iron cot. Pow collapses on the iron cot, unable to take another step. His thirst is sharp and pointed, it's overwhelming and all encompassing, it leaves little room inside him for anything else. All around him he can sense moisture, but he himself is parched.

He shakes his head, feeling the tendons in his neck wheeze and burn. There a rattling sound inside of his skull—his brain perhaps, now shrunken to a desiccated nubbin. That would account for the thickness of his thoughts. Something falls into his lap; at first he thinks it's a piece of jerky, then he realizes it's his ear. He tries to stick his ear back onto his head, but it won't stay, so he puts it in his pocket for safekeeping.

A shadow slinks in the corner of the room; two silver eyes glitter. Freddie, Pow's pet gila monster, which he raised from an egg, is peeking out of its den, a hole in the adobe wall. The lizard waddles across the floor and nips at the toe of Pow's boot, its usual method for requesting a treat. Lacking anything else, Pow gives the gila monster his ear—his hearing seems fine without it—and Freddie nibbles daintily. Pow reaches for the lizard; Freddie spits a shiny squirt of silvery poison at him. Pow licks the slippery venom off his fingers—it's lovely wet.

The lizard is fat with moisture; underneath that scaly skin, it's heavy with wetness, its meat saturated with blood, bile, venom, juice. Pow makes a dry clucking noise with his splintery tongue and reaches for Freddie again. As if sensing his intent, the gila monster scuttles away, but desperation makes Pow quick. He snatches.

III. Dry

Pow's retreat from the hog ranch to his quarters did not go without notice; indeed, when he had staggered onto Fort Gehenna's parade ground, a long file had straggled behind him. In addition to the habitués of the hog ranch, who gave him a respectable head start before following, the brigade included the herd guard, a couple of privates who were loitering in the shade of the sinks watching an ant fight, the tame broncos (as the soldiers call Arivaipa's natives) who live behind the remuda corral, and the dog pack, tempted out of the arroyo by Pow's smell, which, now that his clothes have dried, is quite strong: a meaty kind of decay.

This crowd now stands outside the SOQ, and it has attracted the attention of Lieutenant Brakespeare, Gehenna's adjutant and current acting quartermaster, and Sergeant Candy, Gehenna's ranking noncom. When they arrive to investigate, a multitude of voices in several languages all begin to babble at once. Lieutenant Brakespeare ignores the shouting and enters the SOQ, only to find Pow's room empty. The contents of his trunk are strewn about the room and every item packed therein that once contained anything moist—boot polish tin, a bottle of Madama Twanky's *Sel-Ray-Psalt Medicine*, fly ointment—lies wrecked upon the floor.

The destruction continues across the hallway and into Lieutenant Brakespeare's quarters—the lieutenant swears horribly when she sees the mess—and on into the kitchen beyond. There Berman, the lieutenants' striker, stands surveying a battlefield of crumpled tin cans, smashed sauerkraut crocks, broken wine bottles, and the splintered remains of a water barrel.

"He went that way," Berman says, *that way* being into the back yard. There Lieutenant Brakespeare and Sergeant Candy find Pow facedown in a laundry tub, sucking up soapy water, while the laundress stands over him, whacking at his shoulders with her washboard. They heave Pow out of the almost empty tub. He burps a giant soap bubble, which pops into an appalling stench of sweet-sour decay, and shakes the soldiers off. He feels deliciously water-logged, heavy and solid. He feels much much better.

The crowd has rushed around the back, and now a rotund figure—Captain de Poligniac, Gehenna's commanding officer—pushes through, almost invisible underneath a huge black umbrella, an item that officers in uniform are strictly forbidden to carry. When he reaches the SOQ back porch and lets drop the shade, Polecat (as the good captain is called even to his face) reveals that he's not in uniform anyway, just a pair of dirty red drawers and a white guayabera. He'd been in his quarters, riding out the furnace of the afternoon on an herbal haze, and he is annoyed at being disturbed.

"What's all that infernal racket, Lieutenant Brakespeare?" Polecat complains. He catches sight of Pow, and his voice trails off. His lips pucker in puzzlement, and he stares at the rapidly dehydrating lieutenant.

"Pow!" Polecat says. "I thought you were dead!"

IV. Arid

Of course, Ist Lieutenant Powhatan Rucker is dead. Not just dead, but drowned. How can you drown in a desert? In an Arivaipa thunderstorm, all too quickly. One minute the sky is as blank as a sheet of paper; the next minute it roils with quicksilver clouds, from which lunge enormous purple-silver prongs of lightning. And then rain bullets down, water floods into the arroyos, and anything not on the high ground is swept away. Ten minutes later the desert is dry as a bone again, and the sky empty.

He died a hero's death, Lieutenant Rucker did, trying to save, not another comrade, but rather the hog ranch's entire supply of beer. The story is short and tragic: the freight train dropped fifteen cases of beer at the hog ranch, before proceeding on to Rancho Kuchamonga; an inexperienced drover off-loaded the beer in the arroyo below the hog ranch; when the storm came up, Pow organized his fellow whist players into a bottle brigade and supervised the shifting of fourteen cases to higher ground; the water was already foaming when Pow went back for the last case—refusing to allow the others to join him in harm's way; Pow heroically managed to shove that case up the bank, just as a wall of water twenty feet high came roaring down the ravine.

After Pow's battered and soggy body was found tangled in an uprooted paloverde tree, he was borne off to Gehenna's sandy cemetery, where he was given a full military funeral and toasted by the entire garrison with bottles from the fateful case that killed him. But now that sandy cemetery has spit Pow back up, a circumstance that no one in Gehenna can ever remember occurring before.

"If Pow is dead, how can he be alive?" Polecat says in bewilderment. They've retired to his office for privacy, although the crowd still loiters outside, hoping that voices will be raised enough to facilitate eavesdropping. Considering that the walls of the office are mud-covered brush, and the ceiling more brush, under which hangs a piece of canvas which keeps centipedes from falling on your head, the voices do not have to be very loud. Polecat plops behind his desk, trying to look official, while the Lieutenants Brakespeare and Rucker stand before him in semi-respectful stances. Lieutenant Fyrdraaca, retrieved from the privy, isn't quite as drunk as she was before, but she's not sober enough to stand at attention, so she has sprawled upon Polecat's well-used daybed.

Polecat puts his spectacles on to examine Pow more closely; the lieutenant is still crusted with a fine silt, but the few bits of skin visible look downright shriveled. He is twenty-two years old, but now he looks a hundred.

"I think alive is stretching it a bit, Polecat," Buck says. "I mean, Pow is animated, but he looks a bit rough to actually be alive. I would say he's definitely dead."

"Then what am I doing here?" Pow asks, bewildered.

"I called you back." Lieutenant Brakespeare says. She sounds rather smug.

"You brought him back from the dead?" Polecat moans. "Why in Califa's name did you do that, Azota?"

"His quartermaster accounts were a mess—and short, too." Lieutenant Brakespeare purses her mouth into a small knot. "I'm not going to be responsible for his shortages, or pay for his mistakes."

At the time of his death, Pow had been Gehenna's quartermaster, and thus responsible for all of Gehenna's rations, uniforms, equipment, ordnance and equipage, for the previous three months. During that time he'd not done a lick of paperwork, preferring instead to while away the days playing mumblety-peg with the QM clerks. To say that Pow's QM accounts were a mess was being charitable. Actually, they were a catastrophe.

When Lieutenant Brakespeare (only shortly graduated from Benica Barracks Military Academy but already well on her way to being a properly stuck-up yaller dog, as staff officers are called) assumed the QM duties upon Pow's death, it had taken her fourteen days of non-stop paper pushing to complete the QM returns properly, and even then she couldn't account for all the shortages in the QM inventories. Since officers in the Army of Califa are personally responsible for items on their inventory returns, someone is to going to have to pay for these shortages. Lieutenant Brakespeare has no intention of being that someone.

Polecat complains: "But you shouldn't summon someone back from the dead just to make up a shortage."

"I didn't," Lieutenant Brakespeare says primly. "Officers are forbidden by *The Articles of War* to attempt or achieve any magickal acts. Article 3, Section I, Sub-section 2."

Buck, from the settee, observes: "Maybe forbidden themselves, but there's nothing in *The Articles of War* about paying someone else to attempt or achieve magickal acts for you, eh? Who'd you get to do it?"

"The curandero," Lieutenant Brakespeare admits. The curandero is an elderly bronco who, having decided he was too old and wise to fight, made peace with the Califians and moved into a wiki-yup near the river, from which he dispenses charms, foul-smelling ointments, and philosophical advice, in return for rations. "Anyway, Lieutenant Rucker can go back where he came as soon as he either produces the inkwell or pays for it. I don't care which."

"Inkwell?" says Polecat.

"Ayah, so. Pow signed a receipt for fifteen glass inkwells, shipped from Fort Ludwig to here—" Lieutenant Brakespeare fishes a sheet of paper out of her sack coat and consults it. "On Martes 12. One arrived broken and was dropped from the inventory. One was issued to Corporal Candy on Martes 15; one was issued to the AG, and one to the CO. Leaving eleven on the return. But there were only ten in the QM store. Where's the missing inkwell?" She looks accusingly at Pow.

"I don't know," Pow says. He has no idea where the missing inkwell is, but there's a burning feeling in his throat, a scratchy roar that is extremely distracting. The dry Arivaipa air has sucked his moisture away, and his thirst has returned with a vengeance. Something wiggles on his neck; despite the canvas a centipede has fallen from the brush. Pow pops the flailing bug into his mouth and it squishes wetly between his teeth. The others don't notice.

"How much is the inkwell valued at?" Polecat asks.

Lieutenant Brakespeare consults the receipt again. "Fifteen lisbys."

"Fifteen lisbys!" Polecat reaches for the cigarillo box on his blotter, which does not contain cigarillos. "Fifteen lisbys! That's pocket change!"

"You always gotta do things the hard way, Tiny Doom," Buck chortles, and Lieutenant Brakespeare gives her a poisonous look.

"Have you got fifteen lisbys, Pow?" Polecat asks.

Pow feels in his pockets, but if he ever had fifteen lisbys, the Arivaipa desert has them now. He tries to answer; his jaw creaks like dry wood, and no words come out, only a puff of dust.

"I'll take that as a no. Here, I'll give you fifteen lisbys, Pow, and you can pay Lieutenant Brakespeare, and that will be that," Polecat says, his head now wreathed in soothing herbal smoke. He fishes around in his top desk drawer. "Buck, do you have two lisbys?"

There's an ink bottle sitting on Polecat's desk, half-full of ink. Pow can smell the dark delicious wetness—

"I don't want your money, Captain," Lieutenant Brakespeare complains. "It's Lieutenant Rucker's responsibility, and he should either find that inkwell or pay up—"

Pow's entire focus is now pointed at that ink bottle and the promise of liquidity within. His thirst burns; his blood has long evaporated, and his veins feel like rawhide thongs, taut and stretched. He reaches a claw-like hand toward the bottle. The ink tastes thick and dark; but most deliciously, it tastes wet.

The others have stopped their squabbling and are staring at him. Pow licks his now black lips and sets the empty bottle back on Polecat's desk.

"Anyway, it's not just the inkwell," Lieutenant Brakespeare says triumphantly. "There's also a small matter of the paymaster funds, which are also missing, and which Pow, as QM, is responsible for."

Polecat blanches. "How much?"

"Five thousand divas."

"Paper or gold?" Polecat asks faintly.

"Gold."

V. Parched

Suddenly Lieutenant Brakespeare's actions no longer seem quite so drastic. Fifteen lisbys is nothing; even a private can probably scrounge up fifteen lisbys, the price of a beer. But five thousand divas in gold—Fort Gehenna's entire payroll for the entire year! If the troopers find out their pay is gone, they'll riot, they'll mutiny, they'll desert. They'll raise a howl that will be heard in the War Department back in Califa, a howl that, since Pow is dead, will thunder down upon the shoulders of his superiors: Polecat and Lieutenant Brakespeare. They'll be court-martialed for sure, and lucky to escape cashiering. And they'll still have to pay back the cash. Five thousand divas in gold is a pretty good reason for raising the dead.

Polecat and Lieutenant Brakespeare pounce on Pow, but their berating questions get nowhere. He can hardly hear them; they are distant mirages in his parchedness. The ink has only whetted his thirst—not quenched it—and now his only interest is in moisture. He can smell the wetness; not in the air, which is as dry as dust, but in the living bodies around him—wet blood, wet bile, wet sweat, wet saliva. They are soggy with wetness, fair dripping, and he can feel himself shriveling for the lack of it.

Pow stares at Polecat, upon whose white brow stand little drops of sweat, whose rosy cheeks are flushed and bedewed. Polecat's lips are moving, opening to display the moist cavern of his mouth—the desire to lunge toward that wetness—tear Polecat's tongue out by the roots, suck out all its moisture—is rising like a dust devil inside of Pow, twisting and turning and—

"Hey," says Buck. She's now standing next to him, a bottle in her hand. "Have a drink, Pow. You look like you could use it."

His hands are too gnarled now to grasp the bottle; creakily he leans back, and Buck pours the coarse whiskey into his mouth; as it flows down his throat he feels his flesh expanding, reconstituting itself, plumping out. Delicious delicious wetness.

Lieutenant Brakespeare turns on Buck: "You could be helping. You signed the receipt for the paymaster. This will hit you, too."

Buck protests: "I am helping. While the two of you shriek like owls, I've been thinking. You know, the night Pow died, I was at the hog ranch, too."

"Where else?" says Lieutenant Brakespeare bitterly. She's never set foot in the place.

"*Callate*, Azota. I wasn't feeling so well, so I left early—*callate*, Azota!—and thus missed Pow's heroism, but I do recall now that when I left Pow was playing cards with the scout, Lotta, Pecos, and some other guy. Pow was losing, and losing in gold, too."

"Who was winning?" Lieutenant Brakespeare asks.

"The scout," says Buck triumphantly.

So Polecat puts his sack coat on and orders Lieutenant Brakespeare to arrest Pow, which she does. Then they all march, under colors, down to the hog ranch to demand the return of the payroll. They find the scout eating pickles and playing mumblety-peg with the ice elemental. He freely admits that he won the divas off Lieutenant Rucker, but he refuses to return them. A bet lost is a bet won by someone else, fair and square.

While Polecat dithers, and Buck and Pow have themselves another drink (or two), Lieutenant Brakespeare puts the screws on the scout. She starts out politely persuasive, then turns to choleric threats, but neither attitude makes the slightest dent. The scout is part-bronco, part-coyote, rumour has it, and a shavetail lieutenant don't scare him at all. Lieutenant Brakespeare sends a detail to search the scout's miserable shebang. No gold. Another detail holds the scout down and searches his greasy-buckskin-clad person. No gold. She's urging Polecat to allow her to tie the scout to a wagon wheel and set his hair on fire—*I'll wager he'll cough up the gold then!*—when Buck offers a lazy solution.

"A wager," Buck says. "Let's make a wager."

Arivaipa Territory is arid and dull; the soldiers must make their own fun and what's more fun than a wager? At Gehenna, they'll bet on anything. *I'll stand you four divas, five lisbys, six glories that you can't*: leap a prickly pear cactus; eat six jars of jalapeño pickles; stand on your head for six hours; ride that strawberry roan; stay in bed two weeks; walk from the hog ranch to the flagpole blindfolded. The inhabitants of Gehenna have bet on ant wars; mule races; tennis matches; foot races; marksmanship; whose bed sheets are whiter; whose corporal is fatter, and whether or not lightning is attracted to a picket pin dangling from the flagpole. (Yes.)

The scout's eyes, deep in red-painted sockets, gleam. "A wager?"

"Ayah," Buck answers. "A bet. You won the divas off Pow, now give him a chance to turnabout fair play. A contest of skill."

"What skill?"

"Who can hold their breath longest?" Buck suggests.

The scout shakes his head. "He's dead. He don't breathe. A foot race?"

Even in life, Pow was pokey; in death, he's moving at a snail's pace. Buck quickly counters: "Who can stay on Evil Murdoch the longest?" Evil Murdoch being the most notoriously un-rideable bite-y mule ever seen in Arivaipa.

The scout shakes his head. "Evil Murdoch kick me in the head, I'm dead. The lieutenant, he's already dead, why should he care? Not good odds."

Lieutenant Brakespeare suggests: "How about a penmanship contest?" This suggestion is so boring that she is ignored.

"A drinking contest, then," says Buck, grinning. She knows that the scout takes particular pride in his ability to consume large quantities of bug-juice, with no outward effect. Only last year he drank the barkeep under the table, and she's a professional.

"Done!" says the scout quickly. "I got five thousand divas in gold. What is he going to put up?" This question is a legitimate stumper. The cumulative value of everything at Fort Gehenna, from Polecat's silver cigarette case to the hay in the hay yard, probably isn't worth five thousand divas in gold. What can Pow wager that even remotely begins to match the value of the gold?

"How about his soul?" the scout says.

"Done!" says Buck.

VI. Drink

By now, night is falling. To the northeast, in a cliché suitable for a yellowback thriller, a storm is forming up over Mount Abraxas, garish purple and pink lightning splitting the iron-blue twilight sky. A dust devil spirals across the parade ground; the howling dog pack chases after it. Fort Gehenna is now mostly deserted; every soldier not currently on duty is at the hog ranch, along with every one else for miles. A drinking contest between the scout and a dead man is probably the most exciting thing ever to happen at Fort Gehenna. The hog ranch is standing room only; slits soon appear in the canvas walls, each rent accommodating an avid pair of eyes. No one wants to miss the show.

The officers have had a whispered conversation regarding Pow's stake, which Pow has objected to. With his body liable to crumble to dust any minute, Pow's soul is all he's got left—he doesn't want to chance losing it And besides, he doesn't care about the five thousand divas, why should he? He's dead. They can't court-martial him or cashier him. No, Polecat agrees, they can't. But they can confine him to the guardhouse, which is a dry place, where the water dipper is offered only twice a day. Here, they are offering Pow an opportunity to drink all he can, *set me up another round, keep 'em coming.* Suffer thirst or quench it. When it's put like that, Pow agrees that getting the money back is his responsibility after all.

As for the value of Pow's soul, how can it match the value of five thousand divas? Strictly speaking, it does not. Pow, in life, was an affable fellow, always good for a laugh and a loan, but he wasn't a famous magician, or a holy man, or anyone else who might have accumulated great animus, a weighty powerful soul. No matter to the scout. He has a little collection of souls; he keeps them in a leather pouch he wears on a cord around his neck. He's got the soul of a baby who died at birth; a dog that could read; a woman who lived to be one hundred and four; a coyote with two heads; a man who was hung for horse-stealing; and a woman who changed into a flamingo during the dark moon. The soul of a man who drowned in the desert would be a nice addition to this collection.

The rumble of thunder is growling nearer, like the distant approach of cannon fire, when Pow and the scout sit down across from each other at the whist table. The peanut gallery—no peanuts, no gallery—crowds around.

The rules, as Buck explains them loudly, are simple: whoever quits drinking first loses.

They start with the rest of the beer that Pow rescued from the flood—the last case, the one that Pow died for. After the funeral, the barkeep had put this case away for a special occasion, and Pow's return is certainly a special occasion. It's very poor beer (the good stuff has no hope of surviving the long journey via steamer and mule train to Arivaipa), but the people who drink at the hog ranch aren't picky. As long as the beer is cheap and wet, they are satisfied.

Pow, of course, only cares that the booze is wet. He and the scout chug down the beers as quickly as Lotta places them on the table. Six bottles each. With each swig, Pow feels his flesh expanding, fattening. The alcohol doesn't effect him at all, only the moisture. His muscles and sinews flex, his jaw relaxes. His brain swells back to its normal size, and he is beginning to think clearly again. The scout starts out strong, matching Pow sip for sip, but Gehenna's officers are not yet worried. The beer is weak stuff; even Lieutenant Brakespeare can drink several bottles of the stuff to no ill effect.

The scout finishes sucking the last few drops of beer out of the last bottle and tosses it over his shoulder. A yelp indicates that his aimless aim still found a mark.

"I gotta piss," he announces.

Pow needs no piss break; so he waits at the table, while the scout saunters out back to the saguaro that became the default urinal after the big storm washed the privy away. He returns a few minutes later and the contest resumes.

Now the beer is gone, and at Buck's bidding, the barkeep brings out the hog ranch's supply of mescal: six large ollas. This mescal is rough and strong; Buck doubts if the scout will make it through the second olla. She winks at Pow. Now that he is better hydrated, his eyes don't feel quite so much like glass marbles, so he winks back.

"Ut!" Pow says, raising his glass. The mescal looks exactly like urine, and it tastes, Pow realizes, almost exactly like soap. By the end of the first olla, a thin glaze is starting to creep across the scout's face. He puts his glass down and burrows into his buckskin jacket. The room stiffens and other hands stray toward hips, shirt fronts, waists, and boot-tops—any place a weapon could be stashed.

But when the scout's hand reappears, it's with a leather cigarillo case. He aims the cigarillo for his mouth, and makes the target on the second try. The scout accepts the trigger that the drover, leaning in, offers.

"Cigarillo?" the scout asks Pow.

Pow shakes his head. He's ready for another drink. And anyway, even when alive he never smoked. The scout gets the cigarillo lit on the third try; his hands are definitely shaking now. He probably won't even make it through the next glass. Gehenna's officers exchange triumphant glances.

But the scout makes it through the next glass, and the next one too. They are into their fourth glass when the scout finishes his cigarillo and casually flicks the butt away. But his aim is impaired, and the flick sends the butt flying, not toward the floor, but directly at Pow. It lands in his hair, which, now well saturated with flammable liquid, immediately ignites into a halo of fire.

The crowd recedes in a squawk of horror. The barkeep has had patrons burst into flames before, and experience has taught her to keep a blanket handy. While Buck and Polecat slap Pow with their hats, she elbows through the crowd and tosses the blanket over Pow, pushes him on the floor, and sits on him.

When they unwrap the blanket, they find Pow a bit charred around the temples but otherwise no worse for wear. They haul him to his feet and sit him back down at the table. The fire has quenched his deliciously moist feeling, and he's ready for another drink.

"No more smoking," Buck warns the scout. She doesn't believe for a minute that the scout's flick was unintentional, but since she can't prove this belief, she's going to watch him like a hawk. Pow's thirst is the insatiable thirst of a desiccated dead man. The scout is neither dead nor desiccated, and he should have long succumbed. Buck is getting suspicious. The scout grins at her, pointy blue-stained teeth gleaming, and raises his glass.

But by the time they've killed the mescal, the scout is looking a bit done. His eyes are tarnished silver coins, and, in between chugs, he's clawed his hair into jagged clumps. The canvas walls are now sucking in and out, as though the hog ranch itself is trying to gasp for breath, stifled by the interior tension and the stench of hair pomade, tallow, dog, and bugjuice. A guttural rumble overhead reminds them the storm is coming in.

But the scout doesn't drop. They finish the mescal and pause so that the barkeep can send Lotta out to the back to dig up the whiskey that's been mellowing in a grave near the corral. The scout staggers off to relieve himself of some of his liquid burden and Gehenna's officers worriedly confer.

"He's cheating. He's got to be," Buck says. "No one can drink that much and live. Even Pow's starting to look water-logged."

Pow *is* looking rough. As he has absorbed the liquid, he's puffed up, ballooning like a sponge. Where he had been stringy and dry, he's now round and plump, but it's a strained kind of plumpness. His skin, burned black with decay, looks shiny and stretched, like the skin of a balloon. The bony claws of his fingers have swollen into fat sausages.

In short, Pow looks about to burst. The scout has an outlet for his excess liquid. Pow is drinking faster than he can absorb. Something is gonna give.

"I know he's cheating," Buck repeats.

"How can he be cheating?" Polecat whispers. "What are we going to do?"

Pow is no longer paying attention to the whispered accusations flying between the officers. Something cold and hard has just bopped him on the beezer: an ice cube. He looks up to see the ice elemental, suspended in its silver cage above the table, waving a small blue hand at him. Pow sloshily waves back.

The elemental grabs at its scrawny neck and pulls, making an agonized face. Then it points to the scout's empty seat. Pow is mystified. The elemental grabs at its neck again—no, it's not grabbing at its neck, it's pretending to pull on a pretend something that is not actually hanging around its neck. The elemental points at the scout's empty seat again, and then mimes chugging a bottle. Pow glances around. The scout has not returned; the spectators have thinned out, some ducking outside for the same reason the scout did, others for a smoke. Buck has also disappeared, but Lieutenant Brakespeare and Polecat are still whispering worriedly. No, Polecat is whispering worriedly. Lieutenant Brakespeare is also staring at the ice elemental, who, seeing her gaze, opens his little blue beak. A few teeny tiny sparkles fly out: Gramatica, the language of magick.

Pow may be dead, and also alive, and therefore somewhat magickal, but he still can't understand Gramatica. But Lieutenant Brakespeare, who is not magickal in the slightest, cannot be magickal at all per *The Articles of War*, upon pain of death (except at remove, of course)—a tiny little flicker of comprehension flits across her face, a flicker that almost instantly is reabsorbed back into her normal mulish scowl. The elemental tugs on the imaginary thing again. Pow and Lieutenant Brakespeare make eye contact, and the lieutenant raises her eyebrow oh-so-very-slightly. Pow is still clueless, but Lieutenant Brakespeare seems to have understood.

A bright blue light briefly electrifies the hog ranch interior, its whip-like *crack* provoking shrieks. The roar of thunder drowns out the shrieks. The storm is almost upon them.

The scout returns and takes his place across the table. Buck returns, and she and Polecat resume their positions of support behind Pow. But Lieutenant Brakespeare has realigned herself until she stands directly behind the scout. Buck gives her a glare, which is ignored. The barkeep pours from a dirt-encrusted bottle.

"Ut!" the scout says, raising his glass.

"Ut!" says Pow. The brief hiatus has left him thirsty. He raises the glass and drinks; the liquid flows like oil down his throat.

The scout sputters and puts his glass down. "This is not whiskey!"

The barkeep holds the bottle up so that the label reading *Madama Twanky's Amber Apple Schnapps* is visible. "The whiskey bottles broke," she explains. "This is all I could salvage. Don't you like apple schnapps?"

The scout sniffs the glass again, suspiciously. "It don't smell like apples."

"If you ain't thirsty anymore, we can stop right now," Buck says. "Call an end, and Pow the winner. Get home before the flood."

Pow swallows; death has ruined his palate pretty good, but even in death he knows the aftertaste of apple schnapps, his mamma's favorite digestif. He also now knows the aftertaste of gun oil. And he knows the difference between the two.

"Finish now and we can be out of here before the storm blows us away," Buck suggests. Her smile is very smug.

In response, the scout raises his glass and bolts its contents. Then he chokes. Coughs and wheezes. His eyes roll upward, and the snake tattoo on his forehead ripples. Tears spring to his eyes, snot dribbles from his nose. He swallows hard and slumps forward.

The hog ranch is silent. The wind has stopped, but the roof brush rustles, and a few drops of rain slip through, an advance guard. Another bolt of electric blue scorches the night. This time the crack sets ears a-ringing, and the accompanying thunder has almost no delay. Lieutenant Brakespeare leans over and jiggles the scout's shoulders, but he doesn't respond.

"I hereby declare—" Buck starts to say, and then the scout lifts his head. His eyes glitter green and gold, and he says: "Set us up again."

The barkeep pours them each another round of gun oil, and this time the scout doesn't hesitate. Smiling, he drains the glass and slams it so hard upon the table top that it shatters. He grins, a rill of amber fluid dribbling down his chin.

"Set me—" The scout's voice turns thick and then trails away. His head flings back and his eyeballs roll up and then roll down. A bubble of foam appears on his lips, and, as he gurgles, this bubble forms a beard, dripping down his chin to cover his chest. The scout begins to vibrate, his arms and legs twitching like he's been hit by lightning. The foam turns reddish brown, as the scout paws at his neck, moaning creakily.

"Looking for this?" Lieutenant Brakespeare dangles a small buckskin bag for all to see. In her other hand, the knife she used to snip the buckskin cord while pretending to be solicitous gleams sharply. She smiles, and that smile, in combination with her jagged scars, one on each cheek, is extremely malevolent.

The scout croaks as she opens the bag, waving his hands weakly. Six wisps of light—the souls the scout has collected—

fly up and out, floating through the brush roof to disappear into lightning-spattered darkness. Lieutenant Brakespeare shakes the bag over the table, and something small and glittery falls out: a scorpion.

"What is that?" Buck asks. The scorpion curls its tail up, stinger gleaming. Arivaipa scorpions are dull brown and white, bland. The carapace of this scorpion is milky green, like translucent jade, and its stinger is a small barb of bright fuchsia.

"Ha!" says Lieutenant Brakespeare. "That scorpion is a Potable Sigil. It makes any liquid drinkable. Pretty useful in the desert, no?"

"I told you he was cheating!" Buck crows.

"You cheated too," the scout says thickly. "That weren't no apple likker."

"Evening the odds," Buck retorts. "And anyway, your cheat cancelled out mine—so that makes your cheat bigger!"

The scout is gagging and retching; Candy thrusts a spittoon toward him just in time. The scout vomits up a copious amount of bad booze and gun oil and then keels over backwards. Lieutenant Brakespeare wenches his head up via a fistful of greasy hair and says: "Where's the gold?"

The scout burbles and Lieutenant Brakespeare nods, satisfied. Candy and the drover carry him off, to recover (if he can) in the guard-house. Lieutenant Brakespeare and Polecat follow, to plan the excavation of the payroll gold as soon as the storm blows through. Outside, the rain is starting to come down, which means inside it is starting to come down as well. The spectacle over, the spectators scatter for cover from the storm.

"Can I have another drink?" Pow asks, but no one refills his glass—they've all disappeared. He's killed the bottle of gun oil (Buck had switched the liquids when everyone thought she was pissing), but, of course, he's still thirsty, and so he's rather sorry the contest is over.

The scorpion-sigil skitters, tail waving frantically, trying to find shelter from the raindrops. Pow's interior is starting to feel rather odd. There's a ticklish feeling in his tummy, a funny rustling that makes him want to giggle. Pow unbuttons his sack coat, and something hard butts his hand. He looks down, and sees a scaly nose poking out from a tear in his shirt.

Freddie. The gila monster erupts from Pow's chest and darts forward to snap up the two insect sigils, then scuttles back to safety. A gust of wind has almost taken down one of the canvas walls; another gust blows off half the roof and Pow's hat. A falling viga narrowly misses Pow's head; it lands instead on the table, smashing it. Then something large drops into Pow's lap: the ice elemental's cage. Inside, the elemental has a death-grip on the bars, tiny sangyn colored sparks flashing from its mouth. Pow doesn't need to speak Gramatica to understand the elemental's shrieks for help. As the rest of the roof blows away, Pow fumbles at the cage's door. The door springs open and the elemental springs out, disappearing into the howling electrified night.

Pow lets drop the cage, and raising his face, opens his mouth to the wet wet rain.

Afterword

A thrilling tale of the Old East! Most of the records of the Republic's War Department burned in fire that followed the Upheaval of '15. However, several years later, a few crates of army papers were found in the storeroom of the Bella Union Melodeon, where they were being used as lav paper. Rescued by a visiting scholar who recognized their import during a visit to the facilities while attending a performance by Weatherhead, they were removed to the City Archives.[7] It was there that this historian examined them and discovered within an incomplete set of Fort Gehenna, Ariviapa Territory's post returns.

Through them, it could be determined a Lieutenant Powhatan Rucker did actually serve at that post, though the return made no mention of his death.[8] Further research into City records finds that a Filena Rucker owned a large fishing fleet during this time, but a further connection could not be established.[9] Lieutenant Brakespeare, of course, is familiar to the reader from history, where she

---

7   Hawkins, C.S. "Stop that Flush!: A Surprising Discovery in a Very Surprising Place." *Journal of Philology, Pedagogy, & Practicum.* Temescal: Society of Philology, Pedagogy & Practicum Press, 11-Acatl-156-17.

8   Post Returns of Ariviapa Territory Garrisons, Record Group 93, Box 17, Ledger 12.

9   Anon. *Directory of Persons & Businesses in the City of Califa, Año Abenfaráx 10.* Califa: Alta Califa Publishing.

is more popularly known as the Butcher Brakespeare.[10] Lieutenant Fyrdraaca went on to a much more heroic career: in 2-Tecaptl-72 she led the rebellion against the Huitzil Occupation and helped restore The Warlady Sylvanna Abenfaráx to the Warlord's chair.[11]

No information whatsoever could be unearthed regarding the officer known as Polecat, but this historian finds it hard to believe that such an ineffectual leader would have lasted long on the frontier. The portrait painted of Lieutenant Brakespeare is an intriguing glimpse of a woman not yet corrupted by power, and still with the potential for greatness, a potential that she chose instead to squander in tyranny and blood.[12]

The legend of the water vampire is a common one in arid Arivaipa. To some extent this affliction can be tied to the iconography of the Flayed Priests of the Huitzil Empire, who are allergic to darkness, not light, and who consume flesh, not blood.

---

10   *General Court Martial Proceedings of Cyrenacia Sidonia Brakespeare ov Haðraaða, Alacran Regiment, Army of Califa.* Califa: Army of Califa Press, Año Abenfaráx 22.

11   Cassidy, K. *Buck's Saber: Juliet Fyrdraaca & The Flamingo Rebellion.* Fishtown: Roswell & Trillian Press, 6-Ocelotl-156-17.

12   *Proceedings of the Capital Trial of Cyrenacia Sidonia Brakespeare ov Haðraaða Before the Duque de Espejo y Ahumado.* Cuidad Anahautl: Privately Published.

Metal More Attractive

QUEEN. *Come hither, my dear Hamlet, and sit by me.*
HAMLET. *No, good mother, here's metal more attractive.*

Hamlet
Act III, Scene II

BOOK I

Thy Baited Hook

I.

So, here we have Hardhands in a bar. It's not exactly entirely a bar, but then he's not exactly entirely Hardhands either, at least not yet. At this moment, he's only fifteen years old and his hands are still white and tender; so too is his conscience. Both hands and head are soon to get much tougher, but right now he's still rather sweet.

Ice cream is the joint yummy, not bugjuice, but to the back there is a bar-like counter, thus a bar in spirit if not in name.

Having strode through the swinging curtain of beads which hides the door, forward to this bar-like counter sails young Hardhands for to get the barkeep's attention. The clientele at Guerrero's Helados y Refrescos is thick both in person and in odor, so Hardhands must push and breathe lightly, but he's not to be stopped once he's started. Eventually he reaches his objective, which is well scarred from digging spoons and sliding glasses.

Achieving his goal, Hardhands-Who-Will-Be leans on the bar, very cool-like, and he says to the barkeep, very cool-like: "Have you seen Jack?" He has to shout because there's a tin-pan band playing in a darkened corner, off-key and whinier than love, and this shouting somewhat scotches his suave effect.

The barkeep can hear Hardhands, but she has not seen Jack. Nor has she seen Hardhands' money, or heard his order, so she pays no never mind to his question, but, rather, spits in the glass she holds, and rubs around the rim with a towel. Thus clean, or at least cleanish, the glass is hung on the rack above and the barkeep spits into an entirely new dirty glass. There's an identical woman hanging on the wall behind her, doing the identical same thing, only somehow that woman seems a bit nicer, as though she'd probably answer Hardhands' question, but facing away, as she is, she doesn't even notice him, so there's no help there. Even staring at his own splendid reflection, he's pretty much on his own.

Someone falls off the balcony with a crash, and the barkeep flicks her towel. An egregore built like canister shot, with tusks the size of plantanos and floppy basset ears, rumbles out of the darkness and hefts the splattered form outward. Too much sugar, not enough catch.

Hardhands glares, a fifteen-year-old glare that has the entire force of being the only grandson of the Pontifexa of Califa behind it. Spit, rub, spit, rub is what he gets for his efforts, and his more urgent repeat of the question, which is really now a demand, gets rub, spit, rub, spit. The drover at the other end of the bar warbles drunkenly for another Choronzon's Delight, heavy on the caramel whip, and the barkeep abandons her spitting and rubbing to bob to his bidding. She's not deaf at all, the tin-pan band is not that loud; she just doesn't like uppity young men who stride into her bar and plunk down attitude instead of cash.

The dangling mirror has suddenly gotten more interesting, and Hardhands is a tad distracted. He came to the most notorious helado joint in the City to try to hire the most notorious plunger in the City to do a dirty deed at a cut-rate price, but he's now mesmerized by the slinky entity in the slinky silk ribbands now slinking before the band. It's not the slinking itself that enthralls, no, it's just that the slinkster seems to have tentacles instead of arms; boneless and tendril-like, they wiggle and wave. Its head is rather pointy, and its eyes rather low set and round, squid-like, its skin glittering like coldfire in the cigarillo smoky darkness—a water elemental way out of its element.

"I've seen Jack."

Hardhands turns sideways, away from the loligo gyrating before him in the mirror, thus behind him by the band. The muleskinner probably hasn't had a bath since the midwife dipped his squalling infant-self in milk minutes after he was born, and his face is a beach of rippling wrinkles, but his little marble eyes are quite alert. He's been sloshing the complimentary bread into the complimentary olive oil, and he's left little oily dribbles on the bar top and squishy black finger marks on the bread. Handhands is pretty darn glad he's already had nuncheon with his beloved grandmamma, whom he is going to hire Springheel Jack to kill.

"But just 'cause I've seen Jack," continues the muleskinner, "don't mean that Jack wants to see you."

"I daresay he'll want to see my money," says Hardhands loftily.

"My throat wouldn't mind seeing your divas." The muleskinner nudges his parfait glass. Whipped cream is just a memorable smear around the top edge of the glass, and there is a little tiny smudge of melted ice cream in the bottom. Another suck on the straw and the glass will be dry, oh dear.

Handhands is stuck now. It's gold or information. He digs reluctantly into his purse, which practically squeals when he pries it open, and, fancy that, the barkeep has suddenly found her ears, and with them her hearing.

"You want?" she asks, sliding back, looking lively. She's abandoned two miners fresh in from the fields, gold dust flecking their eyelashes and hair, blisters raw on their hands, who are playing a friendly game of mumblety-pegas they sip their sodas at the far end of the bar.

"Pink Lady Parfait," says the muleskinner, who'd been drinking something cheaper before, but the Pontifexa's grandson can hardly expect to fandango into a bar, even one that doesn't serve booze, and not pay for what he gets, and pay well, too.

The preparation of the Pink Lady Parfait is temporarily halted by a dust-up. The mumblety-peg knife has slipped, and one of the miners is now very friendly with the wooden bar top. She wrenches her hand free with a whistle of pain, and cracks foreheads with her friend. For a moment things look pretty rough, and Handhands wishes he had not worn white. But when the barkeep raps her blackjack down on the counter, the reverberating whackety-whack noise is enough to make the pugilists reconsider their fun. They sheepishly thump fists together in apology and go back to digging for the cherries in their Cheery Cherry Freezie-Slurps. The music continues to whine, but the loligo elemental has slithered off.

"So, Jack," says Hardhands, who has now patiently sat through the stirring and shaking of the Pink Lady Parfait, the dipping of the spoon, the slurping of the straw, the chewing of the soggy caramel corn that always sinks to the bottom of the glass. Lacking the requisite teeth, this last action really qualified as gumming, not chewing, but the old muleskinner gets the job done, and then he's feeling pretty darn frisky. Not frisky enough to actually give Springheel Jack's location up to this uppity young pup who just swirled in like he owns the place (which technically he does, well, at least his grandmamma does, as she owns every square inch of the City), all champagne shiny boots and gleaming bone-white hair, expensive as hell. But frisky enough to continue to pretend that he knows where Springheel Jack is, even though he has hell-all of a clue.

"Sew buttons," says the muleskinner. His straw slurps air with a forlorn rasp. The barkeep is ready with another Pink Lady; she knows this game by heart, string along the sucker until his money runs out. She knows exactly who Hardhands is, of course—Banastre Micajah Haðraaða, Duke of Califa—but she's a Radical Chaoist and likes to skate on political thin ice, so she plunks the Pink Lady down and gives Hardhands a bit of a smarmy grin. Hardhands returns the smarmy grin with an ice blue stare, a thin cold look that suddenly remembers the barkeep that the Pontifexa's grandson is both quick on the trigger and pretty much above the law. She's used to the first, she and her bulletproof bouncer can handle that just fine, but that second—she sidles back to the miners. The muleskinner is on his own.

II.

So, here we have Hardhands at home, if you can call a four-hundred-room monstrosity, all soaring blue minarets and towering arches, fifty bathrooms with fifty ice-cold floors, home, which he does, quite happily. Bilskinir House, looking out over a lazy ocean, its back to the City and thus to the known world.

Hardhands leaves his horse carelessly cropping daisies on the front lawn, vaults front steps, and races into the Entrada, the bang of the door behind him, thunderously. He tears by Paimon, in a rush, in a hurry, in a snit the size of the deep blue sea, scattering the Butler's brushes and leaving elegantly smeared boot tracks on the Butler's foamy white floor. His braids are crackling with annoyance, his sack coat flaps like the wings of an irritated bird, he's pissed because he bought that muleskinner five Pink Lady Parfaits and two plates of jamon y guava sandwies and all he got for his philanthropy was the sobbed story of the death of Evil Murdoch, a mule who had been the very epitome of mules, the beauty of the world and a fantastic spitter with teeth the size of dinner plates. The story had been sad, all right—flippy ears, shifting earth, skittering hooves and a long long fall to a very large splat—but Hardhands is interested not in dead mules but in living outlaws and soon-to-be-dead grandmammas, and he had sat through the woeful tale impatient and annoyed. Afterwards, he and the bereft muleskinner had strolled to the cruddy sinks at the back of the bar, where strenuous exercise (on Hardhands' part) then elicited from the weepy skinner the admission that he had only once seen Springheel Jack at a distance, in a bagnio long ago closed, and never again.

Now Hardhands is late, and he's in a fury because he's late, and his visit South of the Slot has been for naught, and he's down twenty-seven divas in gold, and the muleskinner has gotten strawberry syrup and blood on his new white sack coat. Also, because if he doesn't find Springheel Jack, he's going to have to kill his grandmamma himself. He's fond of the old girl and would rather not, really, but she has given him no choice. Regretful, but true.

He races up the wide marble steps, two-by-two, and happily they are already dry, not that he cares, as washing them is someone else's job, someone else's knees. A sheaf of staff officers are descending downward, the Pontifexa's afternoon briefing is done, and they are laden down with redboxes, round files, lapdesks, and dispatch cases. Hardhands tears through the yaller dogs, sending skirts and lovelocks flying, barking at them mockingly. The officers, wary of Hardhands' stunningly perfect aim and hair-trigger temper, do not dare yip back, but continue down the stairs, mumbling derisively under their breaths.

It is sixteen hundred and Hardhands is supposed to be at the Blue Duck by seventeen for sound check, yet he still needs to bathe, to change, to redo his hair, to kiss his grandmamma good evening. Cursing the muleskinner, he storms up the second flight of stairs and down the narrow hallway, his urgent shadow rippling off glass cases, the woven roses beneath his feet muffling his tread. In his bedroom, he chucks his hat on the red velvet bolster, disturbing the cat curled in a circle on his pillow. He flings his shoulder holster on the dresser and hops out of his skirts, into his dressing gown. The cat has awakened, irritated at the noise, and is now scratching at a carved pineapple on the four-hundred-year old bed. Hardhands was born in that bed, fifteen years before, but if he continues down his path, he certainly will not die there.

"Paimon!" he hollers, ceilingward. "I need you to arrange my hair!"

Back down the hall he goes, not quite as fast, unfastening his braids, snarling the skeins of ivory hair with clawing fingers. He's thinking hard, young Hardhands is. If not Springheel Jack, then who? He once had to shoot a horse that broke its neck trying to jump a cow, but that's not the same as killing a sweet little grandmamma with imperious red hair and a darling pink smile. Can he do it? Can he not?

At the bathroom door, above the happy noise of blessed hot water, Hardhands' consideration is arrested by a piping voice, a wispy little lisp, the high-pitched sound of doom, of gloom, of bloody destiny, of horrific fate, of—

"Bwaaaan!" He turns reluctantly, and a fat little whiteness is hurtling through the air upon him, all bubbling curls and floaty lace. He catches, awkwardly, a fat little chin hitting his own square chin, a bare white foot connecting hard with his kidneys.

"You should be in bed," he says, gritting through fifty fathoms of thundering pain.

"Baftime is funtime," says his Little Tiny Doom. Little Tiny Doom smells like milk and toast, is somewhat grubby, and Hardhands will be damned if he will marry her, not a wit of it. Not a jot, not a tiddle, not at all. Period. Finale. Punto. That's it. The end.

"Quack quack!" adds Little Tiny Doom, in case Hardhands has missed her point.

Hardhands has been on this boat before, and he's eager to get off before he gets soaked. Bathtime is not funtime when it involves red rubber ducks, slippery soap, and shampoo wigs. He doesn't have time for this; the band will be waiting for him, the show is sold right out, and he still has to evoke a drummer to replace their previous percussion dæmon, which spontaneously combusted during The Tygers of Wrath's last gig. He tries to disengage from Little Tiny Doom, but Little Tiny Doom has arms of steel and toes of clinginess and she will not let go of him.

Little Tiny Doom—that is to say, Cyrenacia Sidonia Haðraaða ov Brakespeare, as she is known on the official documents she is too young to sign—adores Hardhands. She loves his height, his splendid glittering clothes, and his splendid shining hair which reminds her of the flossy white candy she gets when she goes to Woodward's Gardens to ride on the Circular Boat. One fat little hand grabs a wad of braid and into her mouth it goes, to see if the shiny white floss tastes good, which thanks to judicious use of bay rum hair oil, it does not.

"Paimon!" Hardhands hollers, and there Paimon is, bearing warm towels and his favorite hairbrush, the one with the badger bristles and the gold loligo crest.

"Sieur Duke?"

"She's eating my hair." A duke should not sound so whiny. Authority is equal parts arrogance and confidence, which Hardhands knows full well but has forgotten in his trauma of being cannibalized by a three-year-old.

"Madama," Paimon says in his dark blue voice. Cyrenacia knows this tone; it is the tone of bed without story, of bread without milk, of bath without duck, and she spits and smiles sweetly in the Butler's direction. She's three years old but she's no fool.

"I'm in a hurry, take her and get her clean or whatever you are going to do with her, and hurry about it because I need you to do my hair. I want a chignon tonight and I haven't got much time— ooff." This ooof has naught to do with time and everything to do grabby hands and dangling gold ear hoops. "Stop it!"

"Bwaaanie—" says Cyrenacia, so cutely. She is a darling child even if she does have only a few wispy curls and a tendency to burp loudly at the dinner table. Her lisping version of Hardhands' name is just darling, too, but darlingness is wasted on Hardhands, who feels it has no place in his carefully cultivated dark mysterious image. Ban, as he is called by his grandmamma, his leman, and the cheap yellow press, is tolerable, but Bannie is beyond the limit.

"Take her—!" Disengaged, and out-thrust, Tiny Doom dangles towards Paimon. Her mouth is starting to squeeze together in a little pink pout. The pout is a prelude to howls and the howls a prelude to a furious grandmamma and then they shall all be in that boat, only it will now be sinking and, battered by grandmamma's ire, they will have forgotten how to swim.

"Sieur—"

The howl is as high pitched as the whistle of steam from a kettle and as hot. Hardhands freezes. He's manifested a Tunnel of Set in his bedroom, he's jumped off Battery Sligo into the boiling sea one hundred feet below, and once he set his hair on fire for a triple dog dare, but now he's stuck like glue. His nerve is being yanked out of his body by the thread of that ghastly sound, and if there were a well nearby, he'd drop Tiny Doom into it and slam the lid shut. Alas, no well, only a brimming bath, toward which, in a burst of desperate creativity Hardhands now turns, but before he can drown the child, Paimon retrieves her from his panicked grasp.

Tap-tap-tap-tap echoes down the stairs like gunshots, the Pontifexa rat-tat-tatting to her great-granddaughter's rescue on high red heels of fire, feathers flying off her wrapper in her rush. She is trailed by seven anxious dogs who are braying in sympathy, and she too is now snapping with anger that her afternoon massage has been interrupted.

"What are you doing to that child, Banastre Haðraaða?" she demands. "You there, sush!" That to the howling dogs, who do sush, for the Pontifexa speaks and is obeyed.

"She was eating my hair!"

"Pah! Why did you let her? Stop that caterwauling, my dove, you are giving Grandmamma a headache and Grandmamma already has enough of a headache, she needs no more." This is said with a suitable guilt-making glance at Hardhands, which guilt it does not induce because he is not going to marry a squalling three-year-old—end of discussion, let us not speak on it again.

Grandmamma's Dove has made her point, and now turns all smiles and sweetness, enough to melt heart, if not hands, of stone.

Paimon peels her nightgown and plunks her in the soapy water, twisting bubbles into a crown and bobbing her red devil duck on a tidal wave of foam.

The Pontifexa beams at her sweet wet little heir. "You were never so cute when you were that age, Banastre."

"Ha! I had more hair and I was never so fat."

"So you say, but I know better." The Pontifexa links one rounded white arm through Hardhands' own sinewy forearm, and together they leave the sloshy bathroom, the mirrors now refracting the pink bobbing child and the blue scrubbing butler.

The Pontifexa and Hardhands have already had the Fight, with the screaming and the cursing and the dire threats: incarceration, exile, defenestration, decapitation. They've had the Pleading, the Urgings of Duty, of Honor, of Sacred Trust, of Love & Debt. They've had the *I Ask So Little of You You Ask The One Thing I Can Not Give.* Now they are having the *I am Ignoring You You Will Do What I Want Anyway Because I said So Damn Your Eyes if I Will We'll See Who is Boss.*

Rub two Haðraaða Wills together and you'll get, well, you'll get nothing at all, cancellation, void, null, stalemate. But the clock is ticking: they've got three days to make up their mind whose Will is to prevail: in three days Julien Brakespeare, Tiny Doom's daddy, is leaving Califa. As Tiny Doom's father he has the right to remove her with him—a nasty court battle has settled that question—and the thought of Julien Brakespeare in final possession of her heir sends the color soaring in the Pontifexa's normally pale face. She is determined that Hardhands' rights as Cyrenacia's husband will prevail over the rights of Cyrenacia's father. The rights of Cyrenacia's mother, she who would have been Georgiana IV, are null and void for Sidonia Haðraaða ov Brakespeare is six months dead. Died in childbed is the official explanation, but the Pontifexa believes that not at all. Julien killed her granddaughter, she is sure of it, but there's no proof.

"Are you still sulking, Banastre?" the Pontifexa demands, stopping in front of Hardhands' bedroom.

"No," he says, although of course he is. He's trying harder not to show it now, though. No point in putting the Pontifexa further up. He's pretending to give in to get exactly what he wants.

"Sulk all you want now, but I expect to see you smile on your wedding day," the Pontifexa says. She is small, but she has incredibly sharp teeth. This wedding day is scheduled for two days hence; dangerously close to the date upon which the Pontifexa must hand her heir over to Julien, but the delay cannot be helped. The Pontifexa, with much consultation with Paimon, has pored over the Almanack to ensure that the wedding occurs on a day in which all the aspects, portents, and sigils align auspiciously and the Magickal Current is high. This delay has caused the Pontifexa no end of knuckle-cracking but has been quite useful for young Ban.

The Pontifexa follows her grandson into his bedroom and begins to fiddle with his hair. She has clever fingers, the Pontifexa does, and soon Hardhands' wayward locks are smoothed and twisted, secured with a wide silver comb. This dressing comes not without its price, and Hardhands' reflection in the mirror is, despite his best efforts, somewhat scowly. The Pontifexa is serene and deft.

"I am sorry, my darling, that I cannot let you do as you will in this matter," she says.

"Um," says Hardhands, for he's already said everything else.

"We can't let Julien Brakespeare have Cyrenacia."

"Why not?"

"Ha!" says the Pontifexa, an explosive *ha* that has a myriad of meanings in it, none of them good. "He's already ruined one of my heirs; I'll not have him ruin the other. Had he not induced your sister to throw over her duty to her city and run off with him, she should be safe within our House still, and the stability of our City not in doubt. He's a crawling serpentine fancy man, and goddess knows what he'll do to her if he keeps her."

She puts the last hair pin in Hardhands' chignon and places narrow hands on his wide shoulders. Their reflections stare back at them, one sullen, the other a tad bit sad. She slides feathered arms around her grandson's broad paisley shoulders and says, in a softer voice: "Don't think, my baby, that I don't know what I am asking you to give up. It is a lot to suddenly ask, when I've asked nothing before."

So she says, and she is right. Until six months ago, Hardhands was nothing but his grandmother's darling boy, who could do whatever he wanted and whom no one dared gainsay. Now suddenly he is the hope of the Haðraaða line, and he wants none of it. Hardhands cannot hold the Steel Fan that is the scepter of the City, for that honor is passed only through female blood, but he can protect the Heir Apparent—which means marrying her so that, during her minority, her father can have no claim of influence over her. Hardhands does not want to marry Little Tiny Doom. He has other plans, in which a dynastic marriage does not figure. He has other loves, too.

However. For the moment, Hardhands wipes the scowl off his face and turns about to pull his sweet little grandmamma, the only parent he has ever known, onto his lap. He kisses her white forehead and says: "I bow to your Will, madama. In this as in all things."

The Pontifexa smiles. "You are my darling boy."

"I am," Hardhands agrees, and they embrace. His grandmamma's hair smells citrusy smooth, like orange blossoms, and this fragrance remembers him when he fit in her lap rather than the other way around. Sometimes he is a wee bit sad those days are gone. For a moment he wavers and then he sternly straightens himself up. He has no choice. Him or her.

The Pontifexa removes herself from Hardhands' lap and clicks to the door. There she pauses, and turns back, patting her mussed coils of sunset-colored hair back into place. Hardhands is leaning over his dressing table stripping a thin line of black paint along his eyelid when she speaks again:

"How is the helado at Guerrero's these days?"

His hand jerks, and he almost puts his eye out with the eyeliner brush. He looks beyond his reflection, to his grandmother's serene steely blue gaze. Paimon has apparently finished with Tiny Doom because he now stands behind his mistress, an enormous blue shadow that seems to darken the room. The Pontifexa is still smiling, but that is not necessarily a Good Thing.

"Yummy, as usual," he says, pleased that his voice does not even quiver.

"With the wedding so near, and Julien still in town, darling, I think it best not to take chances in such a questionable neighborhood. Perhaps I should ask Godelieve to detail you a guard." The Pontifexa is very subtle, but our boy gets her drift.

"I go armed," he says. "And anyway, Julien has no reason to challenge you now. He knows that he has won."

"Still, there is always the possibility that he could learn of our plans, darling, and in desperation take desperate measures. Don't underestimate him."

Hardhands smiles his most boyish carefree smile. "Never mind Julien. He'll never know what hit him. And it would look very odd if suddenly I was bristling with armed lackeys everywhere I went. We don't want to put his nose up, do we?"

"Of course, you are right, Banastre, but still, I cannot rest until the baby is safe. I do so worry. You will be careful, no? I have borne all the loss I can." The Pontifexa's expression, however, belies her words. He's being warned, and he knows it. But a warning will not change his mind.

"Of course, Grandmamma."

"Thank you, sweetness—yes, Paimon, I can hear you breathing down my neck. What do you want?'"

Paimon says, in his gentle rolling voice, "Madama Brakespeare is in bed, awaiting her goodnight story."

"Thank you, Paimon. I shall come. Have a wonderful show, Banastre. I will see you in the morning at breakfast." The Pontifexa sends a kiss winging its way through the air, which her grandson does not try to catch. She closes the door gently behind her. Hardhand grimaces at his own reflection and goes back to his toilette.

When Hardhands finally gets to the Blue Duck, his resolve is stuck as tightly to his Will as a whore sticks to cash. Forget Springheel Jack. Hardhands has thought of metal more attractive. He has remembered in his readings, always eclectic, a receipt for a topical poison. Made from a variety of esoteric ingredients, this poison is fast and furious when it touches the skin, and it leaves not even the tiniest trace, death seeming wholly natural, although a bit surprising. Along with the receipt for the poison is receipt for an antidote that will allow the poisoner to infect without being infected. Hardhands may not be able to stab his grandmamma, drown her in her bath, shoot her in the head, or crack her soft white neck with his soft white hands, but he has full confidence he can kiss her, having done so a thousand times before.

III.

So, here we have Hardhands in the Magick Box. Today he has an entourage suitable to his exalted state: there's Hardhands' leman, lips somewhat compressed, and Hardhands' two hounds, gray as seasalt, and, annoyingly, Hardhands' Little Tiny Doom, along because the Pontifexa has court cases to sit in on and Paimon is making teaberry jam and does not want sticky fingers messing with his sugar. Since she has dressed herself with minimal adult supervision, Cyrenacia is the flashiest of the trio: pink velvet dress, scuffed cowboy boots, and one of the Pontifexa's discarded weasel tippets. Hardhands is in a good enough mood to admit that she does look rather doll.

He is in a good mood because the Tygers of Wrath's gig the previous night had been incredible, fantastic, amazing, their Best Show Ever. The band had practically engulfed the Blue Duck in an inferno of explosive rhythm. The Siege of San Quentin was not as cataclysmically loud. Hardhands' evocation was spot-on, terrific, sharp as a scalpel, and the percussion dæmon that had ensued had been an egregore of least the sixth level, as tall as a horsecar, wide as a street. Such a noise had rolled out of its enormous mouth that the avid ears closest to its maw would probably be bleeding for the next week. If the Blue Duck had had any windows, surely they would have shattered. If the Blue Duck had had a roof, surely it would have raised. Ah, what a show. Even being ordered to babysit Little Tiny Doom cannot spoil the afterglow.

The Magick Box is all darkness and boo-spooky atmosphere, with the usual boo-spooky magickal type stuff hanging on the walls: dried bats, twisted galangal root, black candles, etc. The stuff of which clichés are made, and Hardhands is not interested in clichés, only in pure hard magick, the stuff of Concentration, of Focus, of Absolute Pinpointed Will. He's spent years working on his Art, and by now it's pretty Artful, so he requires not the silly props. He doesn't need dried bats or twisted galangal or black candles, and so he strides by these objects to what he does need, which is kept locked behind the counter, away from amateurs, novices, and greenhorns. The Good Stuff. Expensive and Dangerous as a riptide.

There's a servitor behind the counter, an egregore so advanced that it looks just like a woman. Her eyes are a bit flat and her hair has a rather vivid grassy sheen to it, but otherwise you'd pass her on the street and not even notice. Most servitors never get this advanced, too dangerous to give them such power, but the owner of the Magick Box is perfectly in control of all her sigils and she's more fond of windsurfing than of standing behind a counter selling chicken feet to Adept-Want-To-Bes, thus this incredibly detailed autonomous servitor doing the dirty work for her.

"Do not touch the Hands of Glory," says the egregore. She is talking to Tiny Doom, not to Hardhands, of course.

"Cyrenacia!" barks her uncle. Cyrenacia is barked at so infrequently that she is immune to the bite, but she is bored with the nasty smelling wax thing anyway, so she quits fiddling. "Keep an eye on her, Relais."

Relais vaguely makes motion towards the child, but his heart's not in it, and she knows it. She disappears around a bookcase and Relais lets her go. He's hung over from the night before, and he is worried that his eyes are looking puffy and red, so he has not the interest in small annoying girls.

Hardhands and the egregore have a brief consultation. He knows what he wants and she gives it to him, measuring strange smells and stranger colors into little twists of paper, small smoked glass jars, and, in one case, a pearly vial that is sealed tight with a tiny but powerful sigil.

Jingle-jangle at the door, and though Hardhands does not turn around, he does not need to turn around, he can tell from the sound of the footfalls, from the scent of the cologne, from the burn in the bottom of his belly exactly who has just walked in.

"A pound of bear grease," Hardhands says calmly. He is not his grandmamma's beloved grandson for naught.

"Black bear or cinnamon bear?" asks the egregore.

"White," says Hardhands.

The egregore looks at Hardhands. Grease from an albino bear is rare and as volatile as a fifteen-year-old-boy, which the egregore has suddenly remembered Hardhands is. For all his concentrated Will, he is not an Adept. But he is the Pontifexa's grandson.

The egregore hesitates.

"Well, have you not got it?" Hardhands asks impatiently.

The egregore decides. "Ayah, I have it so, but it is locked. I must dish out, wait here."

The egregore disappears into the darkness at the back of the store. Hardhands then realizes voices behind him: a tiny lisping voice and a lighter adult voice engaged in conversation regarding the sweetness of little puppies.

He jerks around, but the voices are hidden by a bookshelf, which he fair vaults around because he had totally forgotten Little Tiny Doom, and obviously so too had Relais, damn his eyes.

On the other side of the bookshelf, Hardhands' small niece and fiancée is sitting on the floor with a slick dog head in her lap, pulling slick dog ears. Next to her a man leans, elegant in blinding white, also petting a slick dog. Child and man have identical brilliant red hair, although Tiny Doom's color riots through squashy curls and her companion's hair is sheared short to his skull, thus sticks up in tiny pinprick spikes. The man is staring down at the child, avid.

"Cyrenacia!" says Hardhands sharply.

Cyrenacia looks up and waves. "Hiwya, Bwannie! This puppy has twenty nears."

Sometimes it is impossible to understand what the hell she is saying; not that Hardhands cares what she is saying, but not caring doesn't make it any less annoying. He would snatch the child up, but he can't because her father is blocking his grab, and also because his knees are somewhat weak.

Julien Brakespeare releases the dog ears he is fondling and smiles at Hardhands: "Ave, your grace."

Hardhands is not, as previously noted, his grandmamma's grandson for nothing. Though Julien's smile makes his heart flip-flop, he returns a wintry frosty cold smile that will later make battle-hard soldiers weep like little babies but which at this moment, on this person, has null effect.

"Ave, Lord Brakespeare."

Relais appears at Hardhands' side, glaring in an ugly way and clutching at Hardhands' white silk elbow. Both Hardhands and Julien Brakespeare ignore him, and he tightens his grip on Hardhands, not that that will make any difference.

"As it is so," Julien Brakespeare replies and the two men bow and touch clenched fists gently together. The only reason that Julien Brakespeare's lungs are still on the inside of his body, instead of flapping around outside, is because the Pontifexa has bound herself to the rule of law. She is a liberal tyrant with specific ideas regarding the self-imposed limits of her own power and her place within the framework of justice. The Superior Court of Califa upheld Julien Brakespeare's right to his own child, and the Pontifexa will not move against that—at least not publicly.

"Grrrrr," Cyrenacia growls, yanking on the hem of Hardhands' kilt. "Grrrrr . . ."

The two men stare at each other. An outside observer could think that their eyes are locked in hate, but they would be wrong.

Cyrenacia growls again, and whines a little, trying to scratch her ear with the tip of her cowboy boot, just like a puppy can. She has decided recently that being a puppy is more fun than being a little girl, and she has been driving Hardhands, her grandmamma, and her grandmamma's suffering staff wild with her yipping, gamboling, barking, and insistence on lapping water out of a dish. Right now her whine is not driving anyone wild; it is being totally ignored.

"How are you, your grace?" Julien asks.

"Well, thank you, and yourself, my lord?" Hardhands says politely.

The two men have not taken eyes off each other. They are in public and must be polite. Then Julien says one word, a harsh guttural word that blossoms a brief burst of dark red fire in the air. The word is in Gramatica, of course, the language of those things which cannot be spoken, and this word would have turned to ashes—literally—in an ordinary mouth. Julien Brakespeare has not an ordinary mouth, though, he's an adept of the rank of $0=II$, the only such Califa has seen since the death of the Georgiana I, some seventy years previously, and in his mouth the word is forceful and compelling. The sea-salt gray dogs flop over, pink noses tipping upward in sleep. The egregore, who was slopping the albino bear grease in a ramekin, stops in mid-glop, eyes suddenly dead and empty. Relais's grip relaxes and he sits down with a thump that no one notices. Cyrenacia's whining stops. A sudden silence cups the Magick Box, a silence then broken by Julien's soft voice: "I must leave in three days or your grandmamma will have my lungs."

"She will not act against the law," Hardhands says. "She'll try to get around it, but she'll not go obviously against it."

Julien sighs, a sigh which holds the weight of the world in it. "I fear that the Pontifexa has blood, not justice, on her mind. I did not kill Sidonia, Ban. I swear it. She died in childbed, died of our son, leaving me alone and bereft. All I wish is to live in my House, peacefully with my daughter, and to forget the past. But the Pontifexa will not realize it, she will not accept my sincerity. I truly rue,

I do, Banastre, and so did Sidonia. She died with Georgiana's name on her lips and wanted nothing more than to see us reconciled."

"I told you, Julien," Hardhands says impatiently. "She plans on moving around the law with this sub-rosa marriage. She is too conscious of her high standing position to move against you any other way. And her plans are worthless now—I will forestall them, as I promised. The marriage will never happen; she'll be dead first."

"Yet she thinks she acts from the best of intentions," says Julien.

"Ha! She says she acts from love—what the hell does she know of love? She is duty and honor and nothing more. She only knows her own Will, the Wills of those around her are invisible and irrelevant to her, she asks for others to sacrifice, but she will give up nothing. Damn her. Damn her to hell!"

"You speak treason," Julien says, grinning.

"Ayah, so? It's the truth and we know it. Anyway, it doesn't matter—none of this matters, for she'll be soon enough dead and you will have nothing to fear, Julien," Hardhands says, breathlessly.

Their hands meet again, only this time, as the avid audience is now blissfully unaware, their fingers intertwine, and then their bodies follow suit. Since the trial began they have seen each other infrequently, and then under the lens of the Pontifexa, the court, or the diva-dreadful newsrags. Secret meetings have been few and far in between, but when so, they have been hot and burning, and full of schemes. Hardhands is riding the rapids of youth, and all he can think of is Julien, and the force and fire of their love. Nothing else seems to matter.

After a few seconds, Julien disengages and says: "What of Springheel Jack?"

Hardhands answers, somewhat distracted: "I couldn't reach him, but it matters not. I have a better plan. Less messy."

Julien frowns. "And this would be, darling?"

Hardhands tells Julien about the poison and his plans for administering it to the Pontifexa. Julien's frown disappears. He kisses Hardhands tenderly, and for a minute Hardhands feels like a shell has exploded inside his skull. Julien's love is that potent. Their reverie is broken by the sound of growling coming from somewhere around their knees. They break apart and look down. Tiny Doom is gamboling around their boots, yipping and growling.

"Get up, Cyrenacia," Hardhands commands. "That floor is filthy."

"Woof-woof!" says Cyrenacia, worrying the hem of his kilt with sharp little teeth.

"Stop that!"

Cyrenacia paws at his boots, begging like a puppy who wants to be petted. This doggie thing is getting out of hand. It was cute for the first five minutes, but those five minutes are long since past. Before Hardhands can do anything to scotch her behavior, Julien reaches with one somewhat unkindly hand and hauls the child upward.

"You were told to stop," he says.

Cyrenacia halts in mid-growl. Her mouth opens, to roar, and then her father says: "Don't you dare," and such is her surprise that no sound actually comes out. "This child has terrible manners, Banastre."

Hardhands wrinkles his white brow. Tiny Doom is annoying, true, but he'd never particularly noticed terrible manners. In fact, both Paimon and the Pontifexa are harridans when it comes to "please," "thank you," and "excuse me," and thus Hardhands and Tiny Doom rarely forget to echo these sentiments appropriately.

"She has been under the Pontifexa's thumb for only six months and look at her." Julien hauls the child up higher, in such a fashion that she cannot possibly wiggle her way free. Her face is screwed up, but she makes no sound, staring up at her father with eyes like little blue marbles. "Why was she permitted to leave Bilskinir dressed like that? She looks like a rag picker, not the Heir to the House Bilskinir and the City of Califa."

Hardhands looks at his niece. "I thought she looked rather swell," he says, somewhat doubtfully. "I mean, she's cute, isn't she?"

He reaches over and takes Tiny Doom out of Julien's grip. She's as rigid as a wooden doll, but as soon as Julien lets go of her, she snatches at Hardhands and holds on to him for dear life, clutching at his shoulders, her knees digging into his sides. Her hair smells orangy; Hardhands is suddenly reminded of his darling grandmamma.

"Tiresome, I think is the word you are looking for," Julien says. He brushes his hands together; he has not taken his gloves off, and now they are slightly grubby, for Hardhands had been right; the floor Cyrenacia had been crawling on is filthy. "Not that it shall matter much, soon."

Cyrenacia is now snuffling into Hardhands' neck, so he digs into the pocket of his frockcoat for a clean hankie and while he mops her nose, he and Julien make their final plans. Then Julien flicks another Gramatica word off his tongue. This word is bright cerise and it fills the room with a jagged light. When the light fades, the hounds roll over and yawn, the egregore finishes glopping, Relais sits up suddenly, and Julien is gone. Tiny Doom howls when Hardhands tries to put her down. Even when they stop for ice cream and pink popcorn—at a place cleaner than Guererro's but not as flavorable—she will not let go.

IV.

So, here we have Hardhands in his parlor, his office, his Conjuring Room. As he does not rely on atmosphere to get his Will off, the room is simple and compact, with none of the falderal so often associated with the magickal arts. The walls are curved and white, the floor soft blue, and at the apex of the domed ceiling a circular window stares like an eye into the night sky. As with most liminal spaces, the room is round.

Handhands stands in the middle of a circle drawn out of blue cornmeal. His eyes are closed, his arms extended outward, as though to catch the magickal Current, and the air surrounding him glitters and sparks from the sound that is humming in his chest. This noise does not throb and blast like the noise from a percussion dæmon, but it's a pretty darn big vibration and from its incredible vibrato all the nasty little flourishes that cluster around the Current, that cluster around the Will, that just plain cluster, evaporate in horror. Hardhands can banish like no other; Aethyr that has been scrubbed clean by his aural vibrations stays clean for days, even when the circle is dropped. He's good at pushing things away, is our boy, and not so perhaps clever at drawing them in, but he is still young.

The last vowel vibrated and the banishing done, Hardhands launches right into the opening of a Vortex. He spins his arms, stopping at each quarter of the circle, to expel an incendiary Gramatica word. These sounds hang in the air, incandescent coldfire flames that flicker brilliant colors off Hardhands' set face, striping him as if with warpaint. When he is done, and the last explosive word burns before him, patterning a burning crosshatch of four arrows, eight points in all, he gathers into himself all of his Force and Fire, his Galvanic Heart, his Steel Will, and flings this mass of energy outward with a flick of opening fists. The force of his fire hits the Vortex, which catches it and holds it in the center of its pointed web. For a minute the energy hangs there in the middle cross-hatching, and then Hardhands reaches out with a casual hand, and gives the topmost arrow point a good spin.

The Vortex begins to spin, slowly first, then gaining momentum, the colors of the arrow points swirling into one sinuous octarine blur. As the Vortex picks up movement, it starts to hum, a low sound that cannot be heard but which rattles the floor beneath, shakes the wall, and slowly turns into a gathering roar that echoes outward. The floor is shivering, the paint on the wall rippling. A crack has appeared in the center of the Vortex, and through this crack spills a dark blackness that is blindingly bright. Anyone outside the circle who looked into the Vortex's heart would find their eyeballs dribbling right out of their sockets.

Hardhands throws his head back, his loosened hair whipping loligo-like around his face and chest. "Χηαψοφαθυε!"

The Vortex sucks into itself with a thunderclap. The window above cracks, and little fragments of glass shower downward, speckling Hardhands' hair like falling stars. Bilskinir shudders once, like a man who has just been drenched with a bucket full of cold water, and drops a full three inches before Paimon, jerked out of his jelly-making, is able to stabilize the House's foundations. Happy for Hardhands that the Pontifexa is attending a performance of Guillermo el Sangre at the Hippodrome and that by the time the ritual's shockwave reaches into the City it has dissipated into a small rumble that is absorbed by the opera's orchestration. The sangyn-colored aiguillettes in the Pontifexa's hair do bob a bit, but she attributes that to the incredibly high range of the soubrette singing the part of the ingénue and does not at all consider that her grandson may be at home ripping apart the Aeythr with his bare hands.

Back in his circle, the explosion has left Hardhands fireblown but unburned. His hair is sparking a bit, though, and there is a faint glow to his skin, the glow of satisfaction, of completion, of a really damn fine evocation. His Vortex has gone from immediately apparent to lingering afterglow, and now he's ready to get down to brass tacks. The Aeythr around him is scrubbed clean of nasties and charged crackling full of Current. Time to begin.

He breaks the circle of cornmeal because he doesn't need it anymore and, wringing his hair back from blood-speckled shoulders, kneels before a small humpback trunk. From this trunk he withdraws a pack of cards and a small mortar and pestle. He takes these things back into the center of the circle, scattering cornmeal with his bare feet, and sits down cross-legged. The air is supercharged, waiting, and as he draws it into his lungs, his blood tingles in his veins. He's feeling spiffy, and he sings *Let me be your salty dog, or I won't be your man at all, let me be your salty dog* just for the sheer joy of watching his own voice snap and crack around him.

The items that he purchased from the Magick Box are already unpacked and waiting. Brushing his wayward hair back, yet again, Hardhands bends to the task at hand. He pours and mixes, whispering fragments of Gramatica that wisp about his face and hands like wiggly little moths. A stray word flutters about his face and he waves it away absently, twists and ties threads into sigils, words into colors, powders into power. It's a dangerous procedure, one wrong move and he could blow a hole right into next week, but he has supreme confidence in his own abilities and he does not falter once. The sigil completed and glittering before him, he takes a pot of Madam Twanky's Fornication-Red lip pomade and squashes its brilliant pigment into the mortar. He adds the glittering sigil and begins mashing. It takes a few minutes of muscle-cracking, teeth-clenching effort to incorporate the sigil into the pomade, but he presses downward, nudging the process forward with a few swear words, and then it is done. He glops the now quivering pomade back into its small pot and puts the lid back on. Madam Twanky's face stares at up him, teeth caught in a grin, her hair piled high on her head like whip cream, surrounded by grinning monkey putti heads. *Let Angels Kiss Your Soul in Bliss!* scrolls underneath Madam Twanky's friendly face. Angels, indeedy.

Hardhands seals the pot and puts it to one side. He sweeps the remnant of his sigil-making into the crumbled paper bag and then, cracking the Aeyther around him slightly, thrusts the evidence through. There is nothing to show for his business but the faint glimmering riming the interior of the mortar and the smirk on Hardhands' face.

Now that the work is done, he's in a cheerie cherry mood, thinking of the fun to come and the joy with Julien, and how once the Pontifexa is removed nothing is going to get in their way. Julien can rule the kid, do the power thing, and Hardhands and his band will do everything else. Wanting to revel in his spiffy mood and anticipate the future happiness ahead of him, Hardhands decides to indulge himself in a little divinatory spelunking and spills the cards out of their stained silk wrapper. They fall like leaves before him, little plackets of bright colored pasteboard whose backs are marked with a six-pointed hexagram. He scatters the cards further with a brush of his hand and says:

"Present!"

A card flips upward in response, turning itself over helpfully. *The Three of Pistols: Mutation.* Hardhands frowns, a wee bit surprised. Mutation is not an auspicious card; it signifies things gone awry, and when you have just done a major working, involving major mojo, you do not want to be told by the Aeyther that anything might possibly have gone awry.

Hardhands flicks his fingers at the scattered cards, and another piece of pasteboard flips to his command. *Eight of Banners: Bombast.* Although the meaning of this card is clear enough, as a clarifier to the first card, its appearance is confusing. Bombast is not a quality that young Hardhands wishes to associate with himself. He gives up on the present and jumps to the happiness to come.

"Future!"

Jack of Pistols: Abandon. The frown becomes a deep line between Hardhands' black-rimmed eyes. *Abandon* is a wishy-washy card—it can mean the release of restriction, but it can also mean betrayal and being left behind. He flips for clarification: *Six of Banners: Skullduggery.* Definitely on the wrong side of wishy-washy. The Pontifexa is going to mess him up, still. What is she up to that he does not know?

"Explain."

Flip. *The Scout.* Hardhands snatches at the card. A coyote dances across pasteboard, pink tongue lolling in a laugh, brushy tail bobbing insultingly. The Scout is the card of deception, of jibes, of mockery. The coyote has green eyes. The Pontifexa's eyes are welkin blue, but Julien, oh Julien, has eyes as green as grapes. Hardhands' lovely dinner (olive and porpoise galantine and coconut fool) is starting to fidget uneasily in his tummy. His lovely dinner does not like these portents any more than Hardhands himself does. He had expected to get all happy cards: *Ten of Pistols: Release* or *Eight of Pearls: Harmony.* Instead, it's all fire and air, which, of course, mix to become lightning, and lightning scorches and destroys all it touches.

Hardhands flips again, this time touching the card with a long finger to hold it still. *Three of Banners: Nuisance.* Although the image is a familiar one, tonight it has a strange resonance: the Three of Banners shows a small child pulling on the tail of a wolf. The wolf is turning its head, slavering jaws yawning wide, and there's no question about what is going to happen next. The child has bobbing red hair.

"Future," Hardhands says again, and now his voice is hoarse.

The Four of Bones shoots upward, and he ducks back. He grabs for it and swears as its edge slices into his fingers. *Chastisement.* The child on this card has red hair, too. And so does the man who is slitting her throat with a razor. A large pink stuffy pig in dancing shoes is watching this operation, dispassionately, from the abandoned crib.

Hardhands puts the card down and stares into the darkness of the room, chewing on his lip, raw still from the ardor of Julien Brakespeare's kiss. He twists his hands together, once, twice, clenching his fingers into crunchy fists. He looks at the cards laid out before him: *Mutation, Abandon, Bombast, The Scout, Nuisance, Chastisement*. He cracks his fingers again; now they are almost bloodless from his clenching.

"Alfonso, front and center."

A jag of darkness opens up and a water elemental squeezes through. It raises its bowler to Hardhands and flips its tail in greeting: "Ayah, jefe? Que quieres? I was having chow."

"I want to talk to my sister. Find her and bring her here."

The elemental frowns, scratches its little head with one tiny hand. "I dunno, jefe, your circle is torn, and—"

Hardhands flicks Alfonso with a short but potent word in Gramatica. The elemental momentarily disappears in a haze of roiling color, and when the color fades he looks a wee bit scorched around the edges. Smoke tendrils up from his little hat. The distinct smell of fried fish floats on the air.

"Now."

The elemental flicks its tail and darts back through the Vortex.

Hardhands puts his gear away, but he leaves the Vortex open for Alfonso's return. He walks around and around the room, but that doesn't make Alfonso return any faster, nor does it calm his beating heart. He keeps looking down at the cards in his hands, as though they might have changed through the sheer force of the hammering of his heart, but each time he looks down, they remain the same. The coyote grins up at him until he flips the card facedown, ignoring the plaintive yipping. The wolf still turns to snap at the child. The stuffy pig still stares. Hardhands' bare feet leave little bloody smears on the floor, from the broken glass, but he ignores the pain. Pain is just weakness leaving the body, and his mind is on other things. A faint fresh breeze, smelling of salt and water, drifts down from the open space above.

His thoughts are piling up on top of each other, and each thought is hotter than the last until he feels as though he might actually be on fire, and he is surprised that his mind can be so warm and yet his flesh so cold and crawling. He looks at *Chastisement* again; Julien is smiling and holding the edge of the bloody razor to his lips. The child lies broken on the floor. The stuffy pig is sodden with blood.

"Alfonso!" He can't wait any longer.

The elemental zips out of the Vortex, his tale flapping like a wind-vane.

"I cannot find her!" he says breathlessly.

"What do you mean?"

"I can't find her," Alfonso says. "I looked everywhere, but she's gone. There's nothing left."

"That's impossible," Hardhands says. He reaches out to grab Alfonso, but the elemental flips away, holding on to his hat. "There is always something left—a shade of ourselves, a fragment, she's only been dead for six months, that is not enough time for her to cross the Abyss and go on. You didn't look hard enough."

"I did, I did!" the elemental protests. "I did. I called and called, but she did not come."

"You mean she is not dead?" A dim hope flickers in Hardhands' throat.

"Neither living nor dead," Alfonso says. "She is No-Where. She is gone."

"That is impossible," Hardhands says again, stubbornly. He snaps a Gramatica word at the elemental, who this time is prepared to dodge, and does.

"Not for some," says Alfonso cunningly, poised for flight. "Not for some."

Julien. Treacherous remorseless kindless Julien. It's as though the top of Hardhands' brain has been yanked off and absolute certainty poured in, and suddenly he knows, he knows. The Pontifexa had been right all along. Julien Brakespeare had killed his sister, and not content with killing Sidonia Brakespeare's body, he had killed her spirit too, sucked up her soul. It's a great trick and one that only a great adept can pull off, to abrogate a person so completely that it is as though she had never even existed. It is a dirty trick, the worst one in the world. Hardhands snatches again, and this time Alfonso does not flick away fast enough. He's caught, trapped, stuck in a grip so tight that if he were real flesh he'd be squeezed into a tiny pulp, a wiggling mass of struggling goo.

The elemental gurgles and twitches—

"Bwannie!"

Holypigface. Hardhands almost drops the squirming elemental. Tiny Doom is standing in the cornmeally wreckage of his circle. How the hell had she gotten in? He always locks the door—not that it would make any difference to Paimon or the Pontifexa, but he locks it anyway, for the symbolic value of the gesture, if nothing else. He's momentarily forgotten that she's the Heir to Bilskinir and therefore no part of the House is closed to her.

"You are supposed to be in bed," he says.

Tiny Doom is clutching a stuffy pink pig as big as her head, and her nightcap is dangling around her neck from its cords. Carpy teeth slice into Hardhands' fingers, and he lets go of Alfonso with another explicitly nasty word. The elemental darts back into the seam of the Vortex and is gone.

"I had a cold dweam," Tiny Doom says. She patters towards him, scattering the cards further with bare sandy feet, and, remembering suddenly the scattered glass, he snatches her up. She puts chubby arms around his neck and says: "A biswuit would make me warm."

Her weight is very heavy in his arms. The pig is slightly damp from drool, but it's nice and cuddly, too. Hardhands' anger has evaporated into a calm dreamy feeling. His love has curdled into something equally as dreamy, but much more hard.

"Hey, I am bloody," she says.

He jerks. "What?"

"My foot is all bleedy."

He twists her around for inspection, and she grabs on to the dangling reins of his hair. The sole of her foot is grubby gray, except where it is smeary red.

"Oww," she says as he pokes the spot from whence the blood wells. His fingernail scrapes and comes away with a tiny shard of glass.

"It was just a piece of glass," he says. "You'll live."

"Kiss and make well," she commands.

Hardhands doesn't really want to kiss her grubby foot, but he doesn't want to listen to her caterwaul either, so he obediently puckers up his lips. Her foot is warm and the blood is slightly sticky. Sweet sticky Haðraaða blood.

"Better?"

"A biswuit would make it better." She smashes a sloppy wet kiss on his cheek.

He sighs. "You are a pain in my ass, baby. Hold your ears."

She covers her ears obediently, dropping the pig in the process. He shuts down the Vortex with a twist of Gramatica (a shortcut he is later going to regret) and kicks the scattered cards out of his way.

"With honey, my biswuit," Tiny Doom adds. "Gimme Pig."

Hardhands dangles her downward; giggling, she snatches at Pig.

"Grab that pot, too."

She grabs obediently, and he swings her aloft, takes the jar of Madam Twanky's Fornication-Red Lip Pomade from her. Then swings her higher, to settle on his shoulders. They gallop downstairs to the kitchen and Paimon's fifteen-mile-high buttermilk biscuits. Hardhands is ravenous and his mind is now made up.

V.

Julien is waiting by the swingset, which moves idly back and forth in the chill night breeze, creaking a little uncomfortably just like a gibbet. He is muffled in a greatcoat, his chapeau du bras pulled low over his forehead, but still he looks rather cold. Hardhands nudges Fleeter forward towards the shadow of the slide. Fleeter doesn't care much for the bulk of the slide and wiggles a bit, but Hardhands' thighs are firm and she settles down quickly. He slides down, and Tiny Doom, who has fallen asleep in her uncle's muffling arms, wakes up at his movement, yawning loudly in his ear.

"Waffles?"

"Soon," promises Hardhands.

"Ayah," she says and puts her head back down on his shoulder. He adjusts his shawl up over her head and then ties Fleeter to the slide.

"You are late," Julien says.

"I'm sorry. I overslept," Hardhands says, who has not actually closed his eyes for two days. He shifts Tiny Doom's heavy weight to his other shoulder. It's the cold edge of morning, and the eucalyptus trees surrounding the small lake drip with wetness. Julien's minions cluster near the picnic tables. They are passing around a bottle of whiskey, and the general complaint that they had to get out of their warm beds to come and stand around in the fog.

Hardhands and Julien touch fists together briefly, aware of decorum, aware of the eyes of the minions.

Julien looks at the bundle in Hardhands' arms and curls his lip. "Why did you bring the child?"

"I thought you would want to see her."

Julien's lip does not uncurl. "It's too cold and damp out here. She should be home in bed."

"Perhaps so we all should be, darling," Hardhands says with a meaningful glance. "But sometimes necessity requires early rising." He jiggles Little Tiny Doom and she opens her eyes reluctantly. She is not a morning person.

"Kiss your father," Hardhands commands Cyrenacia. She wrinkles her nose, and her father follows suit. But when Hardhands leans her towards Julien, she obediently purses her lips. Her kiss leaves a little red smear on his cheek, which he wipes away distastefully with a snowy white hankie.

"Is it done?" Julien asks.

"Ayah," Hardhands answers. "It is done."

"I have saved you then, Banastre." The two men walk together to the statue of the Goddess Califa. Her gleaming golden skin is slick with glittery moisture, and the dog crouching at her feet looks somewhat bedraggled and in need of a good shake. Legend has it that the Goddess Califa was born from the little lake, which is the City's only natural body of water. This spot, then, is the most sacred place in Califa, the City's secret center, its heart, the wellspring of its Current.

"What did you save me from, Julien?"

Rather than answering, Julien fishes in his pocket. He spins a gold coin upward. It lands neatly in the Goddess's quiver. "The Pontifexa's whims. The patents of mediocrity. Ah, the arrows of desire," he says, looking upward at the Archer, "and the bow of burning gold. What fun we shall have, Ban. No one will hold us now. It is hard to be patient now, when we are so close. How long shall it take, do you think?"

"Not long, not long."

"We must remain discreet, Banastre."

"I know."

"That puppy is cold," Cyrenacia says. She has made no movement to get down from Hardhands' arms, and that is just as well as he has no desire to let her go, even if she does feel as though she weighs one hundred pounds and her knees are grinding into his hipbones.

"He's not a real dog," her father says. He rubs his cheek absently.

"Not now he is not," Hardhands says. "But on the full moon, you know, he and the Goddess get down off the plinth and they hunt."

"Bunnies?"

"No. Not bunnies. What do they hunt, Julien?"

"I have no idea, Ban. This is a story that I haven't heard." Julien has lit a cigarillo, and he blows a twist of smoke upward. "Do tell. If not bunnies, what?"

"Faithless lovers, of course," Hardhands says. "Those who say that they love, but lie. Spit." This is to Cyrenacia, not Julien. She spits into his hankie, giggling, and he rubs the rouge off her lips, then wads the hankie up and flicks it away.

Julien had turned from the statue, looking out over the lake. Now he turns back to Hardhands, just in time to see the spitting operation. He frowns.

"I would hunt bunnies," says Cyrenacia. "What is the puppy's name?"

"Justice," says Hardhands. He is talking to Julien, now, not Cyrenacia.

"What do you mean?" Julien says. His voice has become a razor wire, and it could cut through glass, through steel, through bone. Hardhands does not answer him. He is smiling, and in that smile he suddenly looks remarkably like the Pontifexa, for all the difference in height, the difference in hair, the difference in sex.

Now it is Cyrenacia who is frowning, a charming little wrinkly frown that turns her lips into a little pink knot. "I would name that puppy Bouncer. I want my waffles."

"So do I," says Hardhands. "Come on, Tiny Doom, let's go home. Grandmamma is waiting."

"I love puppy," says Tiny Doom. She waves. "Bye puppy!"

"What have you done, Banastre?" Julien says. He touches his cheek again. It has gone numb, and there is a spreading darkness slowly seeping into the edges of his vision. "What have you done?"

"Changed my mind," Hardhands says.

So, here we have Hardhands walking away from Julien, who has sat suddenly down on the damp ground, his legs as empty as air. Hardhands is fifteen years old and his hands are still white and tender, but his conscience is now hard as bone. He's on his way.

Afterword

As the author of the only complete history of Califa, this historian can state with complete authority that this story is utter balderdash.[13] Readers who wish an accurate accounting of these events are referred to the pertinent volume of *Califa in Sunshine & Shade* for a more judicious rendering.[14] This story was obviously generated by the Abenfaráx propaganda machine and designed to present the House of Haðraaða in the worst possible light, thus helping to justify the usurper Florian Abenfaráx de la Carcaza.

This grubby little tale is presented as artifact only. It is true enough that both Julien Brakespeare and Banastre Haðraaða were adepts of no small accomplishment.[15] But no such plotting against the Pontifexa Georgiana IV's life ever took place. Georgiana IV's affection for her granddaughter and her husband is well documented, and there was never any question that Julien would not take custody of the Pontifexina upon her mother's death. As

---

13   A Lady of Quality. *Califa in Sunshine & Shade: A History in Ten Volumes.* Inverfarigag, Elsewhere: Bilskinir Press.

14   A Lady of Quality. *Califa in Sunshine & Shade, Volume Three: Metal More Attractive (The Long Version.)* Inverfarigag, Elsewhere: Bilskinir Press.

15   Carroll, Peter J. *Liber Kaos: The Psychonomicon.* Privately Published, N.D. Keegan ov Admoish, Nyana. *The Eschatanomicon or Rangering for Everyone.* Califa: Bilskinir Press, n.d.

a famed musician (a detail inexplicably omitted from this story), Julien's touring schedule was far too onerous for a small child. Most certainly young Hardhands was not responsible for Julien Brakespeare's untimely death. That sad event, which took place some days after Julien left the city for an engagement at the Hoot Bar in Nicashio, was attributed by the attending doctor to a surfeit of green peach confit.[16]

Oddly, the only character in this story who is well drawn is Denizen Paimon, the Butler of Bilskinir House. Several years back, this historian interviewed one of the last praterhuman revenants still residing in the Waking World, and his accounting of Denizen Paimon matches up well with this one. Clearly, Paimon was an egregore of taste and distinction.

---

16   "Violin Virtuoso Jams on Jam & is Jammed." *Califa Police Gazette*, 4th of Lluvia, Año Pontifexa 112.

The Lineaments of Gratified Desire

> "Abstinence sows sand all over
> The ruddy limbs & flaming hair
> But Desire Gratified
> Plants fruit of life & beauty there."
> —William Blake

I: Stage Fright

Here is Hardhands up on the stage, and he's cheery cherry, sparking fire, he's as fast as a fox-trotter, stepping high. Sweaty blood dribbles his brow, bloody sweat stipples his torso, and behind him the Vortex buzzsaw whines, its whirling outer edge black enough to cut glass. The razor in his hand flashes like a heliograph as he motions the final Gesture of the invocation. The Eye of the Vortex flutters, but its perimeter remains firmly within the structure of Hardhands' Will and does not expand. He ululates a Command, and the Eye begins to open, like a pupil dilating in sunlight, and from its vivid yellowness comes a glimpse of scales and horns, struggling not to be born.

Someone tugs at Hardhands' foot. His concentration wavers. Someone yanks on the hem of his kilt. His concentration wiggles, and the Vortex wobbles slightly like a run-down top. Someone tugs on his kilt hem, and his concentration collapses completely, and so does the Vortex, sucking into itself like water down a drain. There goes the Working for which Hardhands has been preparing for the last two weeks, and there goes the Tygers of Wrath's new drummer, and there goes their boot-kicking show.

Hardhands throws off the grasp with a hard shake, and looking down, prepares to smite. His lover is shouting upward at him, words that Hardhands can hardly hear, words he hopes he can hardly hear, words he surely did not hear a-right. The interior of the club is toweringly loud, noisy enough to make the ears bleed, but suddenly the thump of his heart, already driven hard by the strength of his magickal invocation, is louder.

Relais, pale as paper, repeats the shout. This time there is no mistaking what he says, much as Hardhands would like to mistake it, much as he would like to hear something else, something sweet and charming, something like: you are the prettiest thing ever born, or the Goddess grants wishes in your name, or they are killing themselves in the streets because the show is sold right out. Alas, Relais is shouting nothing quite so sweet.

"What do you mean you cannot find Tiny Doom?" Handhands shouts back. He looks wildly around the congested club, but it's dark and there are so many of them, and most of them have huge big hair and huger bigger boots. A tiny purple girl-child and her stuffy pink pig have no hope in this throng; they'd be trampled under foot in a second. That is exactly what Hardhands had told the Pontifexa earlier that day; no babysitter, he, other business, other pleasures, no time to take care of small children, not on this night of all nights: the Tygers of Wrath's biggest show of the year. Find someone else.

Well, talkers are no good doers, they say, and talking had done no good, all the yapping growling barking howling in the world had not changed the Pontifexa's mind: it's Paimon's night off, darling, and she'll be safe with you, Banastre, I can trust my heir with no one else, my sweet boy, do your teeny grandmamma this small favor and how happy I shall be, and here, kiss-kiss, I must run, I'm late, have a wonderful evening, good luck with the show, be careful with your invocation, cheerie-bye my darling.

And now see:

Hardhands roars: "I told you to keep an eye on her, Relais!"

He had, too; he couldn't exactly watch over Tiny Doom (so called because she is the first in stature and the second in fate) while he was invoking the drummer, and with no drummer, there's no show (no show, damn it!), and anyway if he's learned anything as the grandson of the Pontifexa of Califa, it's how to delegate.

Relais shouts back garbled defense. His eyes are whirling pie-plates. He doesn't mention that he stopped at the bar on his way to break the news and that there he downed four Choronzon Delights (hold the delight, double the Choronzon) before screwing up the courage to face his lover's ire. He doesn't mention that he can't exactly remember the last time he saw Little Tiny Doom except that he thinks it might have been about the time when she said that she had to visit El Casa de Peepee (oh cute) and he'd taken her as far as the door to the loo, which she had insisted haughtily she could do alone, and then he'd been standing outside, and gotten distracted by Arsinoë Fyrdraaca, who'd sauntered by, wrapped around the most gorgeous angel with rippling red wings, and then they'd gone to get a drink, and then another drink, and then when Relais remembered that Tiny Doom and Pig were still in the potty and pushed his way back through the crush, Tiny Doom and Pig were not still in the potty anymore.

And now here:

Up until this very second, Hardhands has been feeling dandy as candy about this night: his invocation has been powerful and sublime, the blood in his veins replaced by pure unadulterated Magickal Current, hot and heavy. Up until this very second, if he clapped his hands together, sparks would fly. If he sang a note, the roof would fall. If he tossed his hair, fans would implode. Just from the breeze of the Vortex through his skin, he had known this was going to be a charm of a show, the very pinnacle of bombast and bluster. The crowded club still hums with cold-fire charge, the air still sparks, cracking with glints of magick: yowza. But now all that rich bubbly magick is curdling in his veins, his drummer has slid back to the Abyss, and he could beat someone with a stick. Thanks to an idiot boyfriend and a bothersome five-year-old his evening has just tanked.

Hardhands' perch is lofty. Despite the roiling smoke (cigarillo, incense, and oil), he can look out over the big big hair and see the club is as packed as a cigar box with hipsters eager to see the show. From the stage Hardhands can see a lot, his vision sharpened by the magick he's been mainlining, and he sees: hipsters, b-boys, gothicks, crimson-clad officers, a magistra with a jaculus on a leash, etc. He does not see a small child or a pink pig or even the tattered remnants of a small child and a pink pig or even, well, he doesn't see them, period.

Hardhands sucks in a deep breath and uses what is left of the Invocation still working through his veins to shout: "**Ou!**"

The syllable is vigorous and combustible, flowering in the darkness like a bruise. The audience erupts into a hollering hooting howl. They think the show is about to start. They are ready and geared. Behind Hardhands, the band also mistakes his intention, and despite the lack of drummer, kicks in with the triumphant blare of a horn, the delirious bounce of the hurdy-gurdy.

"**Oo!**" This time the shout sparks bright red, a flash of cold-fire that brings tears to the eyes of the onlookers. Hardhands raises an authoritative hand towards the band, crashing them into silence. The crowd follows suit, and the ensuing quiet is almost as ear-shattering.

"Oɩ.." This time his words provide no sparkage, and he knows that his Will is fading under his panic. The club is dark. It is full of large people. Outside it is darker still, and the streets of South of the Slot are wet and full of dangers. No place for a Tiny Doom and her Pig, oh so edible, to be wandering around, alone. Outside it is the worst night of the year to be wandering alone anywhere in the City, particularly if you are short, stout, and toothsome.

"Oɩ!" This time Hardhands' voice, the voice which has launched a thousand stars, which has impregnated young girls with monsters and kept young men at their wanking until their wrists ache and their members bleed, is scorched and rather squeaky:

"Has anyone seen my wife?"

II: Historical Notes

Here's a bit of background. No ordinary night, tonight, not at all. It's Pirates' Parade, and the City of Califa is afire—in some places actually blazing. No fear, tho', bucket brigades are out in force, for the Pontifexa does not wish to lose her capital to revelry. Wetness is stationed around the things that the Pontifexa most particularly requires not to burn: her shrines, Bilskinir House, Arden's Cake-O-Rama, the Califa National Bank. Still, even with these bucket brigades acting as damper, there's fun enough for everyone. The City celebrates many holidays, but surely Pirates' Parade ranks as Biggest and Best.

But why pirates and how a parade? Historians (oh fabulous professional liars) say that it happened thusly: Back in the day, no chain sealed the Bay of Califa off from sea-faring foes, and the Califa Gate sprang wide as an opera singer's mouth, a state of affairs good for trade and bad for security. Chain was not all the small city lacked: no guard, no organized militia, no bloodthirsty Scorchers regiment to stand against havoc, and no navy. The City was fledgling and disorganized, hardly more than a village, and plump for the picking.

One fine day, pirates took advantage of Califa's tenderness and sailed right through her Gate and docked at the Embarcadero, as scurvy as you please. From door to door they went, demanding tribute or promising wrath, and when they were loaded down with booty they went well satisfied back to their ships to sail away.

But they didn't get far. While the pirates were shaking down the householders, a posse of quiet citizens crept down to the docks and sabotaged the poorly guarded ships. The pirates arrived back at the docks to discover their escape boats sinking, and suddenly the docks themselves were on fire, and their way off the docks was blocked, and then they were on fire too, and that was it.

Perhaps Califa had no army, no navy, no militia, but she did have citizens with grit and cleverness, and grit and cleverness trump greed and guns every time. Such a clever victory over a pernicious greedy foe is worth remembering, and maybe even repeating, in a fun sort of way, and thus was born a roistering day of remembrance when revelers dressed as pirates gallivant door to door demanding candy booty, and thus Little Tiny Doom has muscled in on Hardhands' evening. With Grandmamma promised to attend a whist party, and Butler Paimon's night off, who else would take Tiny Doom (and the resplendently costumed Pig) on candy shakedown? Who but our hero, as soon as his show is over and his head back down to earth, lucky boy?

Well.

The Blue Duck and its hot dank club-y-ness may be the place to be when you are tall and trendy and your hearing is already shot, but for a short kidlet, big hair and loud noises bore, and the cigarillo smoke scratches. Tiny Doom has waited for Pirates' Parade for weeks, dreaming of pink popcorn and sugar squidies, chocolate manikins and jacksnaps, praline pumpkin seeds and ginger bombs: a sackful of sugar guaranteed to keep her sick and speedy for at least a week. She can wait no longer.

Shortness has its advantage; trendy people look up their noses, not down. The potty is filthy and the floor yucky wet; Tiny Doom and Pig slither out the door, right by Relais, so engaged in his conversation with a woman with a boat in her hair that he doesn't even notice the scram. Around elbows, by tall boots, dodging lit cigarettes and drippy drinks held low and cool-like, Tiny Doom and Pig achieve open air without incident and then, sack in hand, set out for the Big Shakedown.

"*Rancy Dancy is no good*," she sings as she goes, swinging Pig, who is of course too lazy to walk, "*Chop him up for firewood . . . When he's dead, boil his head and bake it into gingerbread . . .*"

She jumps over a man lying on the pavement, and then into the reddish pool beyond. The water makes a satisfying SPLASH and tho' her hem gets wet, she is sure to hold Pig up high so that he remains dry. He's just getting over a bad cold and has to care for his health, silly Pig he is delicate, and up past his bedtime, besides. Well, it is only once a year.

Down the slick street Tiny Doom galumphs, Pig swinging along with her. There are shadows ahead of her and shadows behind, but after the shadows of Bilskinir House (which can sometimes be *grabby*), these shadows: So what? There's another puddle ahead, this one dark and still. She pauses before it, and some interior alarum indicates that it would be best to jump over, rather than in. The puddle is wide, spreading across the street like a strange black stain. As she gears up for the leap, a faint rippling begins to mar the mirror-like surface.

"Wah! Wah!" Tiny Doom is short, but she has lift. Holding her skirt in one hand, and with a firm grip upon Pig, she hurtles herself upward and over, like a tiny tea cosy levering aloft. As she springs, something wavery and white snaps out of the stillness, racing towards her, whip-crack fast. She lands on the other side and keeps scooting, beyond the arm's reach. Six straggly fingers, like pallid parsnips, waggle angrily at her, but she's well beyond their grip.

"Tell her, smell her! Kick her down the cellar," Tiny Doom taunts, flapping Pig's ears derisively. The scraggly arm falls back, and then another emerges from the water, hoisting up on its elbows, pulling a slow rising bulk behind it: a knobby head, with knobby nose and knobby forehead and a slowly opening mouth that shows razor-sharp gums and a pointy black tongue unrolling like a hose. The tongue has length where the arms did not, and it looks gooey and sticky, just like the salt licorice Grandmamma loves so much. Tiny Doom cares not for salt licorice one bit and neither does Pig, so it seems prudent to punt, and they do, as fast as her chubby legs can carry them, farther down the slickery dark street.

III: Irritating Children

Here is Hardhands in the alley behind the club, taking a deep breath of brackish air, which chills but does not calm. Inside, he has left an angry mob who've had their hopes dashed rather than their ears blown. The Infernal Engines of Desire (opening act) has come back on stage and is trying valiantly to suck up the slack, but the audience is not particularly pacified. The Blue Duck will be lucky if it doesn't burn. However, that's not our hero's problem; he's got larger fish frying.

He sniffs the air, smelling: the distant salt spray of the ocean; drifting smoke from some bonfire; cheap perfume; his own sweat; horse manure. He closes his eyes and drifts deeper, beyond smell, beyond scent, down down down into a wavery darkness that is threaded with filaments of light which are not really light, but which he knows no other way to describe. The darkness down here is not really darkness, either; it's the Magickal Current as his mind can envision it, giving form to the formless, putting the indefinable into definite terms. The Current bears upon its flow a tendril of something familiar, what he qualifies, for lack of a better word, as a taste of obdurate obstinacy and pink plush, fading quickly but unmistakable.

The Current is high tonight, very high. In consequence, the Aeyther is humming, the Aeyther is abuzz; the line between In and Out has narrowed to a width no larger than a hair, and it's an easy step across—but the jump can go either way. Oh, this would have been the very big whoo for the gig tonight; musickal magick of the highest order, but it sucks for lost childer out on the streets. South of the Slot is bad enough when the Current is low: a sewer of footpads, dollymops, blisters, mashers, cornhoes, and others is not to be found elsewhere so deep in the City even on an ebb-tide day. Tonight, combine typical holiday mayhem with the rising magickal flood and Goddess knows what will be out, hungry and yummy for some sweet tender kidlet chow. And not even regular run-of-the-mill niblet, but prime grade-A-best-grade royalty. The Pontifexa's heir; it doesn't get more yummy than that—a vampyre could dare sunlight with that bubbly blood zipping through his veins, a ghoul could pass for living after gnawing on that sweet flesh. It makes Hardhands' manly parts shrivel to think upon the explanation to Grandmamma of Tiny Doom's loss and the blame sure to follow.

Hardhands opens his eyes; it's hardly worth wasting the effort of going deep when everything is so close the surface tonight. Behind him, the iron door flips open and Relais flings outward, borne aloft on a giant wave of disapproving noise. The door snaps shut, cutting the sound in a brief echo which quickly dies in the coffin-narrow alleyway.

"Did you find her?" Relais asks, holding his fashionable cuffs so they don't trail on the mucky cobblestones. Inside his brain is bouncing with visions of the Pontifexa's reaction if they return home minus Cyrenacia. Actually, what she is going to say is the least of his worries; it is what she might do that really has Relais gagging. He likes his lungs exactly where they are: inside his body, not flapping around outside.

Hardhands turns a white-hot look upon his lover and says: "If she gets eaten, Relais, I will eat you."

Relais' father always advised saving for a rainy day and though the sky above is mostly clear, Relais is feeling damp. He will check his bankbook when they get home, and reconsider Sweetie Fyrdraaca's proposition. He's been Hardhands' leman for over a year now: blood sacrifices, coldfire-singed clothing, throat-tearing invocations, cornmeal-gritty sheets, murder. He's had enough. He makes no reply to the threat.

Hardhands demands, not very politely: "Give me my frock-coat."

Said coat, white as snow, richly embroidered in white peonies and with cuffs the size of tablecloths, well, Relais had been given that to guard too, and he now has a vague memory of hanging it over the stall door in the pisser, where hopefully it still dangles, but probably not.

"I'll get it—" Relais fades backward, into the club, and Hard-hands lets him go.

For now.

For now, Hardhands takes off his enormous hat, which had remained perched upon his gorgeous head during his invocation via a jeweled spike of a hairpin, and speaks a word into its upturned bowl. A green light pools up, spilling over the hat's capacious brim, staining his hand and the sleeve below with drippy magick. Another commanding word, and the light surges upward and ejects a splashy elemental, fish-tail flapping.

"Eh, boss—I thought you said I had the night off," Alfonso complains. There's lip rouge smeared on his fins and a clutch of cards in his hand. "It's Pirates' Parade."

"I changed my mind. That wretched child has given me the slip and I want you to track her."

Alfonso grimaces. Ever since Little Tiny Doom trapped him in a bowl of water and fed him fishy flakes for two days, he's avoided her like fluke-rot.

"Why worry your good luck, boss—"

Hardhands does not have to twist. He only has to look like he is going to twist. Alfonso zips forward, flippers flapping, and Hardhands, after draining his chapeau of Current and slamming it back upon his grape, follows.

IV: Who's There?

Here is the Roaring Gimlet, sitting pretty in her cozy little kitchen, toes toasting on the grate, toast toasting on the tongs, drinking hot ginger beer, feeling happily serene. She's had a fun-dandy evening. Citizens who normally sleep behind chains and steel bolts, dogs a-prowl and guns under their beds, who maybe wouldn't open their doors after dark if their own mothers were lying bleeding on the threshold, these people fling their doors widely and with gay abandon to the threatening cry of "Give us Candy or We'll Give you the Rush."

Any other night, at this time, she'd still be out in the streets, looking for drunken mashers to roll. But tonight, all gates were a-jar and the streets a high tide of drunken louts. Out by nine and back by eleven, with a sack almost too heavy to haul, a goodly load of sugar, and a yummy fun-toy, too. Now she's enjoying her happy afterglow from a night well-done. The noises from the cellar have finally stopped, she's finished the crossword in the *Alta Califa*, and as soon as the kettle blows, she'll fill her hot water bottle and aloft to her snuggly bed, there to dwell the rest of the night away in kip.

Ah, Pirates' Parade, best night of the year.

While she's waiting for the water to bubble, she's cleaning the tool whence comes her name: the bore is clotted with icky stuff and the Gimlet likes her signature clean and sharply shiny. Clean hands, clean house, clean heart, the Gimlet's pappy always said. Above the fireplace, Pappy's flat representation stares down at his progeny, the self-same gimlet clinched in his hand. The Roaring Gimlet is the heir to a fine family tradition, and she does love her job.

What's that a-jingling? She glances at the clock swinging over the stove. It's almost midnight. Too late for visitors, and anyway, everyone knows the Roaring Gimlet's home is her castle. Family stays in, people stay out, so Daddy Gimlet always said. Would someone? No, they wouldn't. Not even tonight, they would not.

Jingle jingle.

The cat looks up from her perch on the fender, perturbed.

Heels down, the Gimlet stands aloft and tucks her shirt back into her skirts, ties her dressing gown tight, bounds up the ladder-like kitchen stairs to the front door. The peephole shows a dimly lit circle of empty cobblestones. Damn it all to leave the fire for nothing. As the Gimlet turns away, the bell dances again, jangling her into a surprised jerk.

The Roaring Gimlet opens the door, slipping the chain, and is greeted with a squirt of flour right in the kisser, and a shrieky command:

"Give us the Candy or We'll Give you the Rush!"

The Gimlet coughs away the flour, choler rising, and beholds before her, knee-high, a huge black feathered hat. Under the hat is a pouty pink face, and under the pouty pink face, a fluffy farthingale that resembles in both color and points an artichoke, and under that, purple dance shoes, with criss-crossy ribbands. Riding on the hip of this apparition is a large pink plushy pig, also wearing purple criss-crossy dance shoes, golden laurel leaves perched over floppy piggy ears.

It's the Pig that the Gimlet recognizes first, not the kid. The kid, whose public appearances have been kept to a minimum (the Pontifexa is wary of too much flattery, and as noted, chary of her heir's worth), could be any kid, but there is only one Pig, all Califa knows that, and the kid must follow the Pig, as day follows night, as sun follows rain, as fortune follows the fool.

"Give us the CANDY or We'll GIVE YOU THE RUSH!" A voice to pierce glass, to cut right through the Gimlet's recoil, all the way down to her achy toes. The straw-shooter moves from present to fire; while Gimlet was gawking, reloading had occurred, and another volley is imminent. She's about to slam shut the door, she cares not to receive flour or to give out yum, but then, door-jamb held halfway in hand, she stops. An idea, formed from an overabundance of yellow nasty novellas and an underabundance of good sense, has leapt full-blown from Nowhere to the Somewhere that is the Roaring Gimlet's calculating brain. So much for sugar, so much for swag: here then is a price above rubies, above diamonds, above chocolate, above, well, Above All. What a pretty price a pretty piece could fetch. On such proceeds the Gimlet could while away her elder days in endless sun and fun-toys.

Before the kid can blow again, the Gimlet grins, in her best granny way, flour feathering about her, and says, "Well, now, chickiedee, well now indeed. I've no desire to be rushed, but you are late and the candy is—"

She recoils, but not in time, from another spurt of flour. When she wipes away the flour, she is careful not to wipe away her welcoming grin. "But I have more here in the kitchen. Come in, tiny pirate, out of the cold, and we shall fill your sack full."

"Huh," says the child, already her husband's Doom and about to become the Roaring Gimlet's, as well. "GIVE ME THE CANDY—"

Patience is a virtue that the Roaring Gimlet is well off without. She peers beyond the kid, down the street. There are people about, but they are: drunken people, or burning people, or screaming people, or carousing people, or running people. None of them appear to be observant people, and that's perfecto. The Gimlet reaches and grabs.

"Hey!" says the Kid. The Pig does not protest.

Tiny Doom is stout, and she can dig her heels in, but the Gimlet is stouter and the Gimlet has two hands free where Tiny Doom has one, and the Pig is too flabby to help. Before Tiny Doom can shoot off her next round of flour, she's yanked and the door is slammed shut behind her, bang!

V. Bad Housekeeping

Here is Hardhands striding down the darkened streets like a colossus, dodging fire, flood, and fighting. He is not upset, oh no indeedy.

He's cool and cold and so angry that if he touched tinder it would burst into flames, if he tipped tobacco it would explode cherry red. And there's more than enough ire to go around, which is happy because the list of Hardhands' blame is quite long.

Firstly: the Pontifexa for making him take Cyrenacia with him. What good is it to be her darling grandson when he's constantly on doodie-detail? Being the only male Haðraaða should be good for: power, mystery, free booze, noli me tangere, first and foremost, the biggest slice of cake. Now being the only male Haðraaða is good for: marrying small torments, kissing the Pontifexa's ass, and being bossed into wife-sitting. He almost got Grandmamma once; perhaps the decision should be revisited.

Secondly: Tiny Doom for not standing still. When he gets her, he's going to paddle her, see if he doesn't. She's got it coming, a long time coming and perhaps a hot hinder will make her think twice about, well, think twice about everything. Didn't he do enough for her already? He married her, to keep her in the family, to keep her out of the hands of her nasty daddy, who otherwise would have the prior claim. Ungrateful kidlet. Perhaps she deserves whatever she gets.

Thirdly: Relais for being such an utter jackass that he can't keep track of a five-year-old. Hardhands has recently come across a receipt for an ointment that allows the wearer to walk through walls. For which, this sigil requires three pounds of human tallow. He's got a few walls he wouldn't mind flitting right through, and at last Relais will be useful.

Fourthly: Paimon. What need has a domicilic denizen for a night off anyway? He's chained to the physical confines of the House Bilskinir by a sigil stronger than life. He should be taking care of the Heir to the House Bilskinir, not doing whatever the hell he is doing on his night off which he shouldn't be doing anyway because he shouldn't be having a night off and when Hardhands is in charge, he won't, no sieur.

Fifthly: Pig. Ayah, so, well, Pig is a stuffy pink plush toy, and can hardly be blamed for anything, but what the hell, why not? Climb on up, Pig, there's always room for one more!

And ire over all: his ruined invocation, for which he had been purging starving dancing and flogging for the last two weeks, all in preparation for what would surely be the most stupendous summoning in the history of summoning. It's been a stellar group of daemons that Hardhands has been able to force from the Aeyther before, but this time he had been going for the highest of the high, the loudest of the loud, and the show would have been sure to go down in the annals of musickology, and his name, already famous, would become gigantic in its height. Even the Pontifexa was sure to be impressed. And now . . .

The streets are full of distraction, but neither Hardhands nor Alfonso is distracted. Tiny Doom's footprints pitty-patter before them, glowing in the gloam like little blue flowers, and they follow, avoiding burning brands, dead horses, drunken warblers, slithering servitors, gushing water pipes, and an impromptu cravat party, and, because of their glowering concentration, they are avoided by all the aforementioned in turn. The pretty blue footprints dance, and leap, from here to there, and there to here, over cobblestone and curb, around corpse and copse, by Cobweb's Palace and Pete's Clown Diner, by Ginger's Gin Goint and Guerrero's Helado, and other blind tigers so blind they are nameless also, dives so low that just walking by will get your knickers wet. The pretty prints don't waver, don't dilly-dally, and then suddenly they turn towards a door, broad and barred, and they stop.

At the door, Hardhands doesn't bother knocking, and neither does Alfonso, but their methods of entry differ. Alfonso zips through the wooden obstruction as though it is neither wooden nor obstructive. Hardhands places palm down on wood and, via a particularly loud Gramatica exhortation, blows the door right off its hinges. His entry is briefly hesitated by the necessity to chase after his chapeau, having blown off also in the breeze of Gramatica, but once it is firmly stabbed back on his handsome head, onward he goes, young Hardhands, hoping very much that something else will get in his path, because he can't deny it: exploding things is fun.

The interior of the house is dark and dull, not that Hardhands is there to critique the décor. Alfonso has zipped ahead of him, coldfire frothing in his wake. Hardhands follows the bubbly pink vapor, down a narrow hallway, past peeling paneling and dusty doorways. He careens down creaky stairs, bending head to avoid braining on low ceiling, and into a horrible little kitchen.

He wrinkles his nose. Our young hero is used to a praeterhuman amount of cleanliness, and here there is neither. At Bilskinir House even the light looks as though it's been washed, dried, and pressed before hung in the air. In contrast, this pokey little hole looks like the back end of a back-end bar after a particularly festive game of Chew the Ear. Smashed crockery and blue willow china crunches under boot, and the furniture is bonfire ready. A faint glow limns the wreckage, the after-reflection of some mighty big magick. The heavy sour smell of blackberries wrinkles in his nose. Coldfire dribbles from the ceiling, whose plaster cherubs and grapes look charred and withered.

Hardhands pokes at a soggy wad of clothes lying in a heap on the disgusting floor. For one testicle-shriveling moment he thought that he saw black velvet amongst the sog; he does, but it's a torn shirt, not a puffy hat.

All magickal acts leave a resonance behind, unless the magician takes great pains to hide: Hardhands knows every archon, hierophant, sorceress, bibliomatic, and avatar in the City, but he don't recognize the author of this Working. He catches a drip of coldfire on one long finger and holds it up his lips: salt-sweet-smoky-oddly familiar but not enough to identify.

"Pigface pogo!" says our hero. He has put his foot down in slide and almost gone facedown in a smear of glass and black goo—mashy blackberry jam, the source of the sweet stench. Flailing unheroically he regains his balance, but in doing so grabs at the edge of an overturned settle. The settle has settled backwards, cockeyed on its back feet, but Hardhands' leverage rocks it forward again, and, hello, here's the Gimlet—well, parts of her anyway. She is stuck to the bench by a flood of dried blood, and the expression on her face is doleful and a little bit surprised.

"Pogo pigface on a pigpogopiss! Who the hell is that?"

Alfonso yanks the answer from the Aethyr. "The Roaring Gimlet, petty roller and barn stamper. You see her picture sometimes in the post office."

"She don't look too roaring to me. What the hell happened to her?"

Alfonso zips closer while Hardhands holds his sleeve to his sensitive nose. The stench of metallic blood is warring with the sickening sweet smell of the crushed blackberries, and together a pleasuring perfume they do not make.

"Me, I think she was chewed," Alfonso announces after close inspection. "By something hungry and mad."

"What kind of something?"

Alfonso shrugs. "Nobody I know. Sorry, boss."

As long as Doom is not chewed, Hardhands cares naught for the chewy-ness of others. He uneasily illuminates the fetid shadows with a vivid Gramatica phrase, but thankfully no rag-like wife does he see, tossed aside like a discarded tea-towel, nor red wet stuffy

Pig-toy, only bloody jam and magick-bespattered walls. He'd never admit it, particularly not to a yappy servitor, but there's a warm feeling of relief in his toes that Cyrenacia and Pig were not snacked upon. But if they were not snacked upon, where the hell are they, oh irritation.

There, in the light of his sigil—sign: two dainty feet stepped in jammy blood, hopped in disgust, and then headed up the back stairs, the shimmer of Bilskinir blue shining faintly through the rusty red. Whatever got the Gimlet did not get his wife and Pig, that for sure, that's all he cares about, all he needs to know, and the footprints are fading, too: onward.

At the foot of the stairs, Hardhands poises. A low distant noise drifts out of the floor below, like a bad smell, a rumbly agonized sound that makes his tummy wiggle.

"What is that?"

A wink of Alfonso's tails and top hat and here's his answer: "There's some guy locked in the cellar, and he's—he's in a bad way, and I think he needs our help—"

Hardhands is not interested in guys locked in cellars, nor in their bad ways. The footprints are fading, and the Current is still rising, he can feel it jiggling in his veins. Badness is on the loose—is not the Gimlet proof of that?—and Goddess Califa knows what else, and Tiny Doom is alone.

VI: Sugar Sweet

Here is Hardhands, hot on the heels of the pretty blue footsteps skipping along through the riotous streets. Hippy-hop, pitty-pat. The trail takes a turning into a narrow alley and Hardhands turns with it, leaving the sputtering street lamps behind. Before, the night was merely dark: now it's darkdarkdark. He flicks a bit of coldfire from his fingertips, blossoming a ball of luminescence that weirdly lights up the crooked little street, broken cobbles and black narrow walls. The coldfire ball bounces onward, and Hardhands follows. The footprints are almost gone: in a few more moments they will be gone; for a lesser magician they would be gone already.

And then, a drift of song:

"Hot corn, hot corn! Buy my hot corn!
Lovely and sweet, Lovely and Warm!"

Out of the shadow comes a buttery smell, hot and wafting, the jingling of bells, friendly and beckoning: a Hot Corn Dolly, out on the prowl. The perfume is delightful and luscious and it reminds Hardhands that dinner was long since off. But Hardhands does not eat corn (while not fasting, he's on an all meat diet, for to clean his system clear of sugar and other poisons), and when the Hot Corn Dolly wiggles her tray at him, her green ribbon braids dancing, he refuses.

The Corn Dolly is not alone; her sisters stand behind her, and their wide trays, and the echoing wide width of their farthingale skirts, flounced with patchwork, jingling with little bells, form a barricade that Hardhands, the young gentleman, cannot push through. The Corn Dolly skirts are wall-to-wall and their ranks are solid and only rudeness will make a breach.

"I cry your pardon, ladies," he says, in feu de joie, ever courteous, for is not the true mark of a gentleman his kindness towards others, particularly his inferiors? "I care not for corn, and I would pass."

"Buy my hot corn, deliciously sweet,
Gives joy to the sorrowful and strength to the weak."

The Dolly's voice is luscious, ripe with sweetness. In one small hand she holds an ear of corn, dripping with butter, fragrant with the sharp smell of chile and lime, bursting up from its peeling of husk like a flower, and this she proffers towards him. Hardhands feels a southerly rumble, and suddenly his mouth is full of anticipatory liquid. Dinner was a long long time ago, and he has always loved hot corn, and how can one little ear of corn hurt him? And anyway, don't he deserve some solace? He fumbles in his pocket, but no divas does he slap; he's the Pontifexa's grandson, and not in the habit of paying for his treats.

The Dolly sees his gesture and smiles. Her lips are glistening golden, as yellow as her silky hair, and her teeth, against the glittering, are like little nuggets of white corn.

"*A kiss for the corn, and corn for a kiss,*

One sweet with flavor, the other with bliss" she sings, and the other Dollies join in her harmony, the bells on their square skirts jingling. The hot corn glistens like gold, steamy and savory, dripping with yum. A kiss is a small price to pay to sink his teeth into savory. He's paid more for less, and he leans forward, puckering.

The Dollies press in, wiggling their oily fingers and humming their oily song, enfolding him in the husk of their skirts, their hands, their licking tongues. His southerly rumble is now a wee bit more southerly, and it's not a rumble, it's an avalanche. The corn rubs against his lips, slickery and sweet, spicy and sour. The chili burns his lips, the butter soothes them, he kisses, and then he licks, and then he bites into a bliss of crunch, the squirt of sweetness cutting the heat and the sour. Never has he tasted anything better, and he bites again, eagerly, butter oozing down his chin, dripping onto his shirt. Eager fingers stroke his skin, he's engorged with the sugar-sweetness, so long denied, and now he can't get enough, each niblet exploding bright heat in his mouth, his tongue, his head, he's drowning in the sweetness of it all.

And like a thunder from the Past, he hears ringing in his head the Pontifexa's admonition, oft repeated to a whiny child begging for hot corn, spun sugar, spicy taco, or fruit cup sold on the street in marvelous array but always denied because: *you never know where it's been*. An Admonition drummed into his head with painful frequency; all the other kidlets snacked from the street vendors with reckless abandon, but not the Pontifexa's grandson, whose tum was deemed too delicate for common food and the common bugs it might contain.

Drummed well and hard it would seem, to suddenly recall now, with memorable force, better late than never. Hardhands snaps open eyes and sputters kernels. Suddenly he sees true what the Corn Dollies' powerful glamour has disguised under a patina of butter and spice: musky kernels and musky skin. A fuzz of little black flies encircles them. The silky hair, the silky husks are slick with mold. The little white corn teeth grin mottled blue and green, and corn worms spill in a white wiggly waterfall from gaping mouths.

"Arrgg," says our hero, managing to keep the urp down, heroically. He yanks and flutters, pulls and yanks, but the knobby fingers have him firm, stalk to stalk. He heaves, twisting his shoulders, spinning and ducking: now they have his shirt, but he is free.

"Απελιγαζε!" he bellows at the top of his magickal lungs. The word explodes from his head with an agonizing aural thud. The Corn Dollies sizzle and shriek, but he doesn't wait around to revel in their popping. Now he's a fleet-footed fancy boy, skedaddling as fast as skirts will allow; to hell with heroics, there's no audience about, just get the hell out. He leaves the shrieking behind him, fast on booted heels, and it's a long heaving pause later, when the smell of burned corn no longer lingers on the air, that he stops to catch breath and bearings. His heart, booming with Gramatica exertion, is starting to slow, but his head, still thundering with a sugary rush, feels as though it might implode right there on his shoulders, dwindle down to a pinprick of pressure, diamond hard.

The sugar pounds in his head, beating his brain into a ploughshare of pain sharp enough to cut a furrow in his skull.

He leans on a scaly wall and sticks a practiced finger down his gullet. Up heaves corn, and bile, and blackened gunk, and more gunk. The yummy sour-lime-butter taste doesn't have quite the same delicious savor coming up as it did going down, nor is his shuddering now quite so delightful. He spits and heaves, and heaves and spits, and when his inside is empty of everything, including probably most of his internal organs, he feels a wee bit better. Not much, but some. His ears are cold. He puts a quivery hand to his head; his hat is gone.

The chapeau is not the only thing to disappear. Tiny Doom's tiny footprints, too, have faded. Oh for a drink to drive the rest of the stale taste of rotting corn from his tonsils. Oh for a super duper purge to scour the rest of the stale speed of sugar from his system. Oh for a bath, and bed, and deep sweet sleep. He's had a thin escape, and he knows it: the Corn Sirens could have drained him completely, sucked him as a dry as a desert sunset, and Punto Finale for the Pontifexa's grandson. Now it's going to take him weeks of purifications, salt-baths, and soda enemas to get back into whack. Irritating. He's also irked at the loss of his shirt; it was brand-new, he'd only worn it once, and the lace on its sleeves had cost him fifty-eight divas in gold. And his hat, bristling with angel feathers, its brim bigger than an apple pancake. He's annoyed at himself, sloppy-sloppy-sloppy.

The coldfire track has sputtered, and no amount of Gramatica kindling can spark it alight; it's too late, too gone, too long. Alfonso, too, is absent of summoning, and when Hardhands closes his eyes and clenches his fists to his chest, sucks in deep lungs of air, until the Current bubbles in his veins like the most sparkling of red wines, he knows why: the Current has flowed so high now that even the lowliest servitors can ride it without assistance, is strong enough to avoid constraint and ignore demand. He'd better find the kid soon. With the Current this high, only snackers will now be out; anyone without skill or protection—the snackees—will have long since gone home, or been eaten. Funtime for humans is over, and funtime for Others just begun.

Well, that's fine, Alfonso is just a garnish, not necessary at all. Is not Tiny Doom his own blood? Does not a shared spark run through their veins? He closes his eyes again, and stretches arms outward, palms upward, and he concentrates every split second of his Will into a huge vaporous awareness which he flings out over Califa like a net. Far far at the back of his throat, almost a tickle, not quite a taste, he finds the smell he is looking for. It's dwindling, and it's distant, but it's there and it's enough. A tiny thread connecting him to her, blood to blood, heat to heat, heartbeat to heartbeat, a tiny threat of things to come when Tiny Doom is not so Tiny. He jerks the thread with infinitesimal delicacy. It's thin, but it holds. It's thin, but it can never completely break.

He follows the thread, gently, gently, down darkened alleys, past shuttered facades, and empty stoops. The streets are slick with smashed fruit but otherwise forlorn. He hears the sound of distant noises, hooting, hollering, braying mule, a fire bell, but he is alone. The buildings grow sparser, interspaced with empty lots. They look almost like rows of tombstones, and their broken windows show utterly black. The acrid tang of burning sugar tickles his nose, and the sour-salt smell of marshy sea-water; he must be getting closer to the bay's soggy edge. Cobblestones give way to splintery corduroy, which gives way to moist dirt, and now the sweep of the starry sky above is unimpeded by buildings; he's almost out of the City, he may be out of the City now, he's never been this far on this road, and if he hadn't absolute faith in the Haðraaða family bond, he'd be skeptical that Tiny Doom's chubby little legs had made it this far, either.

But they have. He knows it.

Hardhands pauses, cocking his head: a tinge suffuses his skin, a gentle breeze that isn't a breeze at all, but the galvanic buzz of the Current. The sky above is now obscured by wafts of spreading fog, and, borne distantly upon that breeze, a vague tune. Musick.

Onward, on prickly feet, with the metallic taste of magick growing thicker in the back of his throat. The musick is building crescendo; it sounds so friendly and fun, promising popcorn, and candied apples, fried pies. His feet prickle with these promises, and he picks up the pace, buoyed on by the rollicking musick, allowing the musick to carry him onward, towards the twinkly lights now beckoning through the heavy mist.

Then the musick is gone, and he blinks, for the road has come to an end as well, a familiar end, although unexpected. Before him looms a giant polychrome monkey head, leering brightly. This head is two stories high, it has flapping ears and wheel-size eyes, and its gaping mouth, opened in a silent howl, is large enough for a gaggle of school children to rush through, screaming their excitement.

Now he knows where he is, where Tiny Doom has led him to, predictable, actually, the most magical of all childhood places: *Woodward's Garden, Fun for All Occasions, Not Occasionally but Always.*

How oft has Hardhands been to Woodward's (in cheerful daylight), and ah the fun he has had there (in cheerful daylight): the Circular Boat and the Mystery Manor, the Zoo of Pets and the Whirla-Gig. Pink popcorn and strawberry cake, and Madam Twanky's Fizzy Lick-A-Rice Soda. Ah, Woodward's Garden and the happy smell of sun, sugar, sweat, and sizzling meat. But at Woodward's, the fun ends at sundown, as evening's chill begins to rise, the rides begin to shut, the musick fades away, and everyone must go, exiting out the Monkey's Other End. Woodward's is not open at night.

But here, tonight, the Monkey's Eyes are open, although his smile is a grimace, less Welcome and more Beware. The Monkey's Eyes roll like red balls in their sockets, and at each turn they display a letter: "F" "U" "N" they spell in flashes of sparky red. Something skitters at our boy's ankles, and he jumps: scraps of paper flickering like shredded ghosts. The Monkey's Grin is fixed, glaring; in the dark it does not seem at all like the Gateway to Excitement and Adventure, only Digestion and Despair. Surely even Doom, despite her ravenous adoration of the Circular Boat, would not be tempted to enter the hollow throat just beyond the poised glittering teeth. Despite the promise of the Monkey's Rolling Eyes, there is no Fun here.

Or is there? Look again. Daylight, a tiara of letters crowns the Monkey's Head, spelling Woodward's Garden in cheery lights. But not tonight, tonight the tiara is a crown of spikes, whose glittering red letters proclaim a different title: *Madam Rose's Flower Garden.*

Hardhands closes his eyes against the flashes, feeling all the blood in his head blushing downward into his pinchy toes. Madam Rose's Flower Garden! It cannot be. Madam Rose's is a myth, a rumor, an innuendo, a whisper. A prayer. The only locale in Califa where entities, it is said, can walk in the Waking World without constraint, can move and do as their Will commands, and not be constrained by the Will of a magician or adept. Such mixing is proscribed, it's an abomination, against all laws of nature, and until this very second, Hardhands thought, mere fiction.

And yet apparently not fiction at all. The idea of Tiny Doom in such environs sends Hardhands' scalp a-shivering. This is worse than having her out on the streets. Primo child-flesh, delicious and sweet, and plump full of such energy as would turn the most mild-mannered elemental into a rival of Choronzon, the Daemon of Dispersion. Surrounded by dislocated elementals and egregores, under no obligation and bound by no sigil, indulging in every depraved whim. Surely the tiresome child did not go forward to her own certain doom

But his burbling tum, his swimming head, knows she did.

If he were not Banastre Haðraaða, the Grand Duque of Califa, this is the point where he'd turn about and go home. First he might sit upon the ground, right here in the dirt, and wallow for a while in discouragement, then he'd rise, dust, and retreat. If he were not himself, but someone else, someone lowly, he might be feeling pretty low.

For a moment, he is not himself, he is cold and tired and hungry and ready for the evening to end. It was fun to be furious, his anger gave him forward motion and will and fire, but now he wants to be home in his downy-soft bed with a yellow nasty newsrag and a jorum of hot wine. If Wish could be made Will in a heartbeat, he'd be lying back on damask pillows, drowning away to happy dreamland.

Before he can indulge in such twaddle, a voice catches his attention.

"Well, now, your grace. Slumming?"

Then does Hardhands notice a stool, and upon the stool a boy sitting, legs dangling, swinging copper-toed button boots back and forth. A pocketknife flashes in his hand; shavings flutter downward. He's tow-headed, and blue-eyed, freckled and tan, and he's wearing a polka-dotted kilt, a redingcote, and a smashed bowler. A smoldering stogie hangs down from his lips.

"I beg your pardon?"

"Never mind, never mind. Are you here for the auction?"

Hardhands replies regally: "I am looking for a child and a pink pig."

The boy says, brightly, "Oh yes, of course. They passed this way some time ago, in quite a hurry."

Hardhands makes a move to go inside, but is halted by the red velvet rope which is action as barrier to the Monkey's mouth.

"Do you have a ticket? It's fifteen divas, all you can eat and three trips to the bar."

Remembering his empty pockets, Hardhands says loftily: "I'm on the List."

The List: Another powerful weapon. If you are on it, all to the good. If not, back to the Icy Arrogance. But when has Hardhands not been on the List? Never! Unthinkable!

"Let me see," says the boy. He turns out pockets, and thumps his vest, fishes papers and strings, candy and fish-hooks, bones and lights, a white rat, and a red rubber ball. "I know I had some-thing—Ahah!" This ahah is addressed to his hat, what interior he is excavating and out of which he draws a piece of red foolscap. "Let me see . . . um . . . *Virex the Sucker of Souls, Zigurex Avatar of Agony, Valefor Teller of Tales*, no, I'm sorry, your grace, but you are not on the list. That will be fifteen divas."

"Get out of my way."

Hardhands takes a pushy step forward, only to find that his feet can not come off the ground. The Boy, the Gatekeeper, smells like human but he has powerful praeterhuman push.

"Let me by."

"What's the magick word?"

"Ουδενβακ." This word should blossom like fire in the sultry air, it should spout lava and sparks and smell like burning tar. It should shrink the boy down to stepping-upon size.

It sparks briefly, like a wet sparkler, and gutters away.

He tries again, this time further up the Gramatica alphabet, heavier on the results.

"ΕΙΟΥΑΕΗ!" This word should suck all the light out of the world, leaving a blackness so utter the boy will be gasping for enough breath to scream.

It casts a tiny shadow, like a gothick's smile, and then brightens.

"Great accent," says the boy. He is grinning sympathetically, which enrages Hardhands even more, because he is the Pontifexa's grandson and there's nothing to be sorry about for THAT. "But not magickal enough."

Hardhands is flummoxed. This is a first; never before has his magick been stifled, tamped, failed to light. Gramatica is tricky, it is true. In the right mouth the right Gramatica word will explode the boy into tiny bits of bouncing ectoplasm, or shatter the air as though it were made of ice, or turn the moon into a tulip. The right word in the wrong mouth, a mouth that stops when it should glottal or clicks when it should clack, could turn his tummy into a hat, roll back time, or turn his blood to fire. But, said right or said wrong, Gramatica never does nothing. His tummy is, again, tingling.

The boy is now picking his teeth with the tip of his knife. "I give you a hint. The most magickal word of them all."

What is more magick than Χηαψοφαθυε? Is there a more magickal word that Hardhands has never heard of? He's an adept of the sixth order, he's peeked into the Abyss, surely there is no Super Special Magickal Word hidden from him yet—he furrows his pure white brow into unflattering wrinkles, and then a tiny, whiny little voice in his head says: What's the magick word, Bwannie, what's the magick word?

"Please," Hardhands says. "Let me pass, please."

"With pleasure," the boy says, "But I must warn you. There are ordeals."

"No ordeal can be worse than listening to you."

"One might think so," the boy says. "You have borne my rudeness so kindly, your grace, that I hate to ask you for one last favor, but I fear I must."

Hardhands glares at the boy, who smiles sheepishly.

"Your boots, your grace. Madama doesn't care for footwear on her clean carpets. I shall give you a ticket, and give your boots a polish, and they'll be nice and shiny for you when you leave."

Hardhands does not want to relinquish his heels, which may only add an actual half an inch in height but are marvelous when it comes to mental stature; who cannot help but swagger in red-topped jackboots, champagne shiny and supple as night?

He sighs, bending. The grass below is cool against our hero's hot feet, once liberated happily from the pinchy pointy boots (ah vanity, thy name is only sixteen years old), but he'd trade the comfort, in a second, for height.

He hops and kicks, sending one boot flying at the kid (who catches it easily) and the other off into the darkness.

"Mucho gusto. Have a swell time, your grace."

Hardhands stiffens his spine with arrogance and steps into the Monkey's Mouth.

VII. Time's Trick

Motion moves in the darkness around him, a glint of silver to one side, then the other, then in front of him: he jumps. Then he realizes that the form ahead of him is familiar: his own reflection. He steps forward, and the Hardhands before him resolves into a Hardhands behind him, while those to either side move with him, keeping pace. For a second he hesitates, thinking to run into the mirror, but an outstretched arm feels only empty air, and he steps once, again, then again, more confidently. His reflection has disappeared; ahead is only darkness.

So he continues on, contained with a hollow square of his own reflections, which makes him feel a bit more cheerful, for what can be more reassuring but an entire phalanx of your own beautiful self? Sure, he looks a bit tattered: bare chest, sticky hair, blurred eyeliner, but it's a sexy tattered, bruised and battered, and slightly forlorn. He could start a new style with this look: After the Deluge, it could be called, or A Rough Night.

Of course Woodward's has a hall of mirrors, too, a horrifying place where the glasses stretch your silver-self until you look like an emaciated crane, or squash you down, round as a beetle. These mirrors continue, as he continues, to show only his perfect self, disheveled but still perfect. He laughs, a sound which, pinned in on all sides as it is, quickly dies. If this is the boy's idea of an Ordeal, he's picked the wrong man. Hardhands has always loved mirrors, so much so that he has them all over his apartments: on his walls, on his ceilings, even, in his Conjuring Closet, on the floor. He's never met a reflection of himself he didn't love, didn't cherish, cheered up by the sight of his own beauty—what a lovely young man, how blissful to be me!

He halts and fumbles in his kilt-pocket for his favorite lip rouge (*Death in Bloom*, a sort-of blackish pink) and reapplies. Checks his teeth for color, and blots on the back of his hand. Smooths one eyebrow with his fingertip and arranges a strand of hair so it is more fetchingly askew—then leans in, closer. A deep line furrows behind his eyes, a line where he's had no line before, and there, at his temple, is that a strand of gray amidst the silver? His groping fingers feel only smoothness on his brow; he smiles, and the line vanishes; he grips the offending hair and yanks: in his grasp it is as pearly as ever. A trick of the poor light then, and on he goes, but sneaking glances to his left and right, not from admiration but from concern.

As he goes, he keeps peeking sideways, and at each glance he quickly looks away again, alarmed. Has he always slumped so badly?

He squares his shoulders and peeks again. His hinder, it's huge, like he's got a caboose under his kilt, and his chin, it's as weak as custard. No, it must just be a trick of the light; his hinder is high and firm, and his chin as hard and curved as granite. He's overstressed and overwrought, and he still has all that sugar in his system. His gaze doggedly forward, he continues down the silver funnel, picks up his feet, eager, perhaps for the first time ever, to get away from a mirror.

The urge to glance is getting bigger and bigger, and Hard-hands has, before, always vanquished temptation by yielding to it, he looks again, this time to his right. There, he is as lovely as ever, silly silly. He grins confidently at himself; that's much better. He looks behind him and sees, in another mirror, his own back looking further beyond, but he can't see what he's looking at or why.

Back to the slog, and the left is still bugging him, he's seeing flashes out of the corner of his eye, and he just can't help it, he must look: his eyes, they are sunken like marbles into his face, hollow as a sugar skull, his skin tightly pulled, painted with garish red cheekbones. Blackened lips pull back from grayish teeth—his pearly white teeth!—He chatters those pearly whites together; his bite is firm and hard. He looks to the right and sees himself as he should be.

Now he knows, don't look to the left, keep to the right and keep focused; the left is a mirage, the right is reality. The left side is a horrible joke and the right side is true, but even as he increases his steps to almost a run (will this damn hallway never end?), the Voice of Vanity in his head is questioning that assertion. Perhaps the right side is the horrible joke, and the left side the truth, per-haps he has been blind to his own flaws, perhaps—

This time he is transfixed by the image that stares back, as astonished as he is: he's an absolute wreck. His hair is still and brittle, hanging about his knobby shoulders like salted sea grass.

His ice blue eyes look cloudy, and the thick black lines drawn about them serve only to sink them deeper into his skull. Scars streak lividly across his cheeks. Sunken chest and tattoos faded into blue and green smudges, illegible on slack skin. He's too horrified to seek reassurance in the mirror now behind him, he's transported by the horror before him: the horror of his own inevitable wreckage and decay. The longer he stares the more hideous he becomes. The image blurs for a moment, and then blood blooms in his hair and dribbles from his gaping lips; his shoulders are scratched and smudged with black, his eyes starting from his skull. He is surrounded by swirling snow, flecks of which sputter on his eyelashes, steam as they touch his skin. The shaft of an arrow protrudes from his throat.

"Oh how bliss to me," the Death's Head croaks, each word a bubble of blood.

With a shout, Hardhands raises his right fist and punches. His fist meets the glass with a nauseous jolt of pain that rings all the way down to his toes. The glass bows under his blow but doesn't crack. He hits again, and his corpse reels back, clutching itself with clawlike hands. The mirror refracts into a thousand diamond shards, and Hardhands throws up his other arm to ward off glass and blood. When he drops his shield, the mirrors and their Awful Reflection are gone.

He stands on the top of stairs, looking out over a tumultuous vista: there's a stage with feathered denizens dancing the hootchie-coo. Behind the hootchie-coochers, a band plays a ferocious double-time waltz. Couples slide and twist and turn to the musick, their feet flickering so quickly they spark. The scene is much like the scene he left behind at the Blue Duck, only instead of great big hair, there are great big horns, instead of sweeping skirts there are sweeping wings, instead of smoke there is coldfire. The musick is loud enough to liquefy his skull; he can barely think over its howling sweep.

The throng below whirls about in confusion—denizens, demons, egregores, servitors—was that a Bilskinir-Blue Bulk he saw over there at the bar, tusks a-gleaming, Butler Paimon on his damn night off? No matter even if it is Paimon, no holler for help from Hardhands, oh no. Paimon would have to help him out, of course, but Paimon would tell the Pontifexa for sure, for Paimon, in addition to being the Butler of Bilskinir, is a suck-up. No thanks, our hero is doing just fine on his own.

A grip pulls at Hardhands' soft hand; he looks down into the wizened grinning face of a monkey. Hardhands tries to yank from the grasp; the monkey has pretty good pull, which he puts into gear with a yank, that our hero has little choice but to follow. A bright red cap shaped like a flowerpot is affixed to Sieur Simian's head by a golden cord, and he's surprisingly good at the upright; his free hand waves a path through the crowd, pulling Hardhands behind like a toy.

The dancers slide away from the monkey's push, letting Hardhands and his guide through their gliding. By the band, by the fiddler, who is sawing away at his fiddle as though each note was a gasp of air and he a suffocating man, his hair flying with sweat, his face burning with concentration. Towards a flow of red velvet obscuring a doorway, and through the doorway into sudden hush, the cessation of the slithering music leaving sudden silence in Hardhands' head.

Now he stands on a small landing, overlooking a crowded room. The Great Big Horns and Very Long Claws etc. are alert to something sitting upon a dais at the far end of the room. Hardhands follows their attention and goes cold all the way to his bones.

Upon the dais is a table. Upon the table is a cage. Within the cage: Tiny Doom.

VIII. Cash & Carry

The bidding has already started. A hideous figure our hero recognizes as Zigurex the Avatar of Agony is flipping it out with a dæmon whose melty visage and dribbly hair Hardhands does not know. Their paddles are popping up and down in furious volley to the furious patter of the auctioneer:

". . . unspoiled untouched pure one hundred percent kid-flesh plump and juicy tender and sweet highest grade possible never been spanked whacked or locked in a closet for fifty days with no juice no crackers no light fed on honey dew and chocolate sauce . . ."

(Utter lie, Tiny Doom is in a cheesy noodle phase and if it's not noodles and it's not orange then she ain't gonna eat it, no matter the dire threat.) Tiny Doom is barking, frolicking about the cage happily. She's the center of attention, she's up past her bedtime, and she's a puppy. It's fun!

The auctioneer is small, delicate, and apparently human, although Hardhands is willing to bet that she's probably none of these at all, and she has the patter down: "Oh she's darling oh she's bright she'll fit on your mantel, she'll sleep on your dog-bed, she's compact and cute now, and ah the blood you can breed from her when she's older. What an investment, sell her now, sell her later, you're sure to repay your payment a thousand times over and a free Pig as garnish can you beat the deal—and see how bright she does bleed."

The minion hovering above the cage displays a long length of silver-tipped finger and then flicks downward. Tiny Doom yelps, and the rest of the patter is lost in Hardhands' roar as he leaps forward, pushing spectators aside: "THAT IS MY WIFE!"

His leap is blocked by bouncers, who thrust him backwards, but not far. Ensues: rumpus, with much switching and swearing and magickal sparkage. Hardhands may have Words of Power, and a fairly Heavy Fist for one so fastidious, but the bouncers have Sigils of Impenetrableness or at least Hides of Steel, and one of them has three arms, and suction cups besides.

"THAT IS MY WIFE!" Hardhands protests again, now pinned. "I demand that you release her to me."

"It's careless to let such a tempting small morsel wander the streets alone, your grace." Madam Rose cocks her head, her stiff wire headdress jingling, and the bouncers release Hardhands.

He pats his hair; despite the melee, still massively piled, thanks to Paimon's terrifically sticky hair pomade. The suction cups have left little burning circles on his chest, and his bare toes feel a bit tingly from connecting square with someone's tombstone-hard teeth, but at least he solaces in the fact that one of the bouncers is dripping whitish ooze from puffy lips and the other won't be breeding children anytime soon; just as hard a kick, but much more squishy. The room's a wreck, too, smashed chairs, crumpled paper, spilled popcorn, oh dear, too bad.

"She's my wife to be, as good as is my wife, and I want her back." He makes movement towards the cage, which is now terribly quiet, but the bouncers still bar the way.

Zigurex upsteps himself, then, looming over Hardhands, who now wishes he had been more insistent about the boots: "Come along with the bidding; it's not all night, you see, the tide is rising and the magick will soon sail."

The other dæmon, who is both squishy and scaly, bubbles his opinion as well. At least Hardhands assumes it is his opinion, impossible to understand his blubbering, some obscure dialect of Gramatica, or maybe just a very bad accent, anyway who cares what he has to say anyway, not Hardhands, not at all.

"There is no bidding, she's not for sale, she belongs to me, and Pig, too, and we are leaving," he says.

"Do you bid?" Madam Rose asks.

"No, I do not bid. I do not have to bid. She is my wife."

"One hundred fifty!" Zigurex says, last-ditch.

The Fishy Thing counters the offer with a saliva spray glug.

"He offers two hundred," says Madam Rose. "What do you offer?"

"Two hundred!" says Hardhands, outraged. "I've paid two hundred for a pot of lip rouge. She's worth a thousand if she's worth a diva—"

Which is exactly of course the entirely wrong thing to say but his outrage has gotten the better of his judgment, which was already impaired by the outrage of being manhandled like a commoner to begin with, and which also might not have been the best even before then.

Madam Rose smiles. Her lips are sparkly pink and her teeth are sparkly black. "One thousand divas, then, for her return! Cash only. Good night good night and come again!"

She claps her hands, and the bouncers start to press the disappointed bidders into removing.

"Now look here—" says Hardhands. "You can't expect me to buy my own wife, and even if you could expect me to buy my own wife, I won't. I insist that you hand her over right this very second and impede me no longer."

"Is that so?" Madam Rose purrs. The other bidders retreat easily; perhaps they have a sense of where this is all going and decide it's wise to get out of the way whilst there is still a way to get out of. Even Sieur Squishy and Zigurex go, although not without several smoldering backways looks on the part of the Avatar of Agony, obviously a sore loser. Madam Rose sits herself down upon a velvet-covered chair and waves Hardhands to do the same, but he does not. A majordomo has uprighted the brazier and repaired the

smoldering damage, decanted tea into a brass teapot and set it upon
a round brass tray. Madam Rose drops sugar cubes into two small
glasses and pours over: spicy cinnamon, tangy orange.

Hardhands ignores the tea; peers into the cage to access
damage.

"Pig has a tummy ache and wants to go home, Bwannie." The
fat little lip is trembling, and despite himself Hardhands is overwhelmed by the tide of adorableness, that he should, being a first-
rate magician and poet, be inoculated against. She is so like her
mother, oh his darling sister, sometimes it makes him want to cry.

He retreats into gruff. "Ayah, so well, Pig should not have had
so much candy. And nor should Pig have wandered off alone."

"He is bad," agrees Doom. "Very bad."

"Sit tight and do not cry. We will go home soon. Ayah?"

"Ayah." She sniffs, but holds the snuffle, little soldier.

Madam Rose again offers Hardhands a seat, which again he
does not sit upon, and a glass, which he waves away, remembering
anew the Pontifexa's advice, and also not trusting Madam's sparkly grin. He's heard of the dives where they slide sleep into your
drink; you gulp down happily and wake up six hours later minus
all you hold dear, and a splitting headache as well. Or worse still,
ginjoints that sucker you into one little sip, and then you have such
a craving that you must have more and more, but no matter how
much you have, it shall never be enough. He'll stay dry and alert,
thank you.

"I have no time for niceties, or social grace," he says, "I will
take my wife and pig, and leave."

"One thousand divas is not so great a sum to the Pontifexa's
grandson," Madam Rose observes. "And it's only right that I should
recoup some of my losses—look here, I shall have to redecorate,
and fashionable taste, as your grace knows, is not cheap."

"I doubt there is enough money in the world to buy you good taste, madama, and why should I pay for something that is mine?"

"Now who owns whom, really? *She* is the Heir to the House Haðraaða, and one day she'll be Pontifexa. *You* are just the boy who *does*. By rights all of us, including you, belong to her, in loyalty and in love. I do wish you would sit, your grace." Madam Rose pats the pillow beside her, which again he ignores.

This statement sets off a twinge of rankle because it is true. He answers loftily, "We are all the Pontifexa's obedient servants, and are happy to bend ourselves to her Will, and her Will in the matter of her Heir is clear. I doubt that she would be pleased to know of the situation of this night."

Madam Rose sets her red cup down. An ursine-headed minion offers her a chocolate, gently balanced between two pointy bear-claws. She opens red lips, black teeth, long red throat, and swallows the chocolate without a chew.

"I doubt," she says, "that the Pontifexa shall be pleased at tonight's situation at all. I do wish you would sit, your grace. I feel so small, and you so tall, so high above. And do sample, your grace. I assure you that my candy has no extra spice to it, just wholesome goodness you will find delicious. You have my word upon it."

Hardhands sits and takes the chocolate he is offered. He's already on the train bound for Purgelandia; he might as well make the journey worth the destination. The Minion twinkles azure bear eyes at him. Bears don't exactly have the right facial arrangement to smirk, but this bear is making a fine attempt, and Hardhands thinks what a fine rug Sieur Oso would make, stretched out before a peaceful fire. In the warmth of his mouth, the chocolate explodes into glorious peppery chocolate yum. For a second he closes his eyes against the delicious darkness, all his senses receding into the sensation of pure bliss dancing on his tongue.

"It is good chocolate, is it not?" Madam Rose asks. "Some say such chocolate should be reserved for royalty and the Goddess. But we do enjoy it, no?"

"What do you want?" Hardhands asks, and they both know that he doesn't just mean for Tiny Doom.

"Putting aside, for the moment, the thousand divas, I want nothing more than to be of aid to you, your grace, to be your humble servant. It is not what I may want from you but what you can want from me."

"That I have told you."

"Just that?"

In the cage, Tiny Doom is silent and staring, she may be a screamer, but she does, thankfully, know when to keep her trap shut.

"I can offer you no other assistance? Think on it, your grace. You are an adept, and you traffic with denizens of the deep, through the force of your Will. I am not an adept, but I also have traffic with those same denizens."

The second chocolate tangs his tongue with the sour-sweet brightness of lime. "Contrary to all laws of Goddess and nature," he says thickly, when the brilliant flavor has receded enough to allow speech. "Your traffic is obscene. It is not the same."

"I didn't say it was the same. I said we might complement each other, rather than compete. Do you not get tired of your position, your grace? You are so close, and yet so far. The Pontifexa's brightest boy, but does she respect you? Does she trust you? This little girl, is she not the hitch in your git-along, the sand in your shoe? Leave her with me, and she'll never muss your hair again, or wrinkle your cravat."

"I don't recall inviting you to comment upon my personal matters," says Hardhands, à la prince. "And I don't recall offering you my friendship, either."

"I cry your pardon, your grace. I only offer my thoughts in the hope—"

He's tired of the game now. If he had the thousand divas he'd fork them over just to be quit of the entire situation; it was fun, it was cool, it's not fun, it's not cool, he's bored, the sugar is drilling a spike through his forehead and he's done.

"I'll write you a draft, and you'll take it, and we shall leave, and that's the end of the situation," Hardhands says loftily.

Madam Rose sighs and sips her tea. Another sigh, another sip.

"I'm sorry, your grace, but if you cannot pay, then I must declare your bid null, and reopen the auction. Please understand my position. It is, and has always been, the policy of this House to operate on a cash basis; I'm sure you understand why—taxes, a necessary evil, but perhaps more evil than necessary." Madam Rose smiles at him, and sips again before going on. "My reputation rests upon my policies, and that I apply them equally to all. Duque of Califa or the lowliest servitor, all are equal within my walls. So you see, if I allow you license I have refused others, how shall it appear then?"

"Smart," answers our hero. "Prudent. Wise."

Madam Rose laughs. "Would that others might consider my actions in that light, but I doubt their charity. No, I'm sorry, your grace. I have worked hard for my name. I cannot give it up, not for you or for anyone."

She puts her tea glass down and clicks her tongue, a sharp snap that brings Sieur Bear to her side. "The Duque has decided to withdraw his bid; please inform Zigurex that his bid is accepted and he may come and claim his prize."

Hardhands looks at Doom in her cage; her wet little face peers through the bars. She smiles at him. She's scared, but she has confidence that Bwannie will save her, Bwannie loves her. Bwannie has a sense of déjà vu; hasn't he been here before, why is it his fate to always give in to her, little monster? Tiny Doom, indeed.

"What do you want?" he repeats.

"Well," Madam Rose says brightly. "Now that you mention it. The Pontifexina is prime, oh that's true, but I know one more so. More mature, more valuable, more ready."

Now it's Hardhands' turn to sigh, which he does, and sip, wetting parched throat, now not caring if the drink be drugged or not. "You'll let her go? Return her safe and sound?"

"Of course, your grace. You have my word on it."

"Not a hair on her head or a drop from her veins or a tear from her eye? Not a scab, or nail, or any part that might be later used against her? Completely whole? Untouched, unsmudged, no tricks?"

"As you say."

Hardhands puts his glass down, pretending resignation. "All right then. You have a deal."

Of course he don't really give in, but he's assessed that perhaps its better to get Doom out of the way. He can play rough enough if it's only his own skin involved, but why take the chance of collateral damage? When she's out of the way, he calculates, and Madam Rose's guard is down, then we'll see, oh yes, we'll see.

Madam Rose's shell-white hand goes up to her lips, shading them briefly behind two slender fingers. Then the fingers flip down and flick a shard of spinning coldfire towards him. Hardhands recoils, but too late. The airy kiss zings through the air like an arrow of outrageous fortune and smacks him right in the middle of Death in Bloom. The kiss feels like a kick to the head, and our hero and his chair flip backwards, the floor rising to meet his fall, but not softly. The impact sends his bones jarring inside his flesh, and the jarring is his only movement, for the sigil has left him shocked and paralyzed.

He can't cry out, he can't flinch, he can only let the pain flood down his palate and into his brain, in which internal shouting and swearing is making up for external silence. He can't close his eyes, either, but he closes his outside vision and brings into inside focus the bright sharp words of a sigil that should suck all the energy from Madam Rose's sigil, blow it into a powderpuff of oblivion.

The sigil burns bright in Hardhands' eyes, but it is also trapped and cannot get free. It sparks and wheels, and he desperately tries to tamp it out, dumping colder, blacker sigils on top its flare, trying to fling it outward and away, but it's stuck firmly inside his solar plexus; he can fling it nowhere. It's caught in his craw like a fish bone, and he's choking but he can't choke because he cannot move. The sigil's force billows through him: it is twisting his entrails into knots, his bones into bows, it's flooding him with a fire so bright that it's black, with a fire so cold that it burns and burns and burns. His brain boils, and then: nothing.

IX. Thy Baited Hook

Here is Hardhands, returning to the Waking World. His blood is mud within his veins, he can barely suck air through stifled lungs, and there's a droning in his ears, no not droning, humming, Tiny Doom:

"Kick her bite her that's the way I'll spite her! Kick her bite her that's the way I'll spite her! Kick her bite her that's the way I'll spite her!"

The view aloft is raven-headed angels, with ebony black wings swooping loops of brocade across a golden ceiling. Then the view aloft is blocked by Tiny Doom's face; she still has the sugar mustache, and her kohl has blurred, cocooning her blue eyes in smoky blackness. Her hat is gone.

"Don't worry, Bwannie." She pats his stiff face with a sticky hand. "Pig will save us."

His brain heaves but the rest of him remains still. The frame of his body has never before been so confining. Diligent practice has made stepping his mind from his flesh an easy accomplishment, are there not times when a magician's Will needs independence from his blood and bones? But never before has he been stuck, nor run up against sigils harder and more impenetrable than his own. Lying in the cage of his own flesh, he is feeling helpless and tiny, and it's a sucky feeling, not at all suited to his stature of Pontifexa's grandson, first-rate magician and—

"I will bite you," says Doom.

"I doubt that," is the gritty answer, a deep rumble: "My skin is thick as steel and your teeth will break."

"Ha! I am a shark and I will bite you."

"Not if I bite you first, little lovely, nip your sweet tiny fingers, crunch crunch each one, oh so delicious, what a snack. Come here, little morsel."

The weight of Tiny Doom suddenly eases off his chest, but not without kicking and gripping, holding on to him in a vice-like grip, oww, her fingers dig like nails into his leg but to no avail. Tiny Doom is wrenched off of him, and in the process he's wrenched sideways; now he's got a nice view of the grassy floor, a broken teapot, and, just on the edge, someone's feet. The feet are shod in garish two-tone boots: magenta upper and orange toe-cap. Tiny Doom screams like a rabbit, high and horrible.

"You'll bruise her," says a voice from above the feet. "And then the Pontifexa will be chuffed."

"I shall not hurt her one jot if she's a good girl, but she should shut her trap, a headache I am getting."

Good for her, Tiny Doom does not shut her trap, she opens her trap wider and shoots the moon, with a piercing squeal that stabs into Hardhands' unprotected ears like an awl, slicing all the way down to the center of his brain. With a smack, the shriek abruptly stops.

Two pretty little bare feet drift into Hardhands' view. "Stop it, you two. She must be returned in perfect condition, an' I get my deposit back. It's only the boy that the Pontifexa wants rid of; the girl is still her heir. Leave her alone, or I shall feed you both into my shredder. Chop chop. The guests are waiting, and he must be prepared."

"She squirms," complains the Minion.

Madam Rose, sternly: "You, little madam, stop squirming. You had fun being a puppy, and cupcakes besides, and soon you shall be going home to your sweet little bed. How sad Grand-mamma and Paimon shall be if I must give them a bad report of your behavior."

Sniffle, sniff. "But I want Bwannie."

"Never you mind Bwannie for now. Here, have a Choco-Sniff, and here's one for Pig, too."

Sniff, sniffle. "Pig don't like Choco-Sniffs."

Hardhands kicks, but its like kicking air, he can feel the movement in his mind, but his limbs stay stiff and locked. And then his mind recoils: What did Madam Rose say about the Pontifexa? Did he hear a-right? Deposit? Report?

"Here then is a jacksnap for Pig. Be a good girl, eat your candy, and then you shall kiss Bwannie good-bye."

Whine: "I want to go with Bwannie!"

"Now, now." Madam Rose's cheery tone tingles with irritation, but she's making a good show of not annoying Tiny Doom into another session of shrieking. "Now, Bwannie must stay here, and you must go home—do not start up with the whining again, it's hardly fitting for the Pontifexa's heir to cry like a baby, now is it? Here, have another Choco-Sniff."

Then more harshly, "You two, get the child ready to be returned and the boy prepared. I shall be right back."

The pretty feet float from Hardhands' view and a grasp attaches to Hardhands' ankle. Though his internal struggle is mighty, externally he puts up no fuss at all. Flipped over by rough hands, he sees above him the sharp face of a Sylph, pointy eyes, pointy nose, pointy chin. Hands are fumbling at his kilt buckles; the Sylph has really marvelous hair, it's the color of fresh caramel and it smells, Hardhands notices, as the Sylph bends over to nip at his neck, like new-mown grass. A tiny jolt of pretty pain, and warm wetness dribbles down his neck.

"Ahhh . . . ," the Sylph sighs, "You should taste this, first-rate knock-back."

"Madama said be nice."

"I am being nice, as nice as pie, as nice as he is. Nice and sweet." The Sylph licks at Hardhands' neck again; its tongue is scrape-y, like a cat's, and it hurts in a strangely satisfying way. "Sweet sweet darling boy. He is going to bring our garden joy. What a deal she has made. Give the girl, but keep the boy, he's useful to us, even if she don't want him anymore. A good trick he'll turn for Madama. Bright boy."

Hardhands is hoisted aloft, demon claws at his ankles and his wrists slinging him like a side of beef on the way to the barbeque pit. His eyes are slitted open, his head dangling downward, he can see only a narrow slice of floor bobbing by. A carpet patterned with entwined snakes, battered black and red tiles, white marble veined with gold. He's watching all this, with part of his attention, but mainly he's running over and over again what Madam Rose had said about the Pontifexa. Was it possible to be true? Did Grandmamma set him up? Sell him out? Was this all a smokescreen to get him out of her hair, away from her treasure? He will not believe it, he will not believe it, it cannot be true!

Rough movement drops Hardhands onto the cold floor, and metal clenches his ankles. The bracelets bite into his flesh as he is hoisted aloft, and all the blood rushes to his head in a explosion of pressure. For a second, even his slit of sight goes black, but then, just as suddenly, he finds he can open his eyes all the way. He rolls eyeballs upward and sees retreating minion backs. He rolls eyes downward and sees polished marble floor and the tangled drape of his own hair, Paimon's pomade having finally given up. The fetters are burning bright pain into his ankles, and he's swaying slightly from some invisible airflow, but the movement is kind of soothing and his back feels nice and stretched out. If it weren't for the immobilization, and being obvious bait, hanging upside-down could be kind of fun.

Our hero tries to wiggle, but can't, tries to jiggle but is still stuck. He doesn't dare try another sigil and risk blowing his brains out, and without the use of his muscles he cannot gymnastic himself free. He closes his internal eyes, slips his consciousness into darkness, and concentrates. His Will pushes and pushes against the pressure that keeps him contained, focuses into a single point that must burn through. After a second, a minute, an eternity, all bodily sensation—the burn of the fetters, the stretch of his back, the pressure of his bladder, the breeze on his face—slips away, and his Will floats alone on the Current.

Away from the strictures of his body, Hardhands' consciousness can take any form that he cares to mold it to, or no form at all, a spark of himself drifting on the Currents of Elsewhere. But such is his fondness for his own form, even Elsewhere, that when he steps lightly from the flesh hanging like a side of beef, he coalesces into a representation of himself in every way identical to his corporeal form, although with lip rouge that will not smudge, and spectacularly elevated hair.

On Elsewhere feet, Hardhands' fetch turns to face its meaty shell and is rather pleased with the view; even dangling upside down, he looks pretty darn good. Elsewhere, the sigil that has caged Hardhands' motion is clearly visible as a pulsating net of green and gold, interwoven at the interstices with splotches of pink. A Coarctation Sigil, under normal circumstances no stronger than pie, but given magnitude by the height of the Current and Hardhands' starchy condition. The fetch, however, is not limited by starch, and the Current just feeds its strength. Dismantling the constraint is the work of a matter of seconds, and after the fetch slides back into its shell, it's a mere bagatelle to contort himself down and free.

Casting free of the fetters with a splashy Gramatica command, Hardhands rubs his ankles, and then stands on tingly feet. Now that he has the leisure to inspect the furnishings, he sees there are no furnishings to inspect because the room, while sumptuously paneled in gorgeous tiger-eye maple, is empty other than a curvy red velvet chaise. The only ornamentations are the jingly chains dangling from the ceiling. The floor is bare stone, cold beneath his bare feet. And now he notices that the flooring directly under the dangle is dark and stained, with something that he suspects is a combination of blood, sweat, and tears.

Places to go and praterhuman entities to fry, no time to linger to discover the truth of his suspicions. Hardhands turns to make his exit through the sole door, only to find that the door is gone, and in its place a roiling black Vortex as black and sharp as the Vortex that he himself had cut out of the Aeyther only hours before. He is pushed back by the force of the Vortex, which is spiraling outward, not inward, thus indicating that Something is coming, rather than trying to make him go.

The edges of the Vortex glow hot-black; the wind that the Vortex is creating burns his skin. He shields his eyes with his hand

and tries to stand upright, but his buzzing feet cannot hold against the force, and he falls. The Vortex widens, like a surprised eye, and a slit of light appears pupil-like in its darkness. The pupil widens, becomes a pupa, a cocoon, a shell, an acorn, an egg, growing larger and larger and larger until it fills the room with unbelievable brightness, with a scorching heat that is hotter than the sun, bright enough to burn through Hardhands' shielding hand. Hardhands feels his skin pucker, his eyes shrivel, his hair start to smolder, and then just as he is sure he is about to burst into flames, the light shatters like an eggshell, and Something has arrived.

Recently, Hardhands' Invocations have grown quite bold, and, after some bitter tooth and nails, he's pulled a few large fish into his circle. But those are as like to This as a fragment of beer bottle is to a faceted diamond. He knows, from the top of his pulsating head to the tips of his quivering toes, that this is no servitor, no denizen, no elemental. Nothing this spectacular can be called, corralled, or compelled. This apparition can be nothing but the highest of the high, the blessed of the blessed: the Goddess Califa herself.

How to describe what Hardhands sees? Words are too simple, they cannot do justice to Her infinite complexity, she's Everything and Nothing, both fractured and whole. His impressions are blurred and confused, but here's a try. Her hair is ruffled black feathers, it is slickery green snakes, it is as fluffy and lofty as frosting. Her eyes—one, two, three, four, maybe five—are as round and polished as green apples, are long tapered crimson slits, they are as flat white as sugar. She's as narrow as nightfall, She's as round as winter, She's as tall as moonrise, She's shorter than love. Her feet do not crush the little flowers, She is divine, She is fantastic.

She simply is.

Hardhands has found his footing only to lose it again, falling to his knees before her, her fresh red smile as strong as a kick to the head, to the heart. Hardhands is smitten—no, not smitten, he's smote, from the tingly tingly top of his reeling head to the very tippy tip of his tingling toes. He's freezing and burning, he's alive, he's dying, he's dead. He's hypmoooootized. He gapes at the Goddess, slack-jawed and tight-handed, wanting nothing more than to reach out and grasp at her perfection, bury himself in the ruffle of her feathers. Surely a touch of Her hand would spark such fire in him that he would catch alight and perish in a blaze of exquisite agony, but it would be worth it, oh it would be worth every cinder.

The Goddess's mouth opens, with a flicker of a velvet tongue and the glitter of a double row of white teeth. The Gramatica that flows from Her mouth in a sparkly ribband is as crisp and sweet as a summer wine, it slithers over Hardhands' flushed skin, sliding into his mouth, his eyes, his ears and filling him with a dark sweet rumble.

"Georgiana's toy," the Goddess purrs. He didn't see Her move but now She is poured over the chaise like silk, and the bear-head minion is offering bowls of snacks, ice cream sundaes, and magazines. "Chewable and sweet, ah lovely darling yum."

Hardhands has forgotten Georgiana, he's forgotten Tiny Doom, he's forgotten Madam Rose, he's forgotten himself, he's forgotten his exquisite manners—no, not entirely, even the Goddess's splendor cannot expunge good breeding. He toddles up onto sweaty feet and sweeps the floor with his curtsy.

"I am your obedient servant, your grace," he croaks.

The Goddess undulates a languid finger and he finds himself following Her beckon, not that he needs to be beckoned, he can barely hold himself aloof, wants nothing more than to throw himself forward and be swallowed alive. The Goddess spreads Her wings, Her arms, Her legs, and he falls into Her embrace, the prickle of the feathers closing over his bare skin electric and hot.

X. Doom Acts

Here is Tiny Doom howling like a banshee, a high-pitched shriek that usually results in immediate attention to whatever need she is screaming for: more pudding, longer story, hotter bath, bubbles. The Minion whose arm she is slung under must be pitch deaf because her shrieks have not the slightest impact upon him. He continues galumphing along, whistling slightly, or perhaps that is just the breeze of his going, which is a rapid clip.

She tries teeth, her fall-back weapon and always effective, even on Paimon whose blue skin is surprisingly delicate. The Minion's hide is as chewy as rubber and it tastes like salt licorice. Spitting and coughing, Tiny Doom gives up on the bite. Kicking has no effect other than to bruise her toes, and her arms are too pinned for hitting, and, down the stairs they go, bump bump, Bwannie getting farther and farther away. Pig is jolting behind them, she's got a grip on one dangly ear, but that's all, and his bottom is hitting each downward stump, but he's too soft to thump.

An outside observer might think that Doom is wailing for more candy, or perhaps is just overtired and up past her bedtime. Madam Rose certainly thought that her commotion was based in overtiredness, plus a surfeit of sugar, and the Bouncer thinks it's based in spoiledness, plus a surfeit of sugar, but they are both wrong. Sugar is Doom's drug of choice; she's not allowed it officially, but unofficially she has her ways (she knows exactly in what drawer the Pontifexa's secretary keeps his stash of Crumbly Crem-O's and Jiffy-Ju's, and if that drawer is empty, Relais can be relied upon to have a box of bon-bons hidden from Hardhands in the bottom of his wardrobe), and so her system can tolerate massive quantities of the stuff before hyperactivity and urpyness sets in.

No. She is wailing because every night, at tuck-in time, after the Pontifexa has kissed her, and kissed Pig and together they have said their prayers, then Paimon sits on the edge of Tiny Doom's big white frilly bed and tells her a story. It's a different story every night, Paimon's supply of fabulosity being apparently endless, but always with the same basic theme:

Kid is told what To Do.

Kid does Not Do what Kid is told To Do.

Kid gets into Bad Trouble with various Monsters.

Kid gets Eaten.

The End, yes, you may have one more drink of water, and then no more excuses and it's lights out, and to sleep. Now.

Tiny Doom loves these stories, whose Directives and Troubles are always endlessly inventively different, but which always turn out the same way: with a Giant Monstrous Burp. She knows that Paimon's little yarns are for fun only, that Kids do not really get eaten when they do not do what they are told, for she does not do what she is told all the time, and she's never been eaten. Of course, no one would dare eat her anyway, she's the Heir to the Pontifexa, and has Paimon and Pig besides. Paimon's stories are just stories, made to deliciously shiver her skin, so that afterwards she lies in the haze of the nightlight, cuddled tight to Pig's squishiness, and knows that she is safe.

But now, tonight, she's seen the gleam in Madam Rose's eye and seen the look she gave her minions and Tiny Doom knew instantly that Bwannie is in Big Trouble. This is not bedtime, there is no Paimon, and no nightlight, and no drink of water. This is all true Big Trouble, and Tiny Doom knows exactly where Big Trouble ends. Now she is scared, for Bwannie and for herself, and even for Pig, who would make a perfect squishy demon dessert.

Thus, shrieking.

"Bwaaaaaaaaaaaaaaaaaaaaaaaanie!"Doomcries. "Bwaaaaaaaaaaaa-nie!"

They jump the last step, Tiny Doom jolting bony hip, oww, and then round a corner. Doom sucks in the last useless shriek. Her top half is hanging half over the servitor's shoulder, and her dangling-down head is starting to feel tight, plus the shrieking has left her breathless, so for a few seconds she gulps in air. Gulping, her nose running yucky yuck. She wiggles, whispers, and lets go of Pig.

He plops down onto the dirty floor, hinder up and snout down, and then they round another corner and he's gone.

She lifts her head, twisting her neck, and there's the hairy interior of a pointy ear.

She shouts: "Hey, minion!"

"I ain't listening," says the Minion. "You can shout all you want, but I ain't listening. Madam told me not to listen, and I ain't."

"I gotta pee!"

"You gotta wait," the Minion says. "You be home soon, and then you can pee in your own pot. And you ain't gotta shout in my ear. You make my brain hurt, you loudness little bit, you."

"I gotta pee right now!" Doom, still shouting, anyway, just in case there are noises behind them. "I'M GONNA PEE NOW!"

The Minion stops and shifts Tiny Doom around like a sack full of flour, and breathes into her face. "You don't pee on me, loudness."

Like Paimon, the Minion has tusks and pointy teeth, but Paimon's tucks are polished white and his teeth sparkle like sunlight, and his breath smells always of cloves. The Minion's tusks are rubbed and worn, his teeth yucky yellow, and he's got bits of someone caught between them.

Doom wrinkles her nose and holds her breath and says in a whine: "I can't help it, I have to go, my hot chocolate is all done."

Her feet are dangling and she tries to turn the wiggle into a kick, but she can't quite reach the Minion's soft bits, and her purple slippers wiggle at empty air.

"You pee on me and I snack you up, nasty baby." The Minion crunches spiny fangs together, clashing sparks. "Delish!"

"You don't dare!" says Tiny Doom stoutly. "I am the Pontifexina and my grandmamma would have your knobby hide if you munch me!!"

"An' I care, little princess, if you piss me wet, I munch you dry—"

"**ХАѰНОВНО**" whispers Tiny Doom and spits. She's got a good wad going, and it hits the Minion right on the snout.

The Minion howls and drops her. She lands on stingy sleepy feet, falls over, and then scrambles up, stamping. The Minion is also stamping, and holding his hairy hands to his face; under his clawing fingers smoke is steaming. He careens this way and that, Doom dodging around his staggers, and then she scoots by him and back the way they had just come.

Tiny Doom runs as fast as her fat little legs will run, her heart pounding because she is now in Big Trouble, and she knows if the Minion quits dancing and starts chasing, she's going to be Eaten, too. The hot word she spit burned her tongue, and that hurts, too, and where's Pig? She goes around another corner, thinking she'll see the stairs that they came down, but she doesn't, she sees another long hallway. She turns around to go back, and then the Minion blunders towards her, his face a melt-y mess, and she reverses, speedily.

"*I dance around in a ring and suppose and the secret sits in the middle and knows,*" she sings very quietly to herself as she runs.

Carpet silent under her feet; a brief glimpse of another running Doom reflected off a glass curio cabinet; by a closed door, the knob turns but the door will not open. She can feel the wind of closing in beating against her back, but she keeps going. The demon is shouting mean things at her, but she keeps going.

"*You dance around in a ring and suppose and the secret sits in the middle and knows.*"

A door opens and a were-flamingo trips out, stretching its long neck out; Doom dodges around its spindly legs, ignoring yelps. Ahead, more stairs, and there she aims, having no other options, can't go back and there's nowhere to go sideways.

At the top of the stairs, Doom pauses and finally looks behind. The Minion has wiped most of his melt off, livid red flares burn in his eye sockets and he looks pretty mad. The were-flamingo has halted him, and they are wrangling, flapping wings against flapping ears. The Minion is bigger but the were-flamingo has a sharp beak—rapidfire pecking at the Minion's head. The Minion punches one humongous fist and down the flamingo goes, in a flutter of pink feathers.

"I snack you, spitty baby!" the Minion howls and other things too mean for Doom to hear.

"*We dance around in a ring and suppose and the secret sits in the middle and knows.*"

Doom hoists herself up on the banister, squeezing her tummy against the rail. The banister on the Stairs of Infinite Demonstration, Bilskinir's main staircase, is fully sixty feet long. Many is the time that Doom has swooped down its super-polished length, flying miles through the air, at the end to be received by Paimon's perfect catch. This rail is much shorter, and there's no Paimon waiting, but here we go!

She flings her legs over and slides off. Down she goes, lickety-split, bumping over splinters but still getting up a pretty good whoosh. Here comes the demon, waving angry arms; he's too big to slide, so he galumphs down the stairs, clumpty clump, getting closer. Doom hits the end of the banister and soars onward another five feet or so, then ooph, hits the ground, owww. She bounces back upward and darts through the foyer and into the mudroom beyond, pulling open her pockets as she goes.

Choco-Sniffs and jacksnaps skitter across the parquet floor, rattling and rolling. Sugarbunnies and beady-eyes, jimjoos and honeybuttons scatter like shot. Good-bye crappy candy, good-bye yummy candy, good-bye.

"I DANCE AROUND A RING AND SUPPOSE AND THE SECRET SITS IN THE MIDDLE AND KNOWS."

Ahead, a big red door, well barred and bolted, but surely leading Out. The bottom bolt snaps back under her tiny fingers, but the chains are too high and tippy-toe, hopping, jumping will not reach them. The Demon is down the stairs, he's still shouting and steaming, and the smell of charred flesh is stinky indeed.

A wall rack hangs by the door, and from it coats and cloaks dangle like discarded skins; Doom dives into the folds of cloth and becomes very small and silent. She's a good hider, Tiny Doom, she's learned against the best (Paimon).

Her heart pounds thunder in her ears, and she swallows her panting. When Paimon makes discovery (if he makes discovery), it means only bath-time, or mushy peas, or toenail clipping. If the demon finds her, Pontifexina or not, it's snicky-snack time for sure. She really did have to potty too, pretty bad. She crosses her ankles and jiggles her feet, holding.

In the other room, out of sight, comes yelling, shouting, roaring, and then a heavy thud that seems to shake the very walls. The thud reverberates and then fades away.

Silence.

Stillness.

Tiny Doom peeks between the folds. Through the archway she sees rolling candy and part of a sprawled bulk. Then the bulk heaves, hooves kicking. The demon's lungs have re-inflated and he lets out a mighty horrible roar—the nastiest swear word that Tiny Doom has ever heard. Doom, who had poked her head all the way out for a better view, yanks back, just in time. The Word, roiling like mercury, howls by her, trailing sparks and smelling of shit.

A second roar is gulped off in mid-growl, and turns into a shriek, which is then muffled in thumping and slurping, ripping, and chomping. Doom peeks again: the demon's legs are writhing, wiggling, and kicking. A thick stain spreads through the archway, gooey and green. Tiny Doom wiggles her way out of the velvet and runs happily towards the slurping sound.

XI. Desire Gratified

Inside the Goddess's embrace, Hardhands is dying, he's crying, he's screaming with pleasure, with joy, crying his broken heart out. He's womb-enclosed, hot and smothering, and reduced to his pure essence. He has collapsed to a single piercing pulsing point of pleasure. He has lost himself, but he has found everything else.

And then his ecstasy is interrupted by another piercing sensation: pain. Not the exquisite pain of a well-placed needle, or perfectly laid lash, but an ugly pain that gnaws into his pleasurable non-existence in an urgent painful way. He wiggles, tossing, but the pain will not go away, it only gnaws deeper, and with each razor nibble it slices away at his ecstasy. And as he is torn away from the Goddess's pleasure, he is forced back into himself, and the wiggly body-bound part of himself realizes that the Goddess is sucking him out of life. The love-torn spirit part of him does not care. He struggles, trying to dive down deeper into the bottomless divine love, but that gnawing pain is tethering him to the Waking World, and he can't kick it free.

Then the Goddess's attention lifts from him, like a blanket torn away. He lies on the ground, the stones slick and cold against his bare skin. The echo of his loss pounds in his head, farrier-like, stunning him. A shrill noise pierces his agony, cuts through the thunder, a familiar high-pitched whine:

"Ya! Ya! Ya!"

His eyes are filled with sand; it takes a moment of effort before his nerveless hands can find his face and knuckle his vision clear. Immediately he sees: Tiny Doom, dancing with the bear-headed Minion. Sieur Oso is doing the Mazorca, a dance which requires a great deal of jumping and stamping, and he's got the perfect boots to make the noise, each one as big as horse's head. Tiny Doom is doing the Ronde-loo, weaving round and round Sieur Oso, her circular motion too sick-making for Hardhands to follow.

Then he realizes: no, they are not dancing, Sieur Oso is trying to squash Tiny Doom like a bug, and she, rather than run like a sensible child, is actually taunting him on. Oh Haðraaða!

Dimly Tiny Doom's husband sparks the thought that perhaps he should help her, and he's trying to figure out where his feet are, so as to arise to this duty, when his attention is caught by a whirl, not a whirl, a Vortex the likes of which he has never before seen, a Vortex as black as ink, but streaked hot pink, and furious furious. Though he can see nothing but the cutting blur of the spin, he can feel the force of the fight within; the Goddess is battling it out with something, something strong enough to give her a run for her divas, something tenacious and tough.

"Bwannie! Bwannie!" cries Doom. She is still spinning, and the Minion is starting to look tuckered, his stomps not so stompy anymore, and his jeers turned to huffy puffs. Foam is dribbling from his muzzle like whipped cream.

Hardhands ignores Tiny Doom.

"ΑΠΕΞ!" Hardhands grates, trying to throw a Word of encouragement into the mix, to come to his darling's aid. The Word is a strong one, even his weakened state, but it bounces off the Vortex, harmless, spurned, just as he has been spurned. The Goddess cares nothing for Hardhands' love, for his desire; he chokes back tears and staggers to his feet, determined to help somehow, even if he must cast himself into the fire to do so.

Before he can do anything so drastic, there is the enormous sound of suction sucking in. For a split second, Hardhands feels himself go as flat as paper; his lungs suck against his chest, his bones slap into ribands, his flesh becomes as thin as jerky. The Current pops like a cork, the world re-inflates, and Hardhands is round and substantial again, although now truly bereft. The Goddess is gone.

The Vortex has blushed pink now, and its spin is slowing, slower, slower, until it is no longer a Vortex, but a little pink blur, balanced on pointy toes, ears flopping—what the hell? Pig?

He has gone insane? In one dainty pirouette Pig has soared across the room and latched himself to the Minion's scraggly throat. Suddenly invigorated, Sieur Oso does a pirouette of his own, upward, gurgling.

"What is going on—!" Madam Rose's voice raises high above the mayhem noises, then it chokes. She has stalled in the doorway, more minions peering from behind her safety. Tiny Doom has now attached to Sieur Oso's hairy ankle, and her grip—hands and teeth—is not dislodged by his antic kicking, though whether the minion is now dancing because Tiny Doom is gnawing on his ankle or because his throat is a massive chewy-mess, it's hard to say. Pig disengages from Sieur Oso and leaps to Madam Rose, who clutches him to her bosom in a maternal way, but jerkily, as though she wants less of his love, not more. Her other slaveys have scarpered, and now that the Goddess is gone, Hardhands sees no particular reason to linger, either.

He flings one very hard Gramatica word edgewise at the antic bear. Sieur Oso jerks upward, and his surprised head sails backwards, tears through the tent wall, and is gone. Coldfire founts up from the stump of his neck, sizzling and sparky. Hardhands grabs Tiny Doom away from the Minion's forward fall, and she grasps onto him monkey-wise, clinging to his shoulders.

"Pig!" she screams. "Pig!"

Madam Rose manages to disentangle Pig, and flings him towards Hardhands and Tiny Doom. Pig sails through the air, his ears like wings, and hits Hardhands' chest with a soggy thud and then tumbles downward. Madam Rose staggers. She is clutching her throat; her hair has fallen down, drippy red. Above her, the tent ceiling is flickering with tendrils of coldfire; it pours down around her like fireworks falling from the sky, sheathing her bones in glittering flickering flesh. The coldfire has spread to the ceiling now, scorching the raven angels, and the whole place is going to go: coldfire doesn't burn like non-magickal fire, but it is hungry and does consume, and Hardhands has had enough consumption for tonight. Hefting Tiny Doom up higher on his shoulder, he turns about to retreat (run away).

"Pig! Pig!" Tiny Doom beats at his head as he ducks under the now flickering threshold. "PIG!"

The coldfire has raced across the roof beyond him, and the antechamber before him is a heaving weaving maelstrom of magick, the Current bubbling and sucking, oh it's a shame to let such yummy power go to waste, but now is perhaps not the time to further test his control. Madam Rose staggers out of the flames; the very air around her is bubbling and cracking, spitting Abyss through cracks in the Current, black tendrils that coil and smoke.

Tiny Doom, still screaming: "Pig!"

Hardhands jumps and weaves through the tentacles of flame, flinging banishings as he goes, and the tendrils snap away. He's not going to stop for Pig, Pig is on his own, Hardhands can feel the Current boiling, in a moment there will be too much magick for the space to contain, there is going to be a giant implosion and he's had enough implosions for one night, too. Through the dining room they run, scattering cheese platters, waiters, cocktails, and conservationists, crunching crackers underfoot, knocking down a minion—there—open veranda doors, and beyond those doors the sparkle of hurdy-gurdy lights. Doom clinging to his head like a pinchy hat, he leaps over the bar, through breaking bottles and scattered ice, and through the doors, into blessed cool air. There ahead—the back of the Monkey's Head—keeping running, through gasps and a pain in his side.

Through the dark throat—for a second Hardhands thinks that for sure the Grin will snap shut, and they will be swallowed forever, but no, he leaps the tombstone teeth and they are clear. The sky above turns sheet white, and the ground shifts beneath his feet in a sudden bass roll. He sits down hard in the springy grass, lungs gasping. Tiny Doom collapses from his grasp and rolls like a little barrel across the springy turf. The stars wink back in, as though a veil has been drawn back, and suddenly Hardhands is limp with exhaustion. The Current is gone. The Monkey's Grin still grins, but his glittering letter halo is gone, and his eyes are dim. Madam Rose's is gone, as well.

Well, good riddance, good-bye, adios, farewell. From the Monkey's Grin, Pig tippy-dances, pirouetting towards Doom, who receives him with happy cries of joy.

Hardhands lies on the grass and stares upward at the starry sky, and he moves his head back and forth, drums his feet upon the ground, wiggles his fingers just because he can. He feels drained and empty, and sore as hell. The grass is crispy cool beneath his bare sweaty back, and he could just lie there forever. Behind the relief of freedom, however, there's a sour sour taste.

He was set up. The whole evening was nothing but a gag. His grandmother, his darling sweet grandmother whom he did not kill out of love, respect, and honor, whom he pulled back from the brink of assassination because he held her so dear, his grandmamma sold him to Madam Rose.

Him, Hardhands, sold!

The Pontifexa has played them masterfully: Relais' incompetence, Tiny Doom's greed, Madam Rose's cunning, and his own sense of duty and loyalty. He'd gone blindly in to save Tiny Doom and she was the bait and he the stupid stupid prey, all along.

He, Hardhands, expendable! Can he believe it?

Tiny Doom is ignored, but she is also insistent: "Bwannie— get up! Pig wants to go home!"

For a second our hero is wracked with sorrow; he takes a deep breath that judders his bones, and closes his eyes. The darkness is sparked with stars, flares of light caused by the pressure of holding the tears back. But under the surface of his sorrow, he feels an immense longing, longing not for the Pontifexa, or hot water, or for Relais' comforting embrace, or even for waffles. Compared to this longing, the rest of his feelings—anger, sorrow, guilt, love—are nothing. He should be already plotting his revenge, his payback, his turn-about-is-fair-play, but instead he is alive with thoughts of sweeping black wings, and spiraling hair, and the unutterable blissful agony of Desire.

"Pig wants a waffle, Bwannie! And I must potty, I gotta potty now!"

Hardhands opens his eyes to a dangly pink snout. Pig's eyes are small black beads, and his cotton-stitched mouth is a bit red around the edges, as though he's smeared his lipstick. He smells of salty-iron blood and the peachy whiff of stale coldfire. He looks satisfied.

"Would you please get Pig out of my face?" Hardhands says wearily. The mystery of how Pig fought and defeated a goddess is beyond him right now; he'll consider that later.

Tiny Doom pokes him. She is jiggling and bobbing, with her free hand tightly pressed. She has desires ungratified of her own; her bladder may be full, but her candy sack is empty. "Pig wants you to get up. He says Get Up Now, Banastre!"

Hardhands, thinking of desire gratified, gets up.

Afterword

More twaddle from the hand of the previous historiographer—nay, that title is wasted on such, rather call hir a fabulist of the worst possible kind. It goes without saying that none of the events in this story can be substantiated; hardly surprising, as *they never happened.* Clearly propaganda. The petulant magicks of the teenage Banastre and the incessant whining of the child Cyrenanica, tagged with a preposterous nickname, are designed to make the reader shudder. The events described are fantastic. Should we believe that the Pontifexina could slip the notice of the Denizen of her House and run riot in the streets alone? That the Pontifexa might well sell her precious grandson, her pride and hope? That a possessed plush pink pig might defeat a deity?[17] Such suppositions are preposterous!

Still, the story does have the saving grace of being inventive and lively, and the Hot Corn girls are truly terrifying. Pirates Parade, of course, is still celebrated today, although its revels are now confined to the children's sphere, and we are happily free of the riotous behavior described here. Woodward's Garden rests beneath the waves; it is said that on still days, the fun-fair's spires

---

17   A moth-eaten plush pig may be seen on display with other Brakespeare artifacts at the Museo Anthropologico in Cuidad Xochi, but the pig's provenance is murky, and so it cannot be determined with certainty that it is the same pig. In any event, it has shown no signs of aggression.

and monkey head can still be seen, deep within the water, their lines grotesquely deformed by barnacles and sea-urchins. All else in this story is puffery.

Lovelocks

I. Skinners

Here sit nine officers in sangyn uniforms behind an oaken table which has been well polished to a gleaming bronzy shine. They are in full dress kit, a gleaming bloody sight. Crimson lips with crimson wigs to match, silver gorgets gleaming around stiff necks. Glittering silver aiguillettes drape in a profusion of flourishes over glossy frock-coat fronts. Livid scars, one to each cheek, slash downward on each officer's grim face; by these marks the members of the Alacrán Regiment are always recognized; from these marks they can never hide. This regiment is the beauty of the Army of Califa, red as blood and as hard as hate.

The cadet who stands before this crimson tribunal is not dressed so bloody, but she is as just as grim. Her cadet uniform is somber blackness, unrelieved by gilt, and her blue eyes smolder with resentment and rage. She is a reluctant novitiate, and if her attitude was tinder, a simple spark would set her ablaze. At birth her mother held her aloft and promised her hand to the Alacrán knife, her heart to the Alacrán vow, and her life to the Alacrán loyalty. Compared to a birth-oath, what is free will? The cadet's cheeks are round, still smooth: uncut. Though ordeals lie behind her which will keep her sleepless for many years to come, there's one still ahead, the last and worst of them all.

"Do you understand the charge?" Colonel Haðraaða asks. In reference to his rank, yards of gilt tangle on his bat-wing sleeves. His wig is the larger than those of his subordinates: an elaborate confection consisting of three tiers of puffy crimson curls, a waist-length red plait, and a frothy scalp-lock studded with black angel feathers.

The cadet's response is a small squeak of sullenness. "I do."

Her eyes flicker sidewise, towards a pole flanking the long table. The long regimental flag droops below its finial, and scraps of color flutter along the length of the staff: bright red, faded yellow, oily black, bark brown. Scraps long and short, braided and looped, queued and rolled, knotted and tailed.

Not scraps, but scalps.

"Return here at dawn, with proof of your devotion to our duty, and you shall take your place among us," the colonel says.

"I will," the cadet says, and if there is a slight spin to her words, as though they mean something different to her than to those who sit before her, it's hard to tell. She flickers her gaze away from the scalp-pole and dips downward, straight-backed, into a motion of respect, the wide pans of her skirts dipping gracefully with the motion. She bows her head slightly, respectfully, and when she looks up there is no trace of anger in her eyes.

She smiles. "I will."

II. What Cheer!

So then sometime later, here's a cadet where no cadet has any right, any leave, to be. Standing boldly in front of the What Cheer House, her tri-colored hair gleaming in the flickering gas lights.

Out of uniform, but no mistaking that regulation hair: three fat braids, three bright colors: red as blood, black as death, gold as glory. Showing an atypical lack of respect for precedent, the cadet has ignored the obvious queue and achieved the top of the line through the sheer force of glare. Only a cadet, but one who has already learned the power of attitude.

"Do you have a pass?" the gothick at the front of the line asks sarcastically as the cadet draws nigh. "Are you absent without leave? South of the Slot is off limits to good little soldiers—"

The cadet turns around and looks with eyes as flat as rock. The gothick looks into those eyes, and his black lips snap shut. The gothick's pallid partner takes his arm, and together they fade back into the throng, leaving the cadet in full possession of the front of the queue. But she has not breached all of the What Cheer House's defenses. Another obstacle still stands between her and a feu de joie.

The majordomo stares down at the cadet from its lofty stork-leg height. It sniffles the air, peers through pink avian eyes. "No singles. Couples night."

The cadet takes this news with no change of expression. Her gloved hand flips back a black leather revere, revealing the nestled swell of a small pistol. The butt of the weapon gleams slightly, a coldfire glow. A weapon no cadet should have, and which the major-domo recognizes by scent alone. But the majordomo is a denizen of the third order, whose sole function is to keep out those who need to be kept out, and it cannot be swayed by force, or at least not by the force of a flashy magickal firearm.

"Couples only," the majordomo repeats. The line is pressing forward, hooting at the hold up. The cadet continues to stare, but now the gloved hand is straying towards percussive argument.

A voice intercedes. "We are together, majordomo."

A dollymop has climbed out of the crowd and now clings to the cadet's arm. Apparently the cadet has already learned the lesson of the Offensive—*seize, retain, and exploit the initiative*—because rather than protest the dollymop's license, she forks over two sunny gold divas. The majordomo whisks the red velvet rope away.

The What Cheer House is a class establishment, no rundown gin-joint or blind tiger. No hanky-panky here, no jimcrackerie, or faldera. *Behave or be gone* is the motto of the What Cheer staff, and if you are unable to do the first, the staff is more than happy to help you with the second. *Dance à La Duo* is the What Cheer House's signature night, and the ballroom is crowded with duos engaged in vigorous dancing. Huge fans whirl high above, and the tall windows are open, letting in a bit of a fresh sea breeze, but the music is sprightly and the crowd of couples thick, so the ballroom is more than a bit warm.

The dollymop continues to cling to her companion's arm. She's learned strategy of her own: *don't let go*. The dolly has been standing outside for two hours trying to find a suitable mark, and she's going to grip promise as long as she can. A cloakroom servitor divests her of her heavily beaded pelerine and offers to check the cadet's fringed leather jacket, which offer is waved away.

"You will excuse me now, madama," the cadet says once they have traversed the foyer and achieved the edge of the Salon Grande. The What Cheer House is done up *à la tropical*, so our mismatched couple look out over a riot of potted plants and creeping jungle vines, into a clearing where couples hop about like popping corn.

"You are in a hurry?" the dolly asks. Cadets are usually broke, it is true, but this cadet had handed over the ticket price without a backwards glance, and the dollymop, ever professional, smells that her purse is not yet empty.

"I have an appointment, madama."

"But you'd not have gotten in if not for me. Surely that is worth a little drink?" The dollymop sweeps her feathery fan dangerously close to the cadet's face. She is fluttering the fan-sign for *you are a darling dear and I like you,* but apparently fan sign is not on the curriculum at Bennica Barracks, for the cadet is being studiously blank to the flattery.

"I am your servant then," the cadet says, still politely. Another reason for the dollymop to hold fast; cadets are almost always perfectly well mannered, for at Bennica politeness is enforced with the lash. As not all her clients are gently behaved, it's a pleasant novelty. The cadet is looking upward, slightly, and the dollymop realizes that the sharp gaze is trained upon her coiffure. Her hair, black as ink and curling as rose petals, is her best feature, and tonight, thick braids trained into an elaborate high sculpture, it looks particularly fabulous. Of course, such splendor is not entirely natural, but even the Goddess Califa was not above improving nature, and why should the dollymop not follow her example?

"I admire your hair very much, madama," the cadet says.

"You do me a kindness," says the dollymop, smiling at the compliment, for now she thinks that she knows the cadet's ticket. It's one she has punched before, and, all things considered, a fairly painless peccadillo. She's done worse.

The music crescendos to a halt, and the dancers quit bobbing. The brief silence that follows explodes into a thunder of clapping hands and chattering voices. Then a stampede for the refreshment fountain. Suddenly there is quite a herd between the dollymop and her drink.

The cadet, however, is up to the challenge; all sharp elbows and stomping feet, and not above slashing spurs if necessity requires it. Their progress is marked by torn skirts and ominous grumbling, but eventually they achieve the refreshment fountain rising glittering high above the pushing crowd. Champagne imperial spills from golden dolphin heads into a long golden trough. The cadet grabs at a glass as it floats by and fills it, then, grip tightening, turns and forces her way back to easy air. The dollymop and her drink are steered towards a palm tree growing out of a red velvet couch. Before our polly can protest, or flutter, or just come straight out with her fee, she is sitting on the sofa, glass in hand—the cadet has left a red lip print on the back of her glove and gone. So much for compliments. So much for lonely soldiers. The dollymop sighs, swigs her champagne imperial and fluffs her cleavage. She has no idea what she has just escaped.

The band, hidden behind a screen of potted orange trees, needs no pause, being completely comprised of aural elementals who get their juice from the jolting of the dancers, but the dancers themselves, being mere flesh, must rest and recover. Hence the supper interval. The main floor is left a forlorn field marred only by the detritus of dancing—stray ribbands, lost collar buttons, crushed flowers, dropped gloves. The cadet like an arrow flies across this field, through an elaborate mirrored hall, scattered with intimate tables and intimate diners, and into the gambling rooms beyond.

The gambling rooms are darker, and hazy with smoke, and here no one has bothered to rest during the interval because the people hunched over the green baize tables do not dance. Some of them don't eat and some of them don't even sleep. Some haven't been out of this room in years, and these you can tell by their pallor and shaky hands. For them, the outside world is null and void, the only real existence is in this small dark room: the roll of the dice, the flip of the cards, the rattle of the ball. The lights in the gambling room are purposely low to hide expression, exhaustion, and tears.

The cadet has not come here to play a game, but rather to interrupt one. In one corner of the room, a cluster of backs lean over a long table, and it is to this table that the cadet marches and it is one of these backs, tall and sheathed in black leather, that the cadet pokes with a short stubby finger. Three pokes, each one harder than the last, are required before the back becomes a front, topped by an annoyed face which breaks into a grin.

"I was going to break that pokey finger, but now I haven't the heart," Kanacheta says. "I had never thought to see you here. Ready to play?"

The cadet ignores the question. "I need to speak with you. Can you come away?"

"Ayah. I'm at the top of the mark, and feeling fresh. I should stop while I still have to spend. Let me buy you a drink. I am flush."

"Privately."

Kanacheta is easy; it's one of his many charms. "All right then. Let us piss."

The pisser continues the tropical motif—there is no urinal, only a meandering stream, and for the potty dainty a few holes screened in by lush bougainvillea. Kanacheta is not potty dainty. He steps to the edge of the stream and begins to splash mightily. The cadet shifts gaze oblique left and studies a palm tree.

Kanacheta waits until they are alone in the pisser and then says amiably: "South of the Slot is off limits to cadets, Tiny Doom. Aren't you taking a risk?"

"Don't call me that," the cadet says, annoyed. She has moved away from the stream, so as not to get splashed, and is holding her hands underneath a flowing waterfall. "Ayah, normally so it is, but tonight I may go where I please."

"Well, *Lieutenant Haðraaða*, why is that?"

She replies with a statement that is not an answer. "I need a Glamour. A good strong one."

A monkey dressed in a green top hat and a spangly purple vest swings down on a vine to offer the cadet a mint, which she waves away. Another monkey tosses a hot towel at Kanacheta. "What for?"

"*To know, to dare, to will, to keep silent,*" says the cadet, waving away a powder puffy monkey. Also not an answer, but Kanacheta's an adept and used to reading meaning from a glimmer of light, from the taste of the wind, from the most oblique of obliqueness. He knows what she means.

"A Glamour is simple. What kind do you want?"

"A kind to make me look other than I am. A disguise."

"Still easy, although, if I recall correctly, that's also forbidden." Kanacheta tosses the towel upward, where it is caught, and accepts a mint. "Only rangers are allowed to use magick, particularly as a disguise. I thought your rangering days were over."

"I was never a ranger. I cannot be a ranger," the cadet says bitterly. The rangers are the secret spies of the army, and they are full of sportive magickal tricks, tricks forbidden to the army's other regiments. The cadet served one summer as a ranger, and she would have liked to continue so. Under the aegis of their colonel, Nyana Keegan, she might just possibly have done so. But Nyana Keegan died in a duel with the colonel of the Redlegs Regiment, and without her pull, the cadet is stuck. "Hardhands will not so allow, bastard."

Kanacheta does not pursue her comment; it is a topic best avoided, because the cadet's tongue can be as pointy as her finger. He's been poked enough for one night. Anyway, he doesn't care if the cadet is up to something; he likes causing trouble and he can smell trouble all over the cadet, as thick as gun-oil on a new rifle. What fun!

"A Glamour I can do. And what then?"

The cadet grins, and Kanacheta, who has looked into the very depths of the Abyss itself, and seen exactly what snippy little nasties live here, shudders. He likes her better when she frowns.

III. A Glamour

A little later incense drifts hazily in the closed air of the narrow room. They are sitting on the floor, on the flat mattress that is the room's only furniture—Kanacheta is sitting, that is. The cadet lies with her head in his lap, and his long fingers explore the planes of her face. She wiggles. She does not like to be touched, which is to say that she is finding his touch to be very soothing and calm and she does not want to be soothing and calm, not tonight. Also, she does not like to be touched.

Kanacheta observes: "You are grinding your teeth."

"*Yo muerdo*," she says. *I bite:* the motto of the Alacráns.

I thought you were going to refuse them."

"I cannot refuse them. But perhaps they can refuse me."

"How so?"

"If I fail their ordeal . . ."

"How so?"

The cadet looks upward; from this perspective Kanacheta's chin looks a wee bit weak, and his eyebrows lowering. "*He who lives will see,*" she quotes.

Kanacheta continues his stroking. Somewhere far away he is humming, and the puffball cat, sitting *couchant* upon our cadet's tum (compressing a quart of café con leche against her bladder) joins in with a steady bass purr. The incense is sweet and druggy, as lulling as the flickering green candlelight, and despite the grinding of her teeth, the cadet is starting to slither into a little dream of coziness.

She doesn't notice when the hum turns into Gramatica, the language of magick; her lashes don't flutter, her breathing hardly murmurs, but her little white teeth suddenly stop clenching a dull ache into her head and her jaw goes slack. Kanacheta's patient massage has smoothed away her edges, and she is asleep.

Kanacheta's Gramatica is slow and slurry, and his sounds are thick as his intent. The words flow like molasses, intertwine with the incense smoke, tickle the cat's quivering pink nose. Some magicians speak Gramatica like crashing thunder, and each word sparks fire out of the Æyther, but Kanacheta likes to bend around the edges of the Current, likes to slide along its supple length, silent and subtle. He cares little for flashy effect, so his magick is quiet, but it is concentrated and intense. The edges of the room have blurred in the darkness; shadows move sinuously on the wall, most thrown by the candles, but not all.

After a long time, the candle sputters into itself and the shadows on the high white walls extinguish. Kanacheta's invocation, which has lingered on the air, although he has long since gone silent, fades. Into this stillness, the cadet's eyes open and she says: "I haven't got all night—"

He bends over her, smoothing a wayward fall of golden braid from her face. "Kiss me."

"What?" She recoils, though she can't go far, trapped against the barrier of his body.

"To seal the sigil."

She grimaces, and puckers pink lips, fishily.

Their lips meet briefly. There is no heat. Just a soft pressure and the thin press of flesh against flesh.

"⬧〰〰〜✣□⤢〜◻〽," he says. The Word sparks like a firefly. It makes the candlelight seem dim and insignificant.

"Am I done?"

Kanacheta turns, reaching an arm into darkness, handing her a mirror. She elbows up on his lap, not too carefully, and peers into the silver circle. She sees herself as she always has: round face and pouty lips. That horrible tri-colored hair. Squinty blue glare which has grown more glare-y at the sight of her unchanged reflection. "But I am no different!"

"To you perhaps, but not to everyone else."

"What will they see?"

"What they expect to. The sigil clouds their perceptions."

"How long will the Glamour last?"

"Till moonrise. After then, you shall be, to everyone, yourself again. But until then, I'll warrant your own mother shall not recognize you."

The cadet touches her fingers to her lips. Her nails are ragged, the cuticles raw.

"It's not my mother I wish to fool," she says. "It's my darling husband."

IV. The Redlegs

Meanwhile, elsewhere: the Redlegs cannot claim to the be oldest regiment in the Army of Califa. Nor can they claim to be the smallest, the meanest, or even the most decorated. Still, they must have a special point of regimental pride, and so, casting about within the Tide of Attributes for a suitable distinguishing trait, they chose two characteristics which they practiced until perfect. And by these characteristics they have ever since been known: Loudness and Drunkenness.

No other regiment can put on the *Rum Tum Tiddy* like the Redlegs, nor do so as noisily. Their gymkhanas and soirées are known for producing revelry so loud that men have been known to faint, horses to stampede, eggs to fry in their shells, flowers melt like wax. The Redlegs are an artillery regiment, and years of standing by their guns has rendered them to a soldier stone deaf, so the loudness does not personally perturb them one bit. Indeed, without the rumble of vibration, they feel lost.

As high the Redleg noise, so deep their punch bowl. Deep as a well, deep as a hole straight to the Abyss, and many a sporter has fallen into this wetness and never been seen again. The Redlegs Regimental Punch packs a wallop no less incendiary than *Florian's Flute*, Califa's largest gun. The ingredients are secret and speculative, but the *Califa Police Gazette* once suggested the following:

Arack
Ginger Rum
Champagne
Whiskey
Pineapple Juice
Camphor
Beef Blood
Orange Slices
Horse's Milk
Cayenne Pepper
Nutmeg
And, of course,
Gunpowder.

This libation is served hot, in little glasses, with a twist of ginger peel and a mescal chaser. It smokes, it burns, it causes sweating, swearing, swinging, singing, singeing, and spooning. It can cure you and kill you, or kill you and cure you. It cuts like a knife, hits like a brick, and makes you put your head to your heels and roll around the room like a hoop. It's only mixed on special occasions, but the Redlegs keep strictly to a calendar laden with Regimental Victories, Regimental Red Letter Days, and Regimental Honors, so special occasions arrive with head-pounding frequency. Tonight, however, is the Most Special Occasion of them All (after the Warlord's Birthday, of course, long may his staff stiffen): the Regimental Birthday.

Thus, on this special night, the entire regiment is drunk, drunk enough to piss on the dead, as the saying goes. The Redlegs' Regimental HQ sits in solitary splendor on a remote section of the Presidio, where sandy shoals are blown against scrubby pines, facing seaward, high on a bluff above the fort that guards the entrance to the Bay. It's a wind whippy night, not unusual, and shreds of fog trail through the sky. The streetlights don't extend this far out along the Hansgen Road, but there's enough light from the stars not yet hidden that the sandy road shows clearly in the darkness. Anyway, there's no missing the HQ—the building itself burns like a pyre, and the revelry has progressed to the point where some particularly festive artillerists have primed the guns which sit normally ornamental on the HQ's front lawn and are firing flickering red feu de joies out over the wine dark sea. Their fire is not aimless, but rather an attempt to peg a fishing boat coming in from trawl. Luckily for the hapless vessel, the cannoniers are too punched to hit their mark.

The rhythmic pounding of the guns plays time-keeping tempo to the Regimental Band, who sit on the front porch, playing a sprightly rendition of "The Siege of Califa." Somewhere behind all this noise—the guns, the band, the wind, the surf, the odd pistol shot—comes the sound of canine howls—the Redleg Dogs, annoyed at being penned for the night, making their unhappiness known. Above this riotous scene, golden fireworks arc, mixing with the shell traceries to trace a lacy pattern on the night sky.

As usual, the Redlegs are celebrating in front-page newsworthy style (the *Califa Police Gazette*, that is; the *Alta Califa* is a family paper). Were the Warlord not the guest of honor, the fun would be more muted, but Florian Abenfaráx de la Carcaza has swung a few soirées in his time as well, and he's not shy when it comes to revelry. There he is now, the majestically tall, gesticulating figure upon the highest balcony of the HQ building, directing the fire below through a megaphone. Burn, gun, shout, shoot as ye will, with the Warlord on board, no one for debt will go to jail, it's all faldera & glory.

Not everyone shares in the Redlegs' Delight. Colonel Banastre Haðraaða does not drink, he does not dance, he does not gamble, he does not spoon, and he does not curse. Those uncharitable to the Warlord's Right Hand are sometimes prone to suggest that Hardhands, as he is called behind his back, also does not smile, love, or even feel, but that is not true at all. At the moment he is feeling quite keenly something which pangs him quite keenly: boredom. He has appeared at the Regimental Ball because good manners so required him, and he is staying because etiquette demands that the Warlord depart first (or at least that no one leaves until the Warlord is too smashed to notice). So here my lord colonel sits in the Redlegs Parlour, a grimly crimson figure. He's a bright blot of blood in an otherwise black and gold room: the sole Alacrán present.

The Alacrán Regiment and the Redleg Regiment are longtime enemies, whose interactions are normally confined to battlefield or dueling ground. Rarely do the two regiments socialize without moving quickly from scorn to outright insult: *Skinners vs. Powderpuffs*, the headlines would say. But that same pesky etiquette that demanded Hardhands' attendance has demanded that the Redlegs unmolest him, and he the same. Although right now, surrounded by sodden soldiers grouped around an out-of-tune pianny, singing

"I Tried to Give Her a Diva, but She Only Wanted My Parts," the colonel is indeed wishing longingly of blood. He's not much for sentiment, and the drunken warbling is giving him a bad headache. And his thoughts keep drifting elsewhere.

He's thinking about a cadet who is out there somewhere in the black night, charged with the black deed required for initiation into his regiment. He's remembering his own such initiation, many years previous, the scrape of the knife on bone and the peculiar sound of tearing flesh. He's remembering nerve and sinew and working up the Will, and he's also remembering that first flush of power, the taste of blood warm off the blade, and the explosion of heart-heat on his tongue, in his head, in his phallus. *Ah . . .*

He is saved from such tingly recollections by Cake. Midnight is soon approaching, and the Redleg Ball will culminate with the Traditional Toast and Cake, after which all semblance of sanity will break down. In the drunken melee which shall surely follow, Hardhands should be able to make his leave. He's had orgies in his time, and now he's done and looks forward to a last pipe and an early bed, rather than the awkward press of faceless flesh. But before escape, raise a glass to regimental piety and pretend happy joy in regimental pride, although privately Hardhands' thoughts about the Redlegs are unprintable, even by the *Califa Police Gazette* standards.

The Cake is massive, borne on the shoulders of burly privates chosen particularly for their height and width. It is shaped like a star battery, with red fondant bricks and sugar soldiers manning marzipan guns. Chocolate dogs poise around the candy-cane sally port, slavering whipped cream froth. The regimental flag flies high above the parapets, and below, meringue peaks into stiff blue waves. Behind the cake comes a sixteen-pound gun made of black sugar, as heavy and round as the real thing. Six lowly privates strive to pull the monstrosity into the room, ropes straining. Once in place, they stow the wheels and quickly go through the loading drill, ramming a papier-mâché ball down the sugar barrel and tamping it home with a cotton-candy-tipped ramrod.

Here comes the Warlord and Colonel Melacton, behind them a tide of blackened powdery officers, sweaty in shirtsleeves, dangling on each other like autumn leaves just about to take the plunge. Colonel Melacton is jiggling fore and aft, and his massive wig is askew, showing a sliver of shiny skin, but the Warlord is steady. It takes more than a couple of bowls of punch to put a wiggle in his walk—unlike some, he can hold his liquor (or so is his cherished belief). He's towing the young Ambassador from the Huitzil Empire, who is up way past his bedtime and who has had far, far too much sugar, and probably a touch too much punch as well.

"Where's Hardhands?" shouts Florian. His voice is louder than the music, and that means a lot. "Where is my Right Hand?"

The Warlord's Right Hand rises from his armchair in elegant response, bends elegant knee and says, oh so elegantly: "I am your grace's servant."

Florian receives this elegant tribute with a slightly uncertain nod. Hardhands has never given his liege any cause to doubt his loyalty—exactly opposite, in fact—yet sometimes the Warlord cannot help but wonder. Had Florian been born to a birthright, he'd have fought to the death to keep it. Hardhands birthright was impeccable; married to the Pontifexa of Califa's heir, he should have, upon the Pontifexa's sudden death some eight years earlier, held Califa in a glove-tight trust until his wife came of age.

Instead, Hardhands gave over his wife's destiny to the first pirate that sailed through the Oro Gate and demanded it, handed over his duty as though handing over a piece of pie, yesterday's newspaper. Swore fealty to a pirate, now warlord, and has since then never by the slightest deed or action made his loyalty suspect.

Florian can't understand the why of Hardhands' actions, and sometimes (usually late at night when sleep refuses to wait upon him) wondering this answer troubles him deeply.

But when well-rested Florian is not one to worry about things he cannot control, and most particularly not while in his cups. Tonight his control of the colonel appears to be well-in-hand, so all right then, banish unhappy thoughts and let's onto Cake. (About the thieved-from wife, Florian has not given one thought; she's a child still, locked safely away somewhere, and how much trouble can a deposed child be?)

"Let us have Cake!" Florian bellows. The band strikes up a chorus of "Glory to the Guns" in prelude to the Toast, and strikers in black jackets circulate, handing out jorums of smoking punch. The burly cake wranglers set the Cake down gently in the middle of the spectacle, and retreat.

"Your grace—will you do the honors?" Colonel Melacton hands a lit taper to the Warlord, who has to juggle his jorum before he can accept. The sparkler spits silver sparks, arcing into the sudden darkness as the lights are snuffed.

Florian shouts, "My darling wife, the Infanta Eliade, often counsels to me to share. Well, I wager, I've never felt such a need before, but now I find myself rich with generosity." The Warlord turns to the Huitzil Ambassador, who is standing next to him, wrapped in a draggle-tailed cape of feathers, his jade mask askew with excitement. "Come on, kid, let her light!"

The Ambassador eagerly grabs at the sparkler. He loves to set things afire—bedding, his hair, his duenna, the cat. Fire is bright and good, the goddess's heart, the throne of the soul. In the Huitzil Empire they adore fire, hot as the Sun they also revere. The Ambassador dances forward, feathers close to smoking, and lights the fuse.

"Fire in the HOLE!" The assemblage shouts, loud enough to shake the stars above. The fuse sputters, and fire races down its length. A sound rolls upward, louder than thunder, louder than bombs, loud enough to ring ear and buzz throat and cause momentary dizziness. The cannon vanishes into a roil of candy-colored smoke, the projectile urges itself aloft in a curving parabola. With another blindingly loud boom, a ball of white light implodes and resolves itself briefly into the sparkling sigil of the Redlegs, hung pendant on darkness's skin like a scar, and then a sugar rain showers down.

Officers and courtiers push and scramble, elbows jabbing and spurs scratching, filling skirts, pockets, hats with sweeties. Another fanfare arrests the scramble, and this time attention is turned towards the Cake. The sugar cannons spit a sweet feu de joie, whose light, although smaller than the previous fireworks, burns the eyes all the brighter. When the afterimage fades away, a figure stands in the Cake's epicenter.

The crowd roars and gasps, snapping palms together in furious clapping, whistling with raw throats, hollering a huge huzza, for the figure is the Goddess Califa, arms a-flung and drapery billowing. Her lips are the blackest adamantine and her eyes the blue of the twilight sky. Snaky curls dangle around her shoulders, spilling down to hide the abundant roundness of her bosom, the strong sinews of her arms.

"*Come now, good Colonel, and receive my kiss,*
And with that favor thy guns shall never miss," she cries.

The Warlord pushes Colonel Melacton forward, and blushing he goes, for although surely the Goddess is only a faux-Goddess, picked up off a corner and then primed with a badly written poem, still, her Authority is Strong. Two of the cake battery lift the Goddess free of Her pastry fortress; although she is short, she seems to tower over the Colonel, or perhaps it is just that today his heels are particularly low, and her hair alarmingly high.

He leans, puckering, she leans, pursing and their lips meet to another roar of approval and a blast of sound from the band. Later, the accounts differ, but those standing close to Colonel Melacton all agree this much: the Goddess kisses the Colonel, her hands holding his face in place, then she reaches upward with one hand, slashing silver downward, and with the other hand, *rips*. Another flash turns into a huge puff of smoke. When the smoke clears, she is gone.

So is Colonel Melacton's hair.

V. A Melee

Then, oh the skittering and skedaddling and the whoop-to-do. The hooting and the hollering and the brouhaha. Confusion reigns down on all and the party gives way to pandemonium. There is running and shouting, a few errant gunshots powdering down plaster, skidding of carpet, crashing of furniture. Colonel Melacton is carried out, prostrate with horror, a sympathetic shawl flung over his now bare, but still bloodless, pate. The Goddess has scalped the Colonel of both his wig and dignity. Once can be replaced, but can the other? The Huitzil Ambassador falls from his sugar high and begins to cry loudly for his duenna, hiccupping and gasping. The Warlord shouts: seal off the gates, let loose the dogs, send for a surgeon, sound the alarum, post a reward, shut down the press! Officers slither, careen and skid to carry out his Will. Others scramble to get out of the way, in case the Goddess should return and claim their wigs next.

Through this rout, Hardhands drifts, a tiny smile hovering around his crimson lips, a teeny tiny smile on the outside. On the inside he's grinning like a skull. Such is Hardhands' status that even in pandemonium, people part before him and let him attain the exit with little trouble. Such is his slipperiness, though, that once through the door he fades into shadow before his aides can follow him, and then, finally blessedly alone, he makes his way through the garden and into the sand dunes beyond.

Behind him the commotion continues, lights flashing upward into the dark sky as the beacons are set afire, the urgent blast of bugles, and the braying of the Redleg dogs. He knows where the path is; he skids down the bluff onto the beach below. Before him stretches a slope of moonlit whiteness, edged by heaving blackness, and beyond that darkness a star-spangled sky. He breathes deep of the salt-heavy air, crisp with night-chill, and feels the pace of the surf fall into time with the pounding behind his eyes.

Eos Espada, Hardhands' aide-de-camp, has his phosphates, but there are a few perks to being a colonel and even more to being an eighth-degree adept. The second is being able to light your own cigarillo with a flick of a forbidden magickal word, and the first is not being written up for *conduct unbecoming* should anyone see you do so. Before Hardhands was a soldier and proscribed from meddling in the unequal advantage that magick can give one, he was an ardent practitioner of the Graceful Art, and even now he likes to keep in tune. Who knows, perhaps someday he'll quit being a soldier and then the craft will come in handy again.

The Gramatica word twinkles and alights on the end of his cigarillo, where it sparks a fragrant flame. He sucks a lungful of spicy smoke, and that feels better in his skull, where the night air did not. The sand scrunches under his boots, slippery under leather soles, and soon he's close enough to the water's edge that the boom of the surf outweighs the boom of the signal guns behind him. All this hullabaloo for a mere wig—and a particularly ugly overdone wig, too. He feels joyful.

The coincidence strikes him that it's interesting that Colonel Melacton should be scalped of wig the same night that a cadet of Hardhands' acquaintance should be on the prowl for a scalp of hair. But such is Hardhands' certainty in the sanctity of his regiment, and his surety of the cadet's obedience, that he doesn't consider that the coincidence might not be a coincidence at all. It must all be just chance. Doesn't the Goddess like her jokes?

On Hardhands ambles, kicking up spray and relishing the image of Melacton's shiny bald head. Ahead, the beach curves, sand turning into rock, rock into cliff, cliff into palisade. Far ahead, the palisade curves outward into a high spit jutting into crashing waves, and upon that spit the minarets and spires of Bilskinir, Hardhands' native home, glitter in the darkness like a hundred fiery eyes. He can't get there from here, but he's not trying to walk home, just to enjoy the uncustomary solitude and the Redlegs' calamity.

He is reluctant to return to his duty, where he shall be called upon to waste time and energies trying to solve a crime whose commission he applauds. The night is unusually warm, and the water, frothing in moonlight, looks refreshing. Of course, this look is deceptive. The currents riding beneath the ocean's placid exterior are swift and ripping, and any swimmer who gets caught in their net will be sucked inexorably towards the Oro Gate, to be pulled into the protective maelstrom that seals off the bay's mouth, and there drowned.

A weak swimmer, that is, and one whose skin is not well oiled by a magickal protection sigil. Grinning at his own audacity, and the thought of risking his life over a silly whim, Hardhands lights his last cigarillo and strips, kicking his boots off, strewing his clothes on the damp sand, and, lastly, throwing his itchy formal wig (how he hates that damned feathery scalp-lock) into darkness. Revealed, his hair is as silver-blonde as the moon above, and released from its knot, it covers his shoulders and back like a cape. The sand is chill beneath his bare feet, and gritty, skidding his steps until he steps out onto the firm plane of the water's edge.

Hardhands whispers an Invocation, gently puffing the bright Gramatica Words outward. The letters twine and entangle, forming one squiggly glowing coldfire Sigil. He catches the Sigil in cupped hands, and it fills the bowl of his palms with an oozy coldfire glow. Raising his hands above his head, he lets the Sigil dribble down, shivering slightly at the exhilarating sensation of magick sliding liquidly over his skin, coating him a coldfire rime. When he is well-coated and thus well-protected, he steps forward into the water's surge.

The cold tide slashes against his ankles, and he whoops his shudder. He knows from experience that hesitation just heightens the pain, and so he plunges in, pushing outward against the inward pull of the water, answering each slap with another yell, until he reaches the point of no return and ducks his head down into the icy stew.

The water surrounds him a lover, a lover who wants to claw his eyes out, to swamp his lungs, to cut his flesh into a thousand tiny ribbands, to suck off his phallus, to rip his hair out by the roots. He knows, from experience, that the only way to placate such a lover is to give in, to lie passive beneath her lust, to acquiesce to her love and bleed. The heart-sound pumping in his ears, he drifts downward, his eyes open to the salt-sting, and gives into the water's terrible embrace.

VI. Hoisted!

Only a bit earlier the dollymop's night had been improving. After the cadet ditched her, she swanned her way into the affections (and purse) of a masher who introduced her to a rum bubbler who then passed her on (sore but not done yet) to a cardsharp who is a poker buddy of Captain Theobald, Colonel Melacton's aide-de-camp.

Thus, the Redlegs' Birthday Bash, and thus caught in the stampede caused by Colonel Melacton's calamity. As small as she is, she is no match for stinging, shouting, shooting officers, and she finds herself stranded on top of a red velvet settee, trying to hold her marvelous hair against the frantic martial tide. From this trap, she is rescued by the sweeping broad arm of a sweeping broad man, drunk as hell, but still a commanding figure. Borne along in these safe arms, her marvelous hair-style bobbing against the Warlord's stubbly, yet firm, chin, the dollymop feels her tide turning and is very, very glad that earlier that evening she had been moved to put on her very best chemise: a bit worn, but with tremendous lace panels on the front. The Warlord's tastes are bland, but his tips (and his parts, rumour has it) are large, his generosity legendary. The dollymop tightens her grip around the Warlord's sturdy neck. Now that she's been lifted, she's not about to let go.

The hullabaloo lasts only shortly. Though signals are called and fires are lit, it quickly becomes apparent that the Redlegs are too damn drunk to be effective agents of search and destroy. And anyway, once Florian gets a good grip, all firm and bouncy, on what he has rescued, his enthusiasm for chasing after Colonel Melacton's hair is transferred into enthusiasm to exploit his role as heroic rescuer as far as exploitation will go.

"I shall put a bounty on the wig," Florian says soothingly to Captain Theobald as they stand on the steps of the Redlegs' HQ. He glances at the dollymop, who is now sitting in his barouche, patting her curls and adjusting her cleavage. He is in a hurry to get to his fun before his drunk runs out. She is just as he likes them: sweet and dainty and a bit the worse for wear.

"A price on the head of the shearer," Captain Theobald says. "We can not let this outrage stand—sire—"

"Ayah, so, tell Hardhands to so advertise, and I am sure that someone hard for flash will answer. There's always a squealer. Come now, go tend to your colonel and leave the rest to Hardhands. Go then, that's an order." The Warlord turns away.

Captain Theobald almost protests, and then realizes herself at the last minute. The Warlord is going down the front steps, he's grinning at his dolly, she's grinning back, and his heart ain't with the Redleg tragedy anymore. The Warlord climbs aboard, and an equerry snaps the door shut handily, and Captain Theobald thinks, *ah hell.* She's loyal to her regiment, but Colonel Melacton is a trite old bastard, and he looks better bald anyways.

The Warlord doesn't wait until they get back to Saeta House. He doesn't even wait until they get off the post. He's hungry, and his evening's appetite is only sharpened by the evening's activities. He dives right in. In a matter of five short minutes, the dollymop finds her head back, her boots aloft, her skirts elevated, bouncing up and down to the Warlord's enthusiastic thumping. The jostling of the carriage accentuates their jumping, and the dollymop holds onto the Warlord's shoulders with a tight grip, ineffectually trying to brace her boots against the bench opposite. With each bump, she slides downward on her silken skirts, until she's lying squashed on the floor of the barouche, with Florian grinding away on top like he is making flour, not love.

The dollymop bites Florian's ear, which only makes him groan. She bites harder, and he tosses his head away, which gives her the necessary leverage to refuse his ardour.

He protests. She says firmly, "You are wasting yourself, my lord. Why take five minutes when you can take five hours?"

Florian's motto is fast and frequent, but there's a promise in the tone of her voice that makes him pause. She takes advantage of this pause by sliding an artful hand between them, and then, suddenly he is on the bottom and she's on the top. Though he normally don't care for the bottom at all, right now there is no place Florian would rather be.

And thus continuing, until he realizes that the dollymop has stopped bouncing because the carriage has stopped jostling, and within this halt is the sound of voices: murmur, protest, murmur, protest. Then a thump, and a thud. The Warlord sits up, the dollymop scrambling off him in a crush of petticoat and skirt, and his saber is trapped beneath them, too, and he can't remember what he did with his pistol, and then he is blinded by lantern light.

"Stand and deliver!" says a happy voice.

"I'll deliver your guts on a toasting fork," Florian roars. The audacity to interrupt his bounce, to disrupt his ride. "Do you dare—"

"Alas, I do dare, sire, but I promise I shall do so quickly. I seek only one small thing from you—"

"Do you know who you bother, you squareheaded pimp?" Florian bellows. He is scrabbling through the dollymop's skirts, but he can't find his saber, and since he traded access to pistol for access to a tool of another kind, his only available weapon is blustery indignation.

"What sort of a jacker knows not the value of her hoist?" the road agentess says agreeably. "Surely, this moment shall be the pinnacle of my career, the very cream in my cake, the jam in my tea, and an anecdote to share with my grandchilder, when the goddess shall bless me so . . . But enough of this repartee . . . I shall conclude my business quickly and then allow you to go on your way. My lord, I only ask one small thing—"

"And that is?" Florian says, a tiny bit mollified by the road agentess's liberal sprinklings of flattery. "I do not carry coin, and I wager that my jewels will be no good to you, for everyone knows the

Warlord's appointments, and you'd be in fetters within five seconds of setting foot through a pawnshop door."

"Ha! What care I for such tawdry trifles?" The lamplight elevates, and an enticing heave of bosom leans into the coach. "I seek a jewel far more expensive, and though, perhaps not particularly rare, still worth the having."

A swift sword, crack aim, and devilish dimples Florian has, and he hasn't climbed from Huitzil stud slave to Warlord just on brawn and blood: he does have brains. But these brains are currently addled by punch-drunk love, and the rest of him is dazzled by the white flesh bouncing in front of him, and thus he does not take the road agentess' meaning immediately. "And that is?"

The road agentess says, all sweet-pea sugar: "A kiss, my lord! Give me one small sweet dainty kiss, as light as love, and petal soft, and then we shall be square and I shall go on my way, the happiest jacker of them all."

This bit of flattery hits Florian right below the belt buckle, or thus it would have hit, had Florian's belt been actually buckled. His anger fizzles into humour. He's never before thought of his kisses being quite so precious, but now that he considers the thought, he enjoys it tremendously.

"My lord—" says the dollymop warningly. She tugs on the tail of Florian's shirt, but it's too late. The road agentess tilts her head and closes her masked eyes, her lips are like a red red rose just barely opened, moist with anticipation, and quivering breathlessly. Florian could no more resist such a perfect pout than he could resist a sharp slice of cheese, or a city ripe for the sacking. He's hypnotized by the ripe red lips, by the bouncing breasts, by the thought that his kiss is worth stealing. He's forgotten all about Colonel Melacton's earlier misfortune, and thus he puckers up his own smackers and leans right into the trap.

"Sire!" says the dollymop frantically, but he's forgotten her too.

WHAM! In an instant, the Sparkage fills the coach with blinding white light and a sharp reverberating sound that rattles the coach and makes the horses jump and shudder. A sharp pink sugary smell fills the air, and when the dazzle clears, the Warlord lies pole-axed on the seat, a thin trickle of smoke drifting up from his lips.

Of course, his wig is gone.

VII. Oops

Some time after that, the cadet stands in the pisser of El Mono Real, staring at her wavery warped reflection in the mirror. The pisser at El Mono Real has none of the tropical glories of the What Cheer House. It's a small dark room, with a swampy toilet and a moist floor. The walls are covered with knotty graffiti, some of which burn dimly with a coldfire afterglow. (For obscure reasons, the pisser at El Mono Real is a favorite conjuring site for the radical chaoist crowd.) Someone has written across the glass, in long swirly letters: *Console your loss with vice and pour vinegar on an open wound.* The word *loss* cancels out the cadet's eyes, and *vinegar* blurs her mouth. *Vinegar* and a scowl.

The Glamour has worn off. Though she looks the same as always, to herself—expecting to see herself, so she sees herself, yet she can tell by the flatness of her blood that the magick is all gone. Before, the bubbly Current had made her buoyant and daring; now she's drained and dull. She should feel triumphant. Her night has come off as planned.

(Almost.)

Nyana Keegan would have been proud. Such stealth, speed, and smartness. She out-snuck them all. Maybe not a ranger, but still ranger-y.

(But not her ultimate target—her nerve failed her there.)

Melacton's bald head, the blank look in Florian's eyes; ha-ha!

(Never flinch, said Nyana—she had flinched.)

She should feel crowned and conquering.

(But what about Hardhands, damn him?)

She has failed the ordeal set to her by the Skinners, but she also has failed the ordeal set to her by herself.

(Confronting Hardhands, blast him.)

Instead of feeling triumphant, she is thinking about the gun on her hip, heavy and comforting. When the cadet draws, the etchings on Bedb's grips glitter with coldfire and the bluing of her barrel shines like quicksilver. The solid bone warms her hand even through her glove. The chamber under the hammer is empty, of course, but she could spin the cylinder just slightly, and death would click into place. If only she had the nerve to do it, to put Bedb's metal mouth to her own, accept the bitter goodnight kiss.

(And leave Hardhands to win?)

She sighs and slides Bedb back into her holster. Primps her hair, tho' there's not much she can do with those hated braids. They make her skull feel tight, and the dye has crisped her curls to straw. Leans around *vinegar* to reapply her lip rouge and exits.

El Mono Real's motif, of course, is monkeys. They cavort on the wallpaper, dangle from the ceiling, scamper on the carpet. Happily for the customers, these monkeys are two-dimensional representations only, otherwise the din would have been deafening and the dung throwing extremely bad for business. Even during the day, El Mono Real tends towards uncrowded; this late at night (or this early in the morning, depending on your perspective) the café is almost completely empty. The barista (thankfully not a monkey) leans against the bar, polishing his tamp; by the door a newsie waits for the early edition to be delivered.

Kanacheta has taken over her table and is slurping down her abandoned xocolatte. He wiggles the straw at her. "Here she is, Girl of My Dreams!"

The cadet drops her sack next to her chair and sits: "What does that mean?"

"It means I hail a job well done."

"Huh. That's my drink you are drinking." But she makes no move to take it back.

"The Glamour worked well, eh?" Kanacheta waves the straw towards the barista, who takes his meaning and begins to grind another round. "You have gotten away free and clear, and now they shall never look for you."

"Huh."

"And the most clever of all—to throw the blame elsewhere so it shall stick, and thus you to get away without a squeak."

"What do you mean?"

The busboy sits the xocolattes, splashily, on the table between them, and takes the coin that Kanacheta flips in his direction. "Didn't you hear the commotion? The Warlord's guard arrested the wig thief—the Scalper, the papers have already dubbed her." Kanacheta grins wolfishly. "The nickname *Skinner* already being taken, of course."

The cadet almost chokes on the cherry she has just popped into her mouth. She swallows hard and says: "What? Who?"

Kanacheta grins. "Some dollymop. After she snatched Melacton's rug, she made a play for the Warlord, but he weren't caught as easy as Old Corn-pie. His guards grabbed her. I reckon she'll go to the block. The Redlegs'll demand it, and the Warlord will be sure of it. No one messes with Florian's hair. He's that vain."

"Where did you hear all this?" the cadet demands.

"It's all over the City, Tiny Doom. No one talks of anything else. The papers are all coming out with special editions. It's the biggest story of the last five years."

In a flash of stomach-turning guilt, the cadet's *poor me* changes to *oh hell!* That wasn't part of her plan, to pin the blame on someone else, particularly not on some poor innocent like the dollymop. The cadet recollects the dolly's spectacular hairdo, and her kind smile, and thinks of that spectacular hairdo wilting atop a head on a pike, the kind smile transformed by torture into a screaming rictus.

"But she didn't mess with Florian's hair," the cadet protests. "She was just a bystander."

"Florian thinks otherwise. Better her than you. I'll finish your drink if you won't."

"But they have no proof—I have the proof."

"Since when did Florian need proof before condemning someone? Count your happiness that it's not you going down, and let it lie," Kanacheta advises.

The cadet lets Kanacheta slide her glass to his side of the table and dig in. She bites her lip, and then a finger's edge of glove. The leather tastes oily, feels tough beneath her teeth. Looks at the sack which sits on the seat between them, which contains the snarl of horse hair and ribbands that is Colonel Melacton's wig, the tangle of blonde-and-green-striped human hair that is the Warlord's. As an ordeal, she was sent to cause someone's death, and in intending to avoid just that, she has done just that. The Goddess, that bitch, loves her jokes.

Kanacheta is watching the cadet brightly. He scoots the straw around the bottom of the glass, sucking up the last little bits of coffee, and then says: "You won't do anything foolish, will you, Tiny Doom?"

So intent upon her own thoughts is the cadet that she doesn't object to the nickname. Nor does she answer.

"Never pick up your own tab," Kanacheta says. "Didn't Nyana Keegan always say?"

"I pay my own bills," Tiny Doom says absently, still nibbling on her leathery finger.

"And how are you going to pay this one? With your own life? It's a good joke, but that is going too far."

"Not with my own life," Tiny Doom says. She's done chewing, done considering. She pats at her waist, the side opposite from Bedb's heavy holster. A scabbard dangles from her belt, short and narrow. The hilt of the knife is the perfect size for her small hand, fitting just right in a way that Bedb does not.

"With what then?"

"More hair."

VIII. Press Darling

Finally: Hardhands emerges from the foam, shaking water dog-like, and he's feeling terrific. It's been long, too long since he's flirted with death just for the hey-ho-hell of it, and he'd almost forgotten that crazy euphoric feeling that comes from knowing that he'd come oh-very-close-but-not-quite-yet. He's been in the water for hours, but it had felt to him, protected by his sigil, like only seconds. The moon has made it to the top of the sky; in its skimpy light the beach shines like a sliver of silver, but the cliffs above are black as smoke. Hardhands glances northward; the lights of Bilskinir are still on, awaiting his return. During his absence, the night has quieted, the alarms silenced, and by this he reckons that either the Redlegs found their quarry or they have all passed out.

The Sigil has washed away, and the night air is cutting cold on his bare skin. He's ravenous now, and his mouth waters at the phantom taste of hot steak sprinkled with hot spice. He could eat an entire cow. He tosses the wet flag of his hair back, curling its length around his hands and wringing as he walks towards where his clothing lies abandoned.

And then pauses, for he sees before him a figure standing firmly over his clothes, a figure all too familiar to him, though he has not seen it in years: his sister, fourteen years ago drowned in the same ocean he has just emerged from. Once such ghostly occurrences were common. Once Sidonia haunted her brother's dreams, his waking moments and everything in between, gibbering of murder, of honor, of revenge. Once he thought of nothing but avenging her death, but upon his success, her visitations ended and his thoughts turned elsewhere.

But now, here she is again—his corpse-y sister, glaring at him with flattened eyes, her hair a snarl of braids, her mouth a thorny rosebud scowl in her blackened face. In her blackened hands she holds a mass of moonlit shadow, which for one stomach lurching moment he takes to be someone's entrails, before realizing it is his Alacrán wig.

"Surprise!" she says.

"What do you want?" he demands. Sidonia's fetch had been quite demanding. He does not want to go down that murderous road again. He disposed of everyone who injured her; what more can she ask of him?

"I want to be the secret that sits in the middle and knows," the Apparition answers.

"What?"

"I want what you have stolen from me, you bastard."

"What?!"

"I want to be on the front page of the *Califa Police Gazette*."

And then Hardhands looks at the Apparition again and realizes in horror: not his dead sister but his oh-so-alive wife, her daughter. The mistake is understandable: Tiny Doom has her mother's eyes, her mother's mouth, her mother's hair, and, thanks to a liberal application of black camouflage greasepaint, her drowned mother's complexion, too. She stinks of magick; a residual rime of the Current fairly coats her.

Hardhands opens his mouth to demand—what the hell is she doing here, with his wig, when she should be out looking for a scalp—*oh*. The events earlier at the Redlegs' Regimental Ball snap into sudden understanding. The coincidence that was not a coincidence at all. *Oh bloody hell, oh blasted bloody hell.*

Hardhands leans into a grab, which is going to turn into a smack, but Tiny Doom has anticipated his reaction. She dances out of his way, scrambling up onto a rock, out of his reach unless he will chance his tender feet upon the rough stone. Before he risks tender feet, Hardhands tries a command:

"Get back down here immediately!"

She tosses the wig up in the air, catches it and places it upon her own head. The wig is too big for her; it drops over her head like a hairy hood, the scalp lock flapping.

"It doesn't really suit me, does it? Red is not my color, or so my horoscope says."

"What are you up to, you moronic girl?"

"I'm only out fulfilling the charge upon me."

"We called for murder, not thievery."

"Isn't murder a kind of theft—surely the man you kill feels robbed."

"You be-spoil the Ordeal—"

"Not my Ordeal—yours!"

"Is that my gun—how the hell did you get Bedb?! Get down here this instant, that's an order—"

"Ya!" Tiny Doom jeers. "Your order! Ya!"

That's it! Now careless of his tender feet, Hardhands scrabbles up the rock after her, but she is too high above him, and the rock is indeed rough, particularly on his more sensitive parts, which are still unprotected by clothing. He does not give in to pain, but the rock is also slick and wet; he can't get a good grip. He starts to fall back; then feels a sudden pressure on his skull, a tightness that turns into a painful pull—she's got a handful of his hair! Hardhands roars, reaches up with one waving arm, trying to break Tiny Doom's hold.

Something metallic and cold skims against his scalp, and he is released. He drops back to the sand, now oblivious to the rough rocks, the sandpaper sand. In horror he gropes at his head, expecting blood, but instead feeling a patch of stubble the size of his hand. He was sheared, not scalped. The distinction is of little consolation.

Hardhands says a word so hot it could ignite ice. Tiny Doom laughs. The knife glitters in her hand, and she flutters the sheaf of hair at him—his hair! His hair! He says another word, a word so nasty that all the soap in the world would not be able to wash his mouth clean.

Tiny Doom says: "That's mean! I only took a lovelock. A token for my affection. I could have had your entire topper. You should thank me for my restraint!"

Now Hardhands opens his mouth to roar a Gramatica Word that is going to make Tiny Doom sorry she ever messed with him, oh yes, indeed—and is arrested by a sudden beam of light playing across the beach, blinding him. From behind the light comes shouting, and the crunching sound of wheels, and bellow of a mule, and the blistering blue sound of swearing, and the anxious cries of Eos Espada, his ADC.

"Get that out of my eyes!" shouts Hardhands, and the beam falters downward, defusing on the sand. Eos skitters out of the darkness, and he's not alone. Right behind him are Hardhands' outriders, a couple of still-standing Redlegs, and, *oh hell*, the entire Califa press corps.

Eos sputters: "Are you . . . all right . . . Colonel? A boy . . . came . . . said you were drowning . . . hurry quick . . ."

"Pigface Psychopomp!" Hardhands shouts. "I am not drowning, get off, Eos—" He shakes off the ADC, who is trying vainly to throw his own blouse over Hardhands' shoulders, a gesture not working out too well because Eos is narrow where Hardhands is broad.

A camera crew skids down the dune and plants the boxy camera firmly on the sand. The photographer disappears behind the cloth to prepare the plate, and the flashman is already filling his flash pan. Normally there is nothing more that Hardhands loves than getting his image in the paper, and his lack of clothing disturbs him not a wit, because he's super-secure in his own manly beauty (*take that, Florian!*), but this doesn't seem quite like the right moment to immortalize—

"Did your life pass before your eyes?" the stringer for the *Califa Police Gazette* shouts, his pencil at the ready.

"Was the water cold?" The stringer for the *Alta Califa* pushes up behind the first, and they tussle, pencils clicking, pads whacking.

"Did your lungs burn?" The stringer for the *Warlord's Wear Weekly* takes advantage of the tussle to get his own question in.

"Get the colonel a blanket!" Eos shouts at the bodyguards, who look at each other helplessly: where are they supposed to get a blanket from? They are gunmen, not picnickers.

"Hey!" Tiny Doom shouts from her rocky perch, for no one is paying attention to her, and she wants to be the real attraction. After all, that's the whole point of this setup, isn't it? She hollers again. "Hey!"

Heads, pencils, pads, cameras and that beam of light turn towards her, and she waves. She takes Hardhands' wig off and shakes it like a tambourine. "HEY HO!"

"It's the Scalper!" The cry goes up and hands spring to heads, clutch at coiffures. The outriders rush to form a line between Hardhands and the Scalper, an admirable action but a little late. The Redlegs howl, hands reaching for pistols, sabres, long knives, batons, and hairpins. The reporters fairly leap with excitement; this beats the hell out of a not-drowned colonel. Hardhands quivers with indignation and shouts more orders:

To his outriders: "Get out of my way, blast it!"

To the Redlegs: "Stand down, blast it!"

To Eos: "Get those reporters out of here, blast it!"

To Tiny Doom: "Give me my wig, blast it!"

None of these orders are obeyed. The Redlegs press forward, scrabbling at the bottom of the rock, but the tide is running in, splashing it slippery, and they can't get a good grip. Eos flaps his hands at the reporters, who ignore him, busily scribbling notes: the camera's almost ready. Tiny Doom dances, hops higher, out of their grasp, laughing.

"*You dance around in a ring and suppose,*" she sings. "*I am the secret who sits in the middle and knows!*"

Hardhands is stuck—he could blast Tiny Doom and the Red-legs to the Abyss with a single word, but dares not breach his military vow never to practice magick, not before such an audience. No escaping a board of inquiry then. And what if the press recognize her? Hardhands does not want to lose his wig, but he doesn't want her caught, either, to face the Redlegs' ire (of the Warlord's ire, he's still happily ignorant.) And what if the press notice his now-asymmetrical coiffure? So far he's managed to keep that side of his head away from inquisitive newspaper eyes, but for how much longer?

"Give me my wig," Hardhands bellows, demanding instead of blasting. He pushes the outriders aside and advances menacingly.

Tiny Doom laughs, wiggles the wig. "This? I think it's my wig now . . . And you, pressmen—you had better make sure to give credit where credit is due—I'll not have my laurels rest on a dollymop's head!"

"Why'd you do it?" shouts the *Califa Police Gazette*.

"How'd you do it?" shouts the *Alta Califa*.

"Wig styles: long bob or the hedgehog—any comment?" shouts the *Warlord's Wear Weekly*.

Hardhands begins to puff. The Gramatica is trying to claw its way up his throat; he can barely hold it down. Hardhands is used to being obeyed, and he doesn't take disobedience easily. In a second, he will explode or implode; which one will depend on his control, or lack thereof.

But before he can do either, a voice cries: "Smile and freeze! Hold the wig up higher!" The camera man dives beneath the camera's cover. The flash man plants the flash pole firmly in the ground and prepares to ignite.

Tiny Doom, who has been cavorting like a matinee idol, freezes. She obligingly holds Hardhands' wig up higher, and in doing so, manages to obscure most of her face. There's a low ear-buzzing grumble, and then with a huge puff of smoke and an arcing spray of sparks, the flashpan explodes. Waves of stinky yellowness billow upward, engulfing the entire farcical scene in choking acrid smoke. The shouts of surprise and alarm quickly devolve into coughing choking coughing. The beach has vanished in coils of foul smoke, which might not all be from the camera flash, but might just have had a little bit of magickal help from an ally currently disguised as the *Warlord's Wear Weekly*.

When the air clears of shouting, screaming, and smoke, the newspapers are clutching at their stomachs, now sore from hacking; the outriders have covered their faces with hankies and hit the sand; Eos's eyes are as red as two wine-poached pears; and the Redlegs have scarpered.

Only Hardhands stands, still vibrating angrily, unaffected.

The rock is empty. Tiny Doom is gone.

IX. Scars

A few days later. Tiny Doom, a cadet no more, once again stands in the pisser at the Mono Real. There's new graffiti on the mirror— *when you take the dæmon on board, you must row him ashore*—but otherwise the room is unchanged. Not so Tiny Doom: she glares at her reflection, at the livid cuts which now mar her cheeks. The marks are thin, but they throb. She pats her hair, trying to smooth the frizz down; the tri-coloured braids have been unbraided and her hair is riotous. It will take some time for the dye to grow out, and until then her hair will look terrible. But she refuses to wear a wig.

Kanacheta and the dollymop sit at a table in the back room. They are playing backgammon and drinking xocolattes, and when Tiny Doom approaches, they both look up and smile. Lying before Tiny Doom's empty abandoned Cheery Cherry Slurp glass is a copy of the *Califa Police Gazette*. The cover image is dark and blurry, but Hardhands' wig is easily identified, if you squint a bit and know what you are looking for. In case you don't, the image's inscription will help you out: *The Scalper Strikes Again!*

"It's not a very good likeness," Kanacheta observes.

"All the better for me," replies Tiny Doom.

"There's a one thousand diva reward on your head. You should be proud. Springheel Jack is only valued at five hundred."

"I'm worth every coin."

"Don't scratch, honey," says the dollymop. "They'll only scar worse."

Tiny Doom puts her hands in her lap, fiddling instead with the silver-blonde braided cord wrapped around her wrist. She won the skirmish, but Hardhands won the battle. (The war is not over yet.) The Skinners should have puffed up in indignation at her joke and then tossed her out on her well-boxed ear. And they would have, too, if Hardhands with barely contained fury (he'd forgotten that he ever found the joke funny) had not argued quite persuasively that the Ordeal was about blood, not hair. (Hardhands' own hair was hidden under a replacement wig; Tiny Doom is pretty sure that she and he alone know he lost more than his wig that night.)

It's the blood, Hardhands had said. *It's about the blood.*

The colonel had then produced evidence that, during her first heist, the feigned swipe of Tiny Doom's not-so-feigned knife when she had feigned to scalp Colonel Melacton's wig had drawn two drops of blood. Tiny Doom, furious, had sworn that the knife had not slipped one bit—*is she a baby that she can't control her own blade?*— but Hardhands had a bloody hankie provided by an internal Redlegs' spy to back up his claim, and her angry swearing was disregarded. And anyway, he is the colonel of the regiment and if he wants to bend the rules no junior officer will oppose him. So Tiny Doom's Ordeal was voted a success, and her induction into the Alacráns unavoidable.

(But don't think she's finished yet.)

"You may not be a ranger, but you acted like one," Kanacheta says, consolingly. "And Nyana Keegan always said it's the action that counts."

"And, I for one, am glad of that action," says the dollymop. She's decided to overlook the fact that Tiny Doom got her *into* the mess that almost saw her head on a pike and her pretty limbs nailed to various Califa landmarks before Tiny Doom rescued her from the same. For professional reasons, the dolly has always made it a policy to look forward, not backwards. Florian's attempts to make amends for his ire have proved quite lavish, so the dollymop's future is looking rosy indeed. From street-girl to the Warlord's leman; in the end, by doing her a disservice, Tiny Doom did her a favor, indeed.

Tiny Doom picks up the paper and reads through it again, her scowl curving into a tiny smile. She may have (for the moment) lost, but she got her licks in first. And those licks were mighty sweet. She still has to face Hardhands privately, but she anticipates that audience with equanimity now that she has a card to play. (Surely Hardhands would prefer some details of his heist remain off the *CPG's* front page?) Tiny Doom tri-folds the paper and stuffs it inside her redingote, to relish later, again tugs on the hairy bracelet around her wrist. She looks longingly at the dollymop's coiffure, a heavy crown of braids on top, corkscrew lovelocks spilling below, the whole gorgeous edifice surmounted by a cerulean blue wagon-wheel hat affixed with a sapphire hat pin.

"Odelie," Tiny Doom says to the dollymop, "will you help me fix my hair?"

Afterword

Little is known about the inner workings of the dreaded Alacrán Regiment, but it seems unlikely that an official branch of the Army of Califa would sanction murder as a form of induction. In fact, this historian was skeptical that any of the events described in this story could possibly be rooted in truth, and was astounded when a search of the *Califa Police Gazette*'s morgue (now residing in the newsprint collection at the Universidad de Coyolzauhqui in Cuidad Anahuatl) turned up the very picture referenced in this story![18]

The paper was faded, but the image of the wig quite clear: it was in the style called the Rumpty Skink, very popular in the years 11 & 12 Xochitl-156.[19] The person waving this wig was indistinct, but clearly small and possibly female. The accompanying article contained a breathlessly overwrought account of the Redleg party, Colonel Melacton's scalping, General Hardhands's almost drowning, the Scalper's sudden advance, and the indemnification of Odelie de Godervya (the dollymop).[20]

18 "Colonel Flips Lid, General Flips Wig & Curly Wolves Howl." The *Califa Police Gazette*, date missing.

19 Fyrdraaca, Valefor. *Wolf-tails, Hedgehogs & the Naked Mole Rat: My Life in Wigs.* Inverfarigag, Elsewhere: Bilskinir Press.

20 "Scorpion Stung!" and "Redleg Colonel Red-faced!" The *Califa Police Gazette*, 31

(Which then begs the question: who authored this accounting? After a great deal of research, this historian believes she has uncovered this person's identity. This bombshell—for bombshell it is—shall be revealed in an upcoming article to appear in the *Journal of the Eschatanomicon* and will forever change our understanding of Califa history.) [21]

Note that Odelie de Godervya became the official leman of Florian Abenfaráx until her death five years later, attributed to poison at the hands of the Warlady Eliade Axacaya y Abenfaráx. [22] Her namesake and granddaughter Odelie Abenfaráx ov Kanacheta (fondly called The Zu-Zu) was well-known as the lead singer of the infamous band Califa's Lip Rouge and the partner of the privateer El Calavera.

As an aside, this historian cautions against recreation of the Redleg Regimental punch.

Calabasas, Año Abenfaráx 5.

21   A Lady of Quality. "An Exploration into Authorial Possibilities of Mss. Fragments in the Collection of the Duqesa de Xipe Totec Segunda." The *Journal of the Eschatanomicon*. Pumpkinville: Ariviapa, upcoming.

22   Letter from Azucarina Fyrdraaca ov Fyrdraaca to Banastre Haðraaða ov Brakespeare, dated 9 Sol, Año Abenfaráx 10.

Hand in Glove

I. The Police

Like bees to honey, they cluster around him, Anibal Aguille y Wilkins, the golden boy of the Califa Police Department, thrice decorated, always decorative. Eyes like honey, skin as rich as molasses, a jaw square enough to serve as a cornerstone. He's a dish, is Detective Wilkins, but that is only half of his charm. More than just ornamental, he gets the job done. When he is on the dog, no criminal is safe. He's taken stealie boys and jackers, cagers and rum padders, sweeteners and dollymops. He's arrested mashers and moochers, b-boys and bully rocks. He's a real hero. Everyone adores him.

Well, not everyone. Not the shady element in Califa, who prefer their unlawful livelihoods and criminal hobbies to go unmolested. Not the families of those he has sent to the drop. They hate and fear Detective Wilkins. But the honest citizens of Califa consider him a real trump. Except for one lone constable, who thinks he is a real jackass. And whose opinion matters to this story as we shall soon hear. Hold that thought; you'll need it later.

It's after hours at the police department's favorite saloon, the Drunken Aeronaut, and jubilation, centering on Detective Wilkins, is in full swing. The PD is celebrating a successful conviction in the detective's biggest case yet, a hard case, the worst crime that Califa has seen in a hundred years. For three months, until Detective Wilkins snared him, the Califa Squeeze had the city in an uproar. He was crafty, and busy, with a modus operandi quite chilling: he crept up on his victims—in the bath, in an alley, at breakfast, weeding the garden—and squeezed the life out of them. Then he stole their jewelry and vanished. The City is not unfamiliar with the petty thief, but normally its murderers confine themselves to those who are asking to be murdered: other criminals, dollymops, street orphans, to name but a few unfortunates.

The Califa Squeeze was a different breed of homicide, shameless and daring. He chose his victims from the ranks of the utterly blameless: a City gardener, a lawyer, a lamplighter, a nanny. Innocent folks who kept to the law and expected, therefore, to die old and happy in their beds. By itself each murder was shocking, but when it became apparent that the heinous crimes had been committed by the same maniac, the City had erupted into a frenzy of fear and shrill indignation: the Califa Squeeze must be stopped!

Well, the great Detective Wilkins stopped the Califa Squeeze. Using his wiles, and his extensive underworld contacts, with a hefty dose of charm, and then some deadly browbeating, Detective Wilkins tracked the Califa Squeeze and caught him, red handed, with the boodle. The terror of the city turned out to be a small mumbling shambling old man known as Nutter Norm, who had been living in a crate not far from the Islais Creek Slaughterhouse. The boodle, no longer quite so shiny after spending so much time in close proximity to offal, was discovered in a sack in the crate. When arrested, Norm protested that he had found the loot, but gentle (and not gentle) pressure from the Great Detective finally persuaded the old man to confess tearfully that he was indeed the dreaded Squeeze, though he couldn't explain exactly why he had done such great crimes for such little reward.

The trial lasted barely an hour. The jury, primed by Detective Wilkins's silky smooth testimony, delivered a verdict after only twenty minutes of deliberation: guilty on all charges. Nutter Norm will hang. The jury went home, pleased to have done their duty. The police adjourned to the Drunken Aeronaut to celebrate their hero, who would no doubt soon be called to Saeta House to be congratulated there by the Warlady Sylvanna Abenfaráx herself. Until then, they are drinking champagne, eating oysters, and boisterously toasting the man of the hour.

Remember how I said not everyone in the department loves Detective Wilkins? Well, here we come to the one who does not: Constable Aurelia Etreyo, not splendid at all, but small and round and scowly. She sits in a dark corner, chewing furiously on a cheese waffle and furiously watching the other police officers pet Detective Wilkins. If Detective Wilkins is the department pride, Constable Etreyo is the department crank. She came to the PD the youngest graduate from the police academy ever, full of fever and fire to do good, catch criminals, make the City a safer, better place. Instead, she patrols the Northern Sandbank, the coldest foggiest most forlorn part of the City, where nothing at all happens, because there is almost nothing there. The Sandbank encompasses a series of tall hills, too tall to build upon, intermixed with sand dunes too sandy to build upon. Only two structures stand in the Northern Sandbank: the Califa Asylum for the Forlorn and the Nostalgically Insane and a windblown octagon-shaped house now abandoned. The Northern Sandbank is the worst beat in the City.

Constable Etreyo's been on the job a year, and she's bitter. Constable Etreyo is an acolyte of the great forensic investigator Armand Bertillo, whose book *A Manifesto of Modern Detection* created the template for modern police work. A modern police officer, says Professor Bertillo, uses facts, not fists, to solve crimes. A modern police officer understands that crime can be measured; that criminals leave behind clues, which, when properly interpreted, make the resolution of the case obvious. Fingerprints, bloodstains, murder weapons, murder scenes, all these help the police answer the only question that truly matters in police work: who did it. The Bertillo System categorizes crimes and criminals into types that can be tracked, anticipated, and caught. It is a thoroughly modern way of solving crime, as aloof from the dark old days as day is from night.

Unfortunately for Constable Etreyo, Califa's is not a modern police force. Sure, the chief of police frowns upon interrogation via thumping, and they've done away with the old dirty overcrowded prison in favor of the clean silent penitentiary system, but otherwise the police force remains old-fashioned. Crimes are solved with a carrot or a stick, and order is kept through intimidation and fear—all practices that Detective Wilkins has made perfect, and the reason he sits at the apex of the list of people that Etreyo hates. Etreyo's attempts to persuade her fellow officers to employ the Bertillo System have gained her only ridicule. Her attempt to get the chief of police to endorse the Bertillo System failed miserably. Banished to the worst beat in the City, Constable Etreyo has grown snappish and mean.

So, snappish and mean, she sits in a corner listening to the jolly police officers bombard the Great Detective with praise and free beer. You probably wonder why she pains herself so. If the sight of Detective Wilkins makes her so sick, why not go where he is not? Well, first, she'll be fiked if she'll quit. And she'll be fiked if she'll be driven from her dinner. Also, she can't afford to quit. She's the second of ten children, and all her paycheck goes to the support of the other nine siblings, her parents, an elderly aunt, and a blind gazehound. She can't afford to eat elsewhere; the Drunken Aeronaut gives a police discount.

So Constable Etreyo sits and stews, cheese waffle growing soggy and heavy in her stomach. Detective Wilkins is recounting for the fourth time how he leaned on Nutter Norm: ". . . said to him, "Dear man, I want to help you, I really do, but I cannot," and here I paused and offered him a cigarillo; he took it, poor soul, I said, "I want to be your friend, but you will not let me," and he began to cry, and I knew he'd crack, the Califa Squeeze—I'd squeezed him—"

"Not!" Constable Etreyo's shouted interruption is so loud that the other officers are startled. Detective Wilkins is astounded by the interruption. He turns his gaze toward Etreyo's dark corner, sees her there, smiles, and says genially, "Ah, Constable Etreyo, welcome. How is your waffle? A bit sandy, maybe?"

The other officers giggle, and one of them slaps Detective Wilkins on the shoulder in a friendly sort of way. This friendly slap cockeyes the detective's straw boater and earns the slapper a most unfriendly look in return.

"Better to have sand in my teeth than sand in my eyes," Etreyo says. She hadn't meant to speak. The word had just exploded out of her, but now that she's said one word, it's easy to say a whole lot more.

"I cry your pardon, what do you mean?" Detective Wilkins asks.

"I mean, you've got the wrong man."

"But, dear Constable Etreyo, Nutter Norm confessed."

"He was scared and hungry and you promised him a bacon supper."

"Who would confess to murder—four murders—for a bacon supper?" Sub-Detective Wynn asks scornfully. He's one of Detective Wilkins's chief cronies.

Constable Etreyo can think of several occasions in her life where she would have happily confessed to murder for one slice of bacon, much less an entire bacon supper. But none of these fat plods looks like he's ever missed a meal, so they have no idea what a driving force hunger can be.

"I never get the wrong man," Detective Wilkins says.

"You've got the wrong man now."

"The jury said not."

"The jury did not know all the facts."

Detective Wilkins says: "What do you know of the facts, you who have spent the last weeks traipsing about sand dunes, looking after the safety of cows and crazies, whereas I have examined every crime scene, interviewed every witness, recovered the stolen goods—"

"Fingerprints," Constable Etreyo says. "Fingerprints."

Her words are met with an indulgent sigh (Detective Wilkins), eye rolls and head wagging (the other officers). Here goes Etreyo, they are all thinking, with her *science*.

"Fingerprints are unique," Etreyo continues. "No two prints are the same."

"So you say," Detective Wilkins says, "but can you prove it? There are millions of people in the world. Have you looked at the fingerprints of all of those people? What is there to say that my fingerprints are not the same as, say, a hide tanner in Ticonderoga, or a fisherman in Kenai?"

More laughter. The very idea!

She's heard this argument before, and so had Professor Bertillo; of course, they haven't looked at the fingerprints of everyone in the world. But Professor Bertillo had examined the fingerprints of more than ten thousand people and found not a match among them, and that is a big enough sample to support his theory that fingerprints are unique. Not that snapperheads like Detective Wilkins or his cronies will ever be convinced.

"In this case it doesn't matter whether or not Norm's fingerprints are unique," Etreyo says. "What matters is that they were not at any of the crime scenes. There were plenty of fingerprints, but none of them was Norm's. Which means he cannot be the Califa Squeeze."

Detective Wilkins now stares at her, smile vanished. He says softly, smoke from his cigarillo fluttering as he speaks: "Someone has been detecting behind my back."

This is true. Detective Wilkins had not ordered any of the crime scenes to be dusted for fingerprints; Etreyo had visited them after Detective Wilkins's exit and had done the dusting herself. She says, "You cannot execute an innocent man! And it's a matter of public safety. The Squeeze has to be stopped."

Against Detective Wilkins's own vanity, public safety has not much of a chance. He says, "I do not like people who detect behind my back."

"And I do not like officers who squabble in public," a new voice says. Ylva Landaðon, the chief of police, has been standing at the bar for the last ten minutes, but the officers have been so absorbed in their drama that they didn't notice. Now, realizing her presence, they begin a mad scramble of doffing hats, saluting. *Fiking great*, thinks Constable Etreyo, *records room, here I come.*

"You seem awfully certain that Norm is not the Squeeze, Constable Etreyo," Captain Landaðon says.

"I am, Captain."

"But you can't prove it."

"Nutter Norm's fingerprints were not at any of the crime scenes."

"What does that prove?" Detective Wilkins says. "Perhaps he wore gloves! Did you think of that, Constable Etreyo?"

The other officers laugh, and Etreyo feels her cheeks flush with murderous rage. She swallows hard. "If he had worn gloves, he would have left smeared marks. But I didn't find any such marks."

Detective Wilkins scoffs. "All of this is irrelevant anyway. Norm confessed."

"Ayah, he did," Captain Landaðon says. "Norm confessed, had a fair trial, and was found guilty. It is not the police's place to criticize the verdict. We uphold the law; we do not rule on it. Do you understand, Constable Etreyo? I will hear no more of these wild theories of yours. The case is closed."

Detective Wilkins and his cronies roar. They don't care if they send an innocent man to the drop. They care only for their reputations. They can laugh at her all they want; she knows she is right. But being right won't save Nutter Norm. Only proof that she is right will do that.

And, other than the fingerprints, she doesn't have any.

II. The Crimes

As you might guess from Etreyo's sudden declaration to Detective Wilkins, she's been following the case since the first murder was discovered. Unofficially, she's examined the crime scenes; unofficially, she's examined the bodies; and, unofficially, she's read Detective Wilkins's reports. The man may be a snapperhead, but his reports are thorough. He doesn't follow the Bertillo Protocols of measuring the crime scenes, or making sketches or photogruves of evidence, nor does he dust for prints, but he looks for evidence, and he interviews witnesses. Now Etreyo feels she knows the case as well as Detective Wilkins does. Better, actually, for her understanding of the case is guided by the evidence. His is guided by his own opinions. There is no room in forensics, says Professor Bertillo, for opinion.

But she's gone over and over the case file a hundred times, and all she can do is eliminate Norm. She knows the answer to who the real killer is must be there, in the file, in the clues, somewhere, but she just can't see it. And so Norm will hang. She'd visited him in jail; a broken old man, crying for his life. He'd reminded her of her grandpa. He'd died, too, because her family couldn't afford the medicine to save him.

The case of the Califa Squeeze is a strange one. Four murders and no witnesses, this despite the fact that three of them took place in the middle of the day, with potential witnesses nearby. How could a murderer gain access to his victims, and yet not be seen? In the case of the nanny, his charges were in the next room coloring when the crime happened, and they didn't hear or see a thing. In the lawyer's case, the only access to the murder room was through a door that was locked from the inside. There is no evidence that anyone had climbed in through the window.

There's no obvious motive, either. The petty nature of the items stolen would seem to preclude theft as a motive, particularly since they were all recovered. The Squeeze hadn't even tried to unload them. Detective Wilkins could find no connection between the victims, and neither could Constable Etreyo, following in his footsteps. According to the Bertillo System, there is *always* a motive. But she has no idea what it could be.

The criminal, said Professor Bertillo, cannot hide himself completely. He leaves traces of himself behind, and his fingerprints are his signature. Etreyo had dusted all the crime scenes for prints. She'd used the prints she'd covertly collected from her colleagues to eliminate their prints, and she was then left with only a few unidentified prints. The same prints keep showing up at all the crime scenes. They don't belong to any of the detectives. Etreyo knows these prints belong to the killer. But that knowledge doesn't bring her any closer to discovering who the killer is.

Constable Etreyo wishes she could consult with Sieur Bertillo himself, but he's a thousand miles away, in Bexar, and she can't afford the price of a heliogram, anyway. Cast down, she returns to the station house to file her end-of-shift report, and change out of her uniform. She should just go home.

Instead, we find Etreyo back at the station, standing outside the door to the Califa City Morgue, smearing the space between her nose and her lips with lavender pomade. No matter how many times she has been on the other side of that door, she cannot get used the smell: decaying meat, quicklime, stale blood. The pomade doesn't erase the smell completely, but it certainly does cut it some. Her nose now armored, she pushes through the heavy wooden doors into the white tile room beyond.

It's late and the morgue is shadowy and quiet. All the marble slabs are empty. The floor, newly cleaned, is slick and wet beneath her feet. Dr. Kuddle sits at the rolltop desk at the far end of the room, eating a donut and writing out a report. Etreyo's footsteps echo alarmingly as she walks past the occupied slab, past the zinc trough where the bodies are washed, past the scales, still faintly rimmed with red, where the organs are weighed. Now, with everything cleaned for the night, the morgue seems peaceful, hospital-like. Of course, during the busy part of the day, it most closely resembles a slaughterhouse.

"I have to finish this report," Dr. Kuddle says peevishly. "That's why I am still here, so late. I thought you were at the 'Naut, blowing your mouth off."

Dr. Kuddle doesn't believe in the Bertillo System, mostly because the system calls for extremely elaborate autopsies, and Kuddle is against anything that might increase her workload. But she likes Etreyo and humors her.

"How did you hear about that?"

"I hear about everything," Kuddle says. She hardly ever leaves the morgue, but she knows everything that is going on. "Don't bait Detective Gorgeous. He's an ass. His day will come."

"He's going to be responsible for an innocent man's death."

"I doubt he'll lose any beauty sleep over it."

"It's not right."

Instead of answering her, Kuddle stands up: "Come on. I have something to show you."

"What?" Etreyo asks, following her.

"You shall see," answers Kuddle, opening the door to the freeze room. "Leave the door open behind you, will you? It's freezing in here, and I'm getting a cold, I'm sure."

The freeze room is indeed freezing, but its occupants don't mind the cold. Constable Etreyo shivers, not because of the cold but because she has a vivid imagination and she can easily imagine herself lying on one of the blocks of ice, her dark skin frosted white, her flesh as hard as stone. She banishes this vision from her imagination and turns her attention to the figure that Dr. Kuddle has just unveiled.

Jacobus Hermosa, lamp-lighter. Throttled as he made his rounds lighting the gas-lamps on Abenfaráx Avenue. His partner had been working the opposite side of the street and hadn't seen a thing. Taken: one signet ring. Kuddle hadn't bothered do an autopsy because the cause of death was so obvious: a crushed throat via manual strangulation.

"I've already looked at him. Twice," Etreyo says.

Kuddle holds up the lamp: "I was getting ready to release the body when I noticed something. Look. You can see how the killer gripped Hermosa by the neck; there's the shape of his thumb under the chin, and then the fingers, here, under the right ear. The killer used his left hand; his dominant hand, for sure, as he would hardly crush the life out of someone with his weaker hand."

"Nutter Norm is right-handed," Etreyo says. "So that proves something, I suppose, but it doesn't tell you who the killer is."

"But this will, or it will help. Look at the thumb mark. See, it's crooked, as though it has been broken and fixed, but the bone didn't set right."

Etreyo bends over the corpse. Hope is beginning to well up inside her. "That's a fantastic identifying mark. I can't believe I didn't see it before!" she says excitedly. "When I find a man with a broken thumb like that, I'll have him. And the fingerprints will prove it; they'll match some of the ones I found at the scene."

They leave Hermosa in the cold darkness. Back in the slicing room, Kuddle pours them both hot coffee. As they sip, and Etreyo contemplates the new lead, her excitement dampens. "It's a good clue, but it won't help Norm. I'm not going to find this guy before tomorrow afternoon."

"I've been thinking. The broken thumb brings to mind a recent corpse I had in here. An actor, he was, young fella. He fell during the rehearsal of that new melodrama that was going to open at the Odeon, the one about the Dainty Pirate."

"Did he fall off the stage?"

"No, out of the rigging. The scene was supposed to be on the ship, you know. Sixty feet down to the stage boards, and that was it for our young ingenue. Pity. He was pretty. He had a crooked thumb. I remember it because it was his only flaw."

"If he's dead, he could hardly be my murderer."

"Thirty years ago, I'd have said you were wrong. But I ain't seen a dead man walk in years. But it's still odd."

"Where's the corpse?"

"Well. No one claimed it, you know, and he wasn't a member of the theatre company, so they wouldn't spring for a funeral. I got no budget for a potters' field; it ain't free, you know." Kuddle sounds a bit defensive. "Anyway, I sold it to a medico, dissection, I suppose."

She gets up, goes over to a filing cabinet, and yanks a drawer open. "Just for laughs, here. I read that Bertillo book you gave me, and it did seem interesting, so I started fingerprinting all the corpses that came in, to see if I ever ran across the same prints more than once." She pulls a card out of the drawer and whips it through the air toward Etreyo. "Pretty boy's prints."

Etreyo catches the card and lays it on the desk. She digs through her case and finds the cards she made of the prints she had taken from the crime scene, the prints she hasn't yet identified. And what do you fiking know?

She finds a match.

III. The Investigation

The case, already strange, is now turning even stranger. Clearly the chorus boy could not be the murderer; his fatal fall happened before the murders started. But the fingerprints match. That's irrefutable. Constable Etreyo remembers, uneasily, Detective Wilkins's gibe that she could not really prove that two people did not have the same fingerprints. Maybe this was the proof. If so, then she is nowhere closer to finding the true murderer. And she has no other leads. Leave no stone unturned, Sieur Bertillo advised. So, although she knows the dead chorus boy is a dead end (literally), she decides to check him out anyway.

The patrol room is empty; the swing shift is already gone to work, and the day shift has not started to trickle in. Constable Etreyo goes to the locker room and exchanges her spiffy uniform for a threadbare sack coat suit. On her way out of the locker room, she tucks her shield into her breast pocket and drops her pistol into her pocket. A shadow blocks her way.

"Well, now, busy bee, where do thou wander?"

"Get out of my way," she says, angling to push by Wilkins, but he does not give way. Detective Wilkins is much taller than she is and not very sober. These two qualities make him a substantial roadblock.

"What were you doing in the morgue so late at night?"

"None of your business."

"The captain said to leave my case alone. I hope you are following her orders, dear Constable. The captain would not be pleased to hear otherwise. You think the Sandbank is bad; there is always worse."

Her answer is a sharp heel to the toe of his mirror-shine polished black boot. While he hops in anger, she breezes by him and out the door. Recklessly, she hails a hansom cab; with the help of a friend in the records division, she'll tab the expense to Detective Gorgeous. The cabbie asks her destination and she glances, for the first time, at the address that Dr. Kuddle gave her. And she discovers it's an address she knows well, for it is on her beat: the abandoned Octagon House. Fike. The medico has given Dr. Kuddle a shill address.

"Where to?" the cabbie asks impatiently, peering into the cab through the little window behind his seat.

It's the only lead she's got.

A good detective always checks out every lead, no matter how paltry.

"415 Sandbank Road," she orders.

The cabbie slides his window shut, and with a jerk and jingle of tack, the cab jolts forward. Normally, the journey to her beat is a long cold one, entailing two cold horse-car rides, one to the end of the line, and then a long trudge along Sandy Road to the intersection of Sandy and Sandbank, where her patrol shack sits.

Today she rides in stylish warmth and gets there in half the time of her normal slog. Still reckless, she orders the cab to wait, and the cabbie, with a shrug that says *it's your diva*, hunches down into the shelter of his great coat and takes out a warming flask and a *Califa Police Gazette*. THE SQUEEZE TO BE SQUEEZED the headline says. Etreyo grimaces as she walks away.

The gaslights of the City are now far behind; the house squats in fog-swirled darkness. As she approaches, a gust of wind flaps the front gate open. She walks up the stone walkway, to the chipped marble stairs. The air smells of damp salt and something else, something that buzzes and crackles in the back of her throat. The brass knocker is missing its clapper; she raps hard on the door with her knuckles, but the sound is muted by the wind and the rubbing wheeze of tree limbs. As she expects, no one answers. She peers through a side window and sees darkness.

She's not supposed to enter a building without permission from the owners, unless it's an emergency, but a police officer can always find an emergency. Silently rehearsing her excuse—*I heard a distant cry of help, I thought I smelled smoke*—she rattles the front door knob. When that doesn't open, she goes back to the side window, but it's stuck. She doesn't want to break the glass and alert anyone who might be inside, so she goes around back to find the coal chute. The iron door hangs ajar; it's a tight squeeze, but sometimes being small has its advantages. Detective Wilkins wouldn't fit, but then Detective Wilkins would probably just kick down the front door and be done with it. She goes feet first, with her pistol drawn, just in case. Five minutes later, she is standing in the kitchen, covered in coal dust.

The kitchen is empty, forlorn, no sign that anyone has cooked in it for years. The iron stove is rusted with salt-moisture; the sink is slick with mold. As the name of the house suggests, the Octagon

House has eight outside walls instead of four. In the center of the octagon, Etreyo finds a spiral staircase; up she goes, cautiously, gun still drawn, slowly, so as to make as little noise as possible. The shape of the house means that the rooms are oddly shaped; each floor has four square rooms and four tiny little triangular rooms, all arranged around the core staircase. The rooms are empty, with cracked floorboards and peeling walls. The house appears empty, but it doesn't feel empty. It looks abandoned, but it doesn't *feel* abandoned. The fog means that the night is lighter than usual, and in this light, Etreyo sees footprints on the dusty floorboards, fresh footprints. She's reached the top floor now, but there is still no sign of habitation. Perhaps they were here before and are gone now.

She's about to head back downstairs when the ceiling shakes and small bits of plaster rain down. She hears the sound of foot-steps and realizes that there must be one more floor above her. Either that or someone is walking on the roof. But the stairs go no farther. She circles through the floor again, each room joining the other, until she's back where she started, and then realizes that one of the windows is actually a door leading to a staircase that spirals around the outside of the house. The footsteps move rapidly; two sets of them: one clompy, the other light.

She exits the door, onto the outside stairway, which is rusty and rickety. It coils around the house, nautilus-like. With one hand she clutches the slickly wet railing. In the other she holds her pistol steady; she's never fired it in the line of duty, but she will if she has to. Fog roils around her; it's so thick now that the house seems to drift in a cloud, unmoored from the rest of the world. A tickle begins in the back of Constable Etreyo's throat, a tickle that becomes a sound, low and humming. The sound spreads from her throat up into her skull, down into her feet, tingling her blood, her bones, her nerves. The stairs rattle beneath her; above her, the fog flashes purple, once, twice. Lightning? But where's the storm? The rain? And no lightning that Etreyo has ever encountered before sounds like this: a high-pitched buzzing whine, like two saws being rubbed together. Her teeth tingle, and purple sparks arc down from above. She comes around the last edged corner of the octagon and sees an open door way to her left. The doorway leads to a solarium: glass walls, glass ceiling, currently open to the foggy night.

In the center of the solarium, a waterfall of purple lightning pours down from a central pillar. The pillar stands on a scaffold; a table lies underneath, a human form stretched out upon it. Purple lightning dances and shimmers around the stretcher, envelops the body in an envelope of eye-scorching purple fire. Etreyo thinks she has never seen anything so beautiful or awe-inspiring. Or so frightening, either.

She shouts, but her words are lost in the high-pitched whine. On the other side of the roof she sees a dark figure silhouetted against the glow. She shouts at it again, and then, as she dashes forward, a strike of lightning flares off the center corona and zaps her. Stunned, she drops the pistol and feels a hand on her shoulder, pulling her back.

"Don't get so close!" a voice roars.

"Stop this right now!" she hollers back. "I order you to stop this right now!"

"I can't stop it! We're almost done!"

"Stop it now!"

"It's running down now! See!"

The lightning is indeed dimming, the purple light sputtering. The high-pitched whine lessens and then ceases as the corona of light flickers one last time and dies. For a moment the solarium is dim, foggy, and then it floods with a bright white light. Etreyo spots her pistol lying on the floor and grabs it before turning to face the figure closest to her. "Califa Police Department. Put your hands where I can see them."

"There's no need for this, really, Officer," the woman says. She's tallish, with a narrow face and wide-set blue eyes. She is wearing one pair of spectacles, another pair perches on her head. A dirty white apron covers her clothes. But when Etreyo repeats the order, she follows it.

"You could have gotten us all killed!" The figure that Etreyo had seen on the other side of the room is now furiously advancing upon her. It takes Etreyo a minute to realize that she is seeing what she thinks she is seeing, but the light in the room is far too bright for her to be mistaken.

The chimpanzee shouts, "Who the fike are you and how dare you break into private property!" It wears a white apron over a yellow embroidered vest and a high starched collar, its shirt sleeves rolled up to display muscular dark forearms. And it is walking upright.

"I am Constable Etreyo of the CPD. And I'd like to know who you are, and what you are doing."

"Show me your badge," the chimp demands.

Keeping her pistol level, Etreyo fishes out her shield and displays it. "Please tell me what is going on here."

"I am Dr. Theophrastus Ehle," the chimp says, "and this is my colleague, Dr. Adelaide Elsinore. We are in the middle of a very important experiment, which you and your blundering almost ruined."

Constable Etreyo has never heard of a chimpanzee with a doctorate, or, for that matter, a chimpanzee who can speak or walk upright. However, just because she hasn't met one before obviously does not mean that they do not exist, for here one is, standing there glaring at her.

"What is that?" Etreyo asks, pointing in the direction of the column, which in brighter light is revealed to be topped with a donut-shaped ring.

"It's a galvanic coil transformer," Dr. Elsinore says. "It concentrates galvanic current and strengthens it."

"And what exactly were you doing with it?"

"Renewing life!" Dr. Ehle says scornfully. "Or we would have been if you had not interrupted us. Now I shall have to start all over again!"

"I cry your pardon," Constable Etreyo says, "but you have to admit that your experiment did appear quite alarming. What kind of doctor are you, anyway?"

"Dr. Elsinore is a surgeon. I am a doctor of galvanic physiology."

"What does that mean?"

"Dr. Ehle studies the galvanic patterns of the body, Officer," Dr. Elsinore answers.

"I study life itself," Dr. Ehle interjects haughtily. "And you haven't yet told me what you are doing sneaking around private property."

"I knocked on the door and got no answer. And the house appeared to be abandoned," Constable Etreyo said. She speaks her rehearsed excuse, but Dr. Ehle does not look as though he believes her. "Did either of you purchase a body from the Califa City Morgue?"

"I did," Dr. Elsinore says. "And what of it? The coroner assured me that the poor soul had no family, no friends. And it's perfectly legal to purchase bodies for scientific reasons."

"And where is this body now?"

The two doctors exchange glances, and then their eyes shift toward the figure lying on the stretcher. They don't answer, but they don't have to. The answer is obvious in their glances.

"Why do you ask?" Dr. Elsinore says.

Etreyo counters the question with one of her own: "Are you familiar with the Califa Squeeze?"

Dr. Elsinore answers her. "No, I fear not, Constable Etreyo. Dr. Ehle and I only arrived in the City two weeks ago. Is that a new kind of a dance? Or a drink? We have been deep in our work and have not had much time to read the newspapers.

"Can this wait until later?" Dr. Ehle says impatiently. "I must see what I can salvage of the experiment."

"No, it cannot wait," Etreyo says.

"Can we at least close the roof? It's very cold in here." Dr. Elsinore is correct; the foggy air flowing in through the open roof is very chilly. Etreyo watches closely as the two doctors crank the roof shut. A small barrel camp stove sits near a table of jumbled scientific equipment: beakers, weights and scales, bottles of mysterious liquid. Dr. Elsinore turns a dial on the stove and heat begins to pour off of it.

"What kind of a stove is that?" Etreyo asks.

"It's an Ehle stove," Dr. Elsinore explains. "It runs on the galvanic current generated by the coil transformer. So do the lights." She indicates the white glowing globes that hang from the glass ceiling trusses.

"How does the current get to the stove?"

"It's conducted through the air."

Etreyo has read, in one of her scientific journals, about a theory that galvanic energy can be transmitted through the air. But she had no idea such a feat had actually been achieved. In fact, as far as she knew, no one had successfully harnessed galvanic energy at all. And yet here is that giant coil. And she had seen with her own eyes the galvanic current it produced.

"Please finish with us and get out, Constable," Ehle says. "I want to get back to my work. What is this Califa Squeeze you were asking about?"

Constable Etreyo gives the two doctors a brief history of the Califa Squeeze. As she speaks, Dr. Elsinore grows more and more pale. Etreyo glances at Dr. Ehle, but his face remains inscrutable. Or maybe she just doesn't know how to read a chimpanzee's face. When she is done, Dr. Elsinore, now perched on the edge of a trunk, as though her knees will no longer support her, says: "Theo, I think I need a drink."

Constable Etreyo waits while Dr. Ehre brings Dr. Elsinore a beaker full of a clear liquid that she's willing to bet is gin. Dr. Elsinore drinks it down and then says, "This is terrible news. I had no idea. This is awful, terrible, awful."

"Don't be histrionic, Adelaide," Dr. Ehle says. He takes back the beaker and shakes his head no to Dr. Elsinore's hopeful look. "They can hardly blame us."

"But who else is to blame? I knew I should have gone after it. I knew it! Oh, blasted hell!"

"Perhaps you would like to share your regrets with me," Constable Etreyo says. She has angled herself so that she is closest to the door, and both doctors are before her. Clearly they do know something about the Califa Squeeze, and in case they are in league with him, she doesn't want to give them the chance to get the jump on her.

"It's my fault. I take full responsibility," Dr. Elsinore says.

"Are you saying you committed these murders?" Constable Etreyo says, her grip tightening on her truncheon.

"No, of course she didn't. Don't be an ass, Adelaide," Dr. Ehle says. "If anyone is responsible, it is me."

"Why don't you tell me what you are talking about," Constable Etreyo says, "and I can decide for myself."

"We will do better. We will show you. Come!"

Constable Etreyo hesitates. Perhaps she ought to arrest them both, take them back to the station, where she can call on backup. But they are here, and the station house is full of eager ears, and she'd prefer to keep whatever the doctors tell her private, until she's had a chance to check out their claims. Dr. Ehle says, "We are not murderers. The exact opposite, as you will see. You may release your death grip on your billyclub, Constable. You are in no danger from us."

Well, they may claim so, but many police officers have ended up dead because they believed they were in no danger, so Constable Etreyo prefers to remain on the skeptical side. "You go and I shall follow."

"As you wish."

Dr. Elsinore has already darted ahead, toward the coil transformer and the stretcher beneath it. They step over a ring of charred wood flooring, still smoking slightly. Constable Etreyo hates to get too close to the coil transformer, but she swallows her trepidation and peers over Dr. Elsinore's shoulder. A narrow figure lies on the stretcher, covered to the neck with a pink sheet. Dr. Elsinore holds a white globe in her hand, and in the dim soft light, Constable Etreyo sees the pale profile of the pretty chorus boy, who has been dead for three weeks. But Constable Etreyo has seen corpses that have been dead for three weeks, and they do not look this dewy and fresh. Their lips are not so full and red, and their cheeks are not so firm and round. Their hair does not curl so romantically over their marble-smooth foreheads.

Nor do their chests rise and fall as they breathe.

"This man is not dead," Constable Etreyo says.

"He was dead. But he is alive now," Dr. Ehle says proudly. "He has been revivified."

"How is this possible? Are you magicians?"

Dr. Ehle snorts. Dr. Elsinore shakes her head, "No, not magicians. scientists. Theo, you should explain. You are the genius behind this."

Dr. Ehle says: "I shall try to put it in layman's terms, Officer. The spark of life, as they call it, is really just a galvanic current that runs through our body, powers our brains, our muscles, our limbs. Upon death, this spark ceases. We can no longer move, no longer think. Our flesh, without the galvanic current to keep it warm, begins to decay, to die. I have simply restored the galvanic spark. And thus he lives again."

Constable Etreyo gingerly touches the chorus boy's cheek. It feels cool, but it also feels alive. "He is the Califa Squeeze," she says.

"No, he is not." Dr. Elsinore lifts the edge of the white sheet, revealing a white muscular arm—that ends in a neat stump.

She says: "His hand is."

IV. The Evidence

Constable Etreyo believes in science, but if she hadn't seen the proof of Dr. Elsinore's story before her own eyes, she would not have believed it, for the story seems more like a fairy tale than science. And yet there the proof lies, breathing faintly.

The body on the cot is not the dead chorus boy. Oh, the head is, and so is the right hand, and the left leg. The torso belongs to a blacksmith from Yucaipa who had an unfortunate accident with an anvil; the left leg came from an Atacasdero cowboy who fell under his horse during a stampede. Apparently, the doctors have been traveling around Califa, collecting body parts.

Dr. Elsinore says, "We would have preferred to use an entire body, of course, and not have to mix and match like this, but it's very hard to find an entire body in suitable condition. Most young fit people die in accidents, in a manner that renders parts of them unusable. Or they die whole, but their bodies are ravaged by disease. So I had to piece our perfect specimen together. The chorus boy provided the last bits."

"Adelaide is a genius with the needle," Dr. Ehle said. "She performed the surgery that allowed me to speak. She did a marvelous job on our boy."

"Isn't he lovely?" Dr. Elsinore makes a move to withdraw the sheet farther, and Constable Etreyo hastily stops her. Seeing a body cut up is bad enough, but seeing it stitched together, like a monstrous crazy quilt, somehow that seems much worse. She is content to use her imagination. As it is, she can now see the small black stitches around the base of the neck where the head has been attached to the trunk, and that's more than enough, thank you.

"The problem remains the blood," Dr. Ehle says musingly. "In a living being, the heart pumps the blood, and the blood circulates through the body, carrying with it oxygen and other vital nutrients. By the time I get my hands on blood, it's always sluggish and thick and will not circulate. So eventually the flesh will begin to decay, anyway, and the galvanic charge weakens down, and he will die again."

"The brain is a problem, too," Dr. Elsinore says. "The galvanic spark revivifies the body but does nothing for the brain. He is alive, but vegetative—"

"I tell you, a fresher brain will be the answer—" Dr. Ehle says.

"I don't think so, Theo. That doesn't solve—"

They sound as though they have had this argument before, and that it is a lengthy one. Etreyo interrupts, "But what about the hand, Doctor? How can it act alone?"

Dr. Ehle says, "A mistake. I always prime the body part with some galvanic current before I attach it, to ensure that the part is still fresh and works. I used too much current and gave the hand such a jolt that it became completely animated. It jumped off the table and skittered away, and though Dr. Elsinore and I tried to catch it, we failed. I thought it didn't matter; the galvanic current would wear off, and the hand would die again. I had no idea that it would prove so indomitable."

"And look what has happened," Dr. Elsinore says sorrowfully.

"Ayah, look what has happened," Constable Etreyo says grimly. "Four people dead, and an innocent man about to be hanged. And more important, the hand still out there. We have to catch it before it kills someone else. And in time to exonerate Nutter Norm."

As far as Etreyo can recall, Bertillo's System has no suggestions for catching murderous revivified hands. However, before Etreyo became a police officer, she worked two summers as a rat-catcher, and it seems to her that the same principles should apply. She needs a trap and bait. The trap will be easy enough; it's the bait that proves perplexing. What would lure in a hand? Etreyo thinks back to the crimes and feels like an idiot not to have seen the connection between the jewelry before: the Squeeze only stole items it could wear. It has a taste for gimcracks. She needs bait that a vain, luxury-loving hand will find irresistible. Dr. Elsinore, eager to help, provides the solution. What would prove more alluring to a hand than a lovely embroidered glove? She has just the thing tucked away in her portmanteau.

Constable Etreyo extracts from the doctors the promise that they will not leave the Octagon House until the case is closed and the hand is caught. Dr. Ehle agrees, but to her surprise, Dr. Elsinore insists on accompanying her. The cabbie still waits outside, asleep in his great coat; the fog is beginning to lift. Dawn is not far away. They ride back into the City and stop at the first hardware store they see, where Etreyo buys a rat-trap with a voucher.

Nutter Norm had claimed he had found the bag of jewelry hidden in a duck's nest near Strawberry Pond in Abenfaráx Park. The cabbie drops them off near the pond; Etreyo pays him with another voucher. In the early morning light, the grass is wet with dew, and the ducks are still in their nests. The pond is not far from the end of the Q horsecar line. Another connection between the murders snaps into place, belatedly; they all occurred within a block of the Q line. The Squeeze had been commuting to its crimes.

"What if it's gone?" Dr. Elsinore asks worriedly as Etreyo tramps around the bushes, looking for a good place to put the trap. In a duck's nest, she finds a small horde of nail polish and emery boards. The Squeeze is also a shoplifter.

"It's still around," she says. "I just hope it's out getting more lacquer and not looking for more jewelry." She drops the glove into the trap and props the door open, then pushes the trap into the bushes.

"Perhaps the galvanic current has worn off," Dr. Elsinore says as they settle onto a park bench to wait.

"For Nutter Norm's sake, I hope not. The captain is not going to believe my report if I cannot present the hand as proof."

"But at least then we shall not have to worry about anyone else getting hurt. I will swear an affidavit," Dr. Elsinore says. "Surely the captain will not doubt me?"

Surely not. Etreyo says, "Let's wait and see."

They wait and see. Foggy dawn fades into a warm blue day. The ducks leave their nests and take to the pond, swimming and diving. A group of small school children parade by, two-by-two, hand-in-hand, and are swarmed by the ducks, looking for stale bread. The chaperones look sideways at Dr. Elsinore and Constable Etreyo sitting so aimlessly on the bench. Eventually, the school-children leave and the ducks go back to the water. The trap, hidden in the bushes, remains unsprung. A red dog arrives, chases a ball into the water, and then swims frantically around, barking at the ducks, until he's whistled away. The sun is getting warm. The trap springs and they rush to it, only to find an angry squirrel catapult-ing around inside. They release the squirrel and reset the trap. Dr. Elsinore goes to the pond chalet snack shop and comes back with two boxes of pink popcorn and two coffees. Etreyo is sweating and not because of the sun. It's almost noon: Norm's execution is scheduled for two p.m. She checks the trap again: nothing.

A horse cop clops by and asks them why are they are loitering. A flash of Etreyo's badge sends him on his way. Dr. Elsinore goes off to find a bathroom. It's almost one. The trap is still empty. Etreyo's imagination keeps sliding back to poor Nutter Norm. He's probably eating his last meal right about now; then he'll be dressed in the coarse sacking of his shroud. He never hurt anyone; his only crime was to be crazy and old. She could have saved him if she'd been smarter—

"Well, what a fine day to sit in the park."

Detective Wilkins sits down next to her. He holds two ice cream cones. He offers her one. He smells of bay rum and roasted almonds, and the slight breeze is blowing his hair into romantic curls, gusting the edges of his cape dramatically.

"What do you want?" she demands, refusing the cone with a shake of her head.

"Just taking the air."

"I thought you'd be at the prison. That you'd want to see the fruits of your labor fulfilled."

"My job is done. I never linger when my job is done. The ice cream is dripping on my hand. I'll toss it."

She takes it. It's a pity to waste good ice cream, and besides, she's starving. She's had nothing to eat since that long ago cheese waffle. The pink popcorn had stuck in her throat when she'd tried to eat it.

"You are not very nice to me, Constable. I only did my job."

"Tell that to Nutter Norm," Etreyo says, licking at her cone: salted caramel with orca bacon. Her favorite. She knows she should not be enjoying the ice cream while a man waits to die, but she is very hungry and the ice cream tastes very good.

"He had a miserable life. He is better off dead."

She tosses the cone away, the taste of the ice cream suddenly slick and sickening in her mouth. "That's not for you to judge—"

"Constable!" Dr. Elsinore says excitedly. She has returned and yanks on Etreyo's sleeve. "The trap has sprung."

"Trap? What trap?" Detective Wilkins asks.

She ignores him and hurriedly follows Dr. Elsinore into the bushes. It's probably just another squirrel, and in twenty minutes Nutter Norm will be dead.

But the thing in the trap is definitely not a squirrel.

The murderous hand has had a hard life since it escaped the doctors. Its nails are broken, rimmed with dirt. Its knuckles are bruised and its fingertips calloused. The wrist ends in a ragged, oozy wound. It looks more pathetic than horrifying. The hand throws itself upon the glove, clutches at it, tosses it up in the air, but, of course, one hand alone cannot put on a glove. Its anger and frustration are palpable.

"Poor thing." Dr. Elsinore says. "I think it needs medical attention."

"It killed four people," Etreyo says, gingerly hoisting the cage up. "Come on—we may still have time to save Nutter Norm."

"What the fike is that?" Once again Detective Wilkins blocks her way. But this time he's not looking at her; his attention is focused on the trap.

"The real murderer!" Etreyo says. "And I can prove it, too! Get out of my way!"

Now, though you may find it hard to believe, the physical perfection that is Detective Wilkins is not without flaw. It's a flaw that he takes pains to hide, and one that he has learned to work around. His eyesight is not very good. He can see distance fine, but up close, things tend to blur, and to bring them into focus, he must get very near indeed. He sees the cage perfectly, but the hand, now clutching at the bars of its prison, is not so distinct. He leans forward to get a better look. Etreyo pivots away from this lean, tries to go around him. Wilkins reaches for the cage; she sidesteps his grip and puts her foot down squarely on a duck that she didn't know was underfoot. The duck quacks angrily, and surprised by the sudden flutter of wings at her feet, Etreyo drops the cage.

The cage pops open, and galvanic-quick the Squeeze leaps from its prison, scuttles on fingertips, crab-like, across the ground, and grabs a hold of Detective Wilkins's perfectly creased trouser leg. Detective Wilkins looks down and sees something crawling rapidly up his leg; he squints, and thinks it's a squirrel, a rabid squirrel probably, for whoever heard otherwise of a squirrel attacking someone? Detective Wilkins stamps his feet, and bats at the hand, trying to dislodge it. The Squeeze knows what it wants: the splendid diamond pinky ring that Detective Wilkins wears on his left hand, and it is not going to be so easily dislodged.

"Hold still!" Etreyo shouts, tearing off her coat.

Detective Wilkins is doing the tarantella now, his feet stepping mighty high, slapping ineffectually. The Squeeze is skittering up Detective Wilkins's splendidly embroidered weskit, heading for his snow-white cravat.

"Get it off!" Wilkins hollers. His straw skimmer falls off and he steps on it, putting his foot through the crown. Now he looks as though he's invented a new dance: the Murdering Hand Fandango. Choking back laughter, Etreyo throws all her weight against the dancing detective. He goes down like a ninepin.

"Use my cloak, it's bigger!" Dr. Elsinore cries.

Etreyo snatches Dr. Elsinore's cloak and throws it over the thrashing detective, hoping to trap the Squeeze in its folds. Detective Wilkins's screams, muffled in the heavy cloak, have become wheezes, and his thrashing is lessening. His head is tangled in the cloth; when Etreyo gets it free, she sees that the Squeeze has Detective Wilkins by the throat.

She grabs at the Squeeze, tries to pry it off, but the Squeeze has a death grip on the detective. His face has turned plum-purple, and his eyes are bulging out. She dares not let go of what grip she has to reach for her pocketknife. Dimly, she hears Dr. Elsinore shouting. Dimly, she hears herself shouting. Wilkins's tongue is protruding; his face is almost blue. Desperately, she leans down and sinks her teeth into the Squeeze. She bites down as hard as she can, until her teeth grate on bone. The hand spasms and slackens its grip, and Detective Wilkins gurgles. A horrible rancid iron taste floods Etreyo's mouth, and she almost gags, but grimly she holds on. Her jaws ache, and the taste is making her want to upchuck. But she holds on. The Squeeze's grip is growing weaker. With one last spasm, it lets go of Wilkins's throat. Etreyo raises up her head, tears the now limp hand out of her mouth, and throws it back into the cage. Dr. Elsinore slams the cage door shut. Someone helps Etreyo crawl off of Detective Wilkins's now limp form; dimly, she hears someone yell that he is still alive. Etreyo staggers over to the bushes, and spits and spits and spits, and rubs her lips against her sleeve until they are raw.

V. The Trial

Like moths to a flame, they cluster around him, the great Detective Wilkins, his muscular throat wrapped in a silken bandage, silver sunshades hiding his bruised eyes. Just back from Saeta House, where he has received a commendation for bravery in subduing and capturing the Hand of Gory (as the press have re-dubbed the murderer). Not every detective is willing to revisit his own case, to admit that he might have the wrong man. Not every detective is willing lay his life on the line to capture a murderer and save an innocent man. The stationhouse throngs with well-wishers, and people are lined up outside to shake his hand.

What a trump!

The Hand of Gory has been booked and now resides, still in its cage, in a cell in the Califa City Jail. How a revivified hand can participate in its own defense, understand the charges against, and make a plea, well, that's not the police's problem. The lawyers will have to figure that out. The police (who love lawyers not a whit) are sure that the lawyers will find a way. Nutter Norm has been released and now resides in the Palace Hotel's best suite, courtesy of the Warlady. Doctors Elsinore and Ehle have had an audience with the Warlady, the end result being that they have been appointed to her medical staff. The Warlady is canny; she sees great potential in galvanic energy, if it is harnessed to Califa's advantage. The not-quite-so dead chorus boy has returned to the Odeon Theater, a chorus boy no longer, but now, with much ballyhoo, recast in the lead role of the Dainty Pirate. The run is already sold out.

But where is the true hero of the hour, Constable Etreyo? She's in the stationhouse bathroom, brushing her teeth for the hundredth time. No matter how hard she scrubs, she can't get the rancid taste of the Hand of Gory out of her mouth. As she brushes, she listens to the sounds of congratulation coming from the other room and tries not to feel bitter. Nutter Norm, standing on the scaffold with a rope around his neck, was reprieved. That's all that matters. Let Detective Wilkins have the glory. He's already been somewhat overshadowed by Doctors Ehle and Elsinore and their fantastic medical experiments, anyway. Once the revivified chorus boy makes his debut, Detective Wilkins will be forgotten.

But Etreyo does feel bitter. To the press, Detective Wilkins has credited his turnaround to the Bertillo System, the very system he had earlier ridiculed. The *CPG* has published a glowing account of his investigation, of his ferocious fight with the Hand. She has not been mentioned at all. Her report, contradicting Detective Wilkins's in almost every detail, has been ignored by Captain Landaðon.

She spits into the basin one last time; she's out of Madama Twanky's *Oh-Be-Joyful* tooth polish. She's gone through two bottles already, and yet the taste still lingers. She should have bitten Detective Wilkins instead. She bets his flesh tastes just like chicken. It's almost midnight: time for her to go on shift. She's already changed into her blue tunic with the brass buttons. She collects her truncheon and her helmet; on the way out of the locker room, she finds herself blocked in again.

"I want to thank you," Detective Wilkins says. He takes his sunshades off. The blue bruising brings out the golden glints in his eyes. "You saved my life."

"That's not what I read in the papers."

"Don't take it personally. The police must always appear as heroes; that is how we keep order. But I am grateful."

"Don't take it personally," she says. "I was after the hand."

"Happy for me, then, that you are so single-minded."

"What do you want?"

"To thank you," he says sweetly, sincerely. "And to invite you to join my team."

"Your team?" she says warily.

"Captain Landaðon has agreed that it is time for the department to modernize. To that end, I'm organizing a team to study the Bertillo System. I thought you might have some interest in joining it. Am I wrong?"

Etreyo is torn. Finally—the Bertillo System is taken seriously. But to work under Detective Wilkins! She'd almost rather continue to patrol the Northern Sandbank. Wouldn't she?

"I'll think about it," she says.

Detective Wilkins grins gorgeously. "Do that. We'll be in the ready room. Oh, and here—a little token of my esteem."

Constable Etreyo waits until he's gone before she opens the beribboned box he has given her. Nestled inside is a small cut-glass flask. She holds the bottle up and reads: *Madama Twanky's Mint-o Mouth Wash: Polish Your Palate Until it Shines!*

VI. The Verdict

Constable Etreyo laughs and takes the bottle to the bathroom. The Mint-O Mouth Wash burns the awful taste away and makes her smile almost blinding. It would be a pity to waste that brilliant smile on the Northern Sandbanks. And anyway, doesn't Detective Wilkins always get what he wants? Who is she to stand in the way of the hero of the hour?

Etreyo puts her truncheon and helmet away, tucks the bottle of Mint-O in her locker, and walks down the hall to the ready room.

Afterword

We turn now to one of early Califa's most infamous crimes. The Califa Squeeze, or as it later became known, The Hand of Gory, kept the city on edge for several months before its capture by Detective Anibal Wilkins y Aguille. The author of this piece clearly consulted Detective Wilkins's autobiography, for the details here match up almost perfectly with his own account, although Detective Wilkins is more modest in his own description and gives his partner, Detective Aurelia Etreyo, more credit than she probably deserves.[23]

The Doctors Ehle & Elsinore were responsible for the invention of the Azimuth Recombinator and the Galvanic Explicator, technology which helped bring Califa into the modern era. (In fact, it was during testing of the Azimuth Recombinator that the line between the Waking World and Elsewhere was severed.) Readers will be pleased to know that Nutter Norm died in a rest home at Niguel Playa, at the age of 106. Detective Etreyo left the Califa Police force four years after this case to found a private security company in Ticonderoga. Today, Zopilotes Ltd., still controlled by the Etreyo family, is the largest private security company in the world, with offices in fifteen countries.

---

23   See Aguille y Wilkins.

Scaring the Shavetail

It's old Arizona again . . .
Full of outlaws and bad bad men . . .

Traditional Army Song

After the war ended, I got a hankering to see the elephant. So I enlisted, in the Regulars this time, and followed the drum west. Back home they were settling into peace, but beyond the Mississippi it was still hot times. There was miners to protect, strikers to bust, bandits to chase, and Indians behind every bush. We were busy in the Dakotas, and busy in Texas, but Arizona Territory really kept us hopping.

Back then, A. T. weren't no pleasure fair, like it is today. Then, it was a hard dry land, full up with bronco bulls and bunco artists, poison toads and rattling snakes. And Apaches. Say what you will about them Sioux, or Cheyenne, or even the fierce Comanche. The Apaches had it over the whole lot. Oh, quiet and mild they were, one minute, sipping government coffee, eating government beef. Then suddenly, they're off the reserve, cutting a trail of blood and death, and you riding right behind them, wishing you weren't. They were dangerous, but not the most dangerous of all.

I'd take old Geronimo over a shavetail any day.

Oh, the green lieutenant, new from the Point, so fresh he smells of fish, with his polished brass buttons and starched paper collar, puffed up on his own authority. It ain't hard to figure how the Apache is going to custerize you: bullet to the brain from a distance, knife to the throat up close. But a shavetail lieutenant, well, you never know how he's going to get you. He'll order you to guard duty in a lightning storm, or to camp in a wash. He'll issue you poisonous beef or lead you too far from water because he's hot on the chase. He'll ride right into a box canyon because he's too mighty to listen to his scout, and then be surprised when Mr. Lo and his savage friends pop out from behind the rocks, yodeling like Rebs. He'll be surprised still when he and his scalp part company, and I don't know about you, but I've always been fond of my hair and wanting to keep it.

But thank the good Lord, a shavetail was as dangerous to himself as he was to the boys and tended to not last much longer than whiskey at a hog ranch. I served under five silly shavetails, and they went this way: Lieutenant Amberson fell into a dry well on his way back from the sinks and broke both his legs. Lieutenant Clarke stared into the sun during an eclipse and burned out his eyes. Lieutenant Mundy mixed river water into his gin and got the squirts so bad that he had to be removed to the hospital at McDowell on a stretcher, the boys crying boo-hoo before him and laughing up their sleeves as the ambulance pulled away in a puff of dust and muleskinner cursing. Lieutenant Brittan lasted the longest. Then the square-headed pimp forgot to check his girth and got bucked into a teddy bear cactus during morning parade. The surgeon got most of the spines out, but he resigned anyway and went back home to sell insurance. As shavetails go, he hadn't been too bad, and some of the boys went on the bum when he left, but I figure that a man who can't remember to check his own girth is a man who eventually is going to forget to check yours. *Fair-thee-well my sweetheart,* says the old song, my sentiments exactly.

But it's the fifth shavetail I am concerned with here, for reason you shall soon see. Like the others, he came to our troop fresh from the Point. Though the captain told me, over drinks in the back of the sutler's store, that our boy graduated dead last in his class. His father was the quartermaster general of the army and a close friend of Uncle Billy's, so that's how he made it through his four years at all. It's grand to have pull, but most of us don't. In '67 and '68, I followed Uncle Billy all over Indian Territory as we chased them Cheyenne—even held his horse a couple of times—and I'll wager he wouldn't know me from Adam.

Well, the shavetail came to Arizona without Uncle Billy to get him through, and even though the captain babied him, he was God's own original Jonah. The boys liked him well enough, for he was amiable and always ready to give a payday loan or overlook a tarnished button, but that's what you want in a comrade, not in a boss. And he did the silliest things: burned green wood in his stove without opening his windows, almost smothering himself and his striker. Sprained his ankle dancing a jig at the Saturday baile. Missed retreat because he was racing frogs with the major's children. Accidentally discharged his pistol while he was mounting up and shot a hole through the major's straw boater.

Through all these misfortunes, the shavetail remained happy and gay. But the boys and I weren't happy and gay at all. We were listening to the telegraph chatter with news of Apache discontent and thinking about riding behind a man who couldn't keep from shooting his own commanding officer. That thought gave us no pleasure.

Git there firstest with the mostest General Forrest said during the War. He was a traitorous son-of-a-bitch, but he was right. The boys and I weren't above making things a bit hot if we needed to, add a little extra encouragement to the shavetail's departure, if he didn't encourage himself quite enough.

So we stepped in. When the shavetail was Officer of the Day, the fire alarm rang at Guard Post Number 5, the post closest to the sinks, and when he arrived to investigate he found an angry skunk pent up in the pisser. Someone let the dog pack into the Adjutant General's office to run all over the papers the shavetail had spread out on the floor to dry, overlaying his painstaking columns of numbers with huge smeary paw prints. His drawers came back from the laundress pink because they'd been washed accidentally with Mrs. Captain McDonough's magenta silk wrapper. His macaroni was replaced with snips of tubing and his oatmeal mixed with sand.

But he had sand, this shavetail did, and he didn't quit. Each misfortune he laughed off, saying *"For this we are soldiers."* The boys were starting to mutter maybe he was all right, maybe he'd be just fine, but I wasn't fooled. I remembered Captain Fetterman and his boast he could ride through the entire Sioux Nation (he could not), and though I was in Texas when Hard Ass Custer got his entire command killed, I could picture the scene perfectly.

The shavetail had to go.

So we hit him with both canister and shot. He woke up to a baby rattler in his bed, and tarantulas in his shoes. He whacked the rattler with an umbrella and carefully carried the tarantula outside. His lavender soap was replaced with lye; he got himself a jar of sweet oil from the sutler's to coat the burns with and came to stable call smelling like a salad. We left the doors to the hay barn open and let five hundred dollars of hay blow away, five hundred dollars he would have to pay back himself. He got a money wire from his mamma.

None of these torments discouraged him in the least. He remained still sweet, still nice, and still with us, and things were heating up. A ranch just outside of Miller's Station had been burned to the ground, its stock driven off, and the mail was jumped twice in one week, strewing bloody letters halfway to Tucson. Our general wasn't one to sit around when there was a chance of getting his name in the New York papers, never being one to miss a trick, and still feeling upstaged by Hard Ass Custer and his heroic end.

It was time to up the ante, to give the shavetail the Old Hurrah. Back in the War, the boys had a way of dealing with a foolish officer. They just shot him when he wasn't looking, but I never held with that solution then and I wasn't going to start with it now. So I turned my mind to a less final trick, but it was hard coming up with perfect coup-de-grace. The shavetail had proven himself to be tenacious, and the setup had to be hard and foolproof.

It was Mickey Free who provided the answer. Mickey wasn't one of the boys. He was part Mexican, part Dutchman, but he'd been captured by the Apaches as a child and brought up among them. Now he was an army scout and interpreter, and none better. Like most Indians he loved a joke, and nothing suited his fancy more than a good prank. And few things soured Mickey faster than a green lieutenant, for 'twas a green lieutenant made such a mess of things in trying to rescue him, back before the War, ruining the peace between Cochise and the white man and causing so much sorrow. When Mickey heard of my conundrum, he proposed a solution immediately, and it was a crackerjack idea, oh yes.

A greenhorn might have been skeptical, but I weren't no greenhorn. It is true that we live in a rational age governed by scientific men, but these men, I do believe, ain't never been to Arizona. There I saw such things that science cannot explain: rain falling from a clear blue sky, a coyote walking up right on two feet and wearing a red hat, the thighbone of a javelina that could sing *Lorena*. Once I was with a patrol that chased Geronimo and his band into a cave up in the Salt River Canyon, and though we blocked the exit for two days, not a one ever came back out again. Finally, the captain went up to investigate, and he found that cave empty as a licked skillet. Geronimo and his people were gone, and I know they didn't sneak out at night for the moon was full, and a full moon in Arizona makes the night as bright as day. Geronimo had used his magic to make them vanish, only to reappear sixty miles south, below the Mexican Line. Or so he boasted later, and we all believed him. Arizona Territory is a strange and terrible place, full of strange and terrible magic, and I wager a man of science wouldn't last long out here.

So when Mickey proposed we put the scare into the shave-tail with a chupacabra, I wasn't skeptical one bit. The white man holds that the chupacabra is just a story to scare children with; in Arizona, most of what the white man holds don't signify. A chupacabra, said Mickey, would be so fearsome and awful, the shavetail would hightail it back to his mamma in Baltimore City pronto.

But we had to catch a chupacabra first. The chupacabra, Mickey said, was a canny clever creature, and could only be caught by a man of great power and integrity, in the light of the full moon. Mickey would take care of that, and in the meantime t'would be my job to put some nervousness into the shavetail, kind of soften him up some.

And with the help of the boys, that's what I did. A shuffle outside the shavetail's quarters, late at night, strange snuffling. An even stranger howling, far off in the distance, eerie and echoing through the high desert night. The shavetail was bewildered, and getting to be a bit flighty, particularly when a trip to the sinks late one night (necessitated by the spoonful of castor Gothic had slipped into his evening coffee) was disturbed by red eyes winking out of the darkness and the sound of gnashing teeth. Later, Pinkey and Spooner

(who'd been on guard that night) reported that the sight of the shavetail's long legs pumping under his nightshirt as he sprinted back
to the safety of his quarters was a one they would cherish fondly
when age forced them into wicker chairs at the Old Soldier's Home
in Washington City, if they were ever allowed inside its doors.

After a couple of days of softening, I met Mickey down at
Maxey's saloon. There, out behind the privy, he showed me a flour
sack, weighty and smelling vaguely of sulphur. He'd tracked and
bagged the chupacabra up near Needle's canyon and drugged it
with laudanum. But never worry, he assured me that the chupacabra
would be lively enough when the time came. I wasn't tempted to
peek in the bag. Thanks to the War, my dreams are horrible enough;
they need no more fuel.

Next night, Pinky and Spooner rousted the entire garrison
with their hysterical chatter. We gathered on the porch of the COQ
to hear them blurt out their story. They'd been out on night guard,
watching over fifty head of prime army beef, when their gentle reverie had been disturbed by an awful figure bounding out of the
darkness, red eyes glittering like bayonets, stinking of brimstone
and salt. This horrible apparition clutched a calf in its hairy paws.
Pinky had fired at the horror, but he missed, stampeding the herd.
In the melee the apparition vanished, unscathed.

Was it Geronimo? the shavetail asked.

At the mention of that name, Mrs. Major, magnificent as a
ship at sail in her enormous pink wrapper, slid to the porch with a
loud thump.

No, not Geronimo, said Al Seiber, our chief of scouts, after Mrs.
Major was hoisted into her parlor, there to be revived with a large
whiskey.

And then Al said an even more dreadful word, which made the
boys clutch at other and shriek with horror.

What's a chupacabra? asked the shavetail. His nightcap was fuzzy and blue; I'd have bet a month of Pinky's pay that the shavetail's mamma had knit it for him. Oh, they are so sweet when they are young.

A devil from hell, Al said darkly. He was in on it, of course, not because he was worried about his skin—no Indian ever put the scare on Al Seiber, but because he liked some fun. And also I'd promised to settle his sutler's tab when the shavetail resigned. Al was a fine fellow, but he could drink until a lesser man would have drowned.

What? asked the shavetail.

Now Al, Colonel Grierson roared, *don't you go filling the lieutenant's head with nonsense. 'Twas nothing more than a rabid coyote.* The colonel was a good man, stalwart in a fight, but he was a solid Presbyterian in his beliefs and willfully blind to anything that fell outside them. He ordered the shavetail to take a detail, track down the coyote that had stampeded the herd, and custerize it.

What's a chupacabra? the shavetail asked again, at form-up, as he was checking our girths before we rode out. He was silly, that shavetail, but I had to admit we'd never caught him in that trick and after a while had not even bothered to try.

It eats babies, said Spooner.

It sucks souls, said Pinky.

It has eyes as red as hot shot and teeth like tombstones, said Henderson.

It can jump fifty feet straight in the air and will suck you dry, said Mickey Free.

Of course, it were all lies. Cabra, of course, means goat in Mexican, and that's what the chupacabra eats: goats. The shavetail was safe as houses as far as any chupacabra was concerned. But, of course, the shavetail didn't know anything about *that,* and he wasn't going to, neither. They study French at the Point, and Latin, too, but Mexican they have none.

The major said it's just a rabid coyote, the shavetail said weakly.

We shall see, Mickey said darkly and to our delight we saw the shavetail shiver. No doubt he was thinking of those red eyes out by the sinks.

So off we went on our chupacabra hunt, the shavetail riding pretty at the head of the company. Al rode next to him, half soused and looking as cozy on that swayback mule as if he sat in his granny's rocker. Next came the boys two by two, and then me. I didn't ride alone, though: a woven basket hung from my saddle. Tucked inside it was the softest sweetest little baby goat bleating forlornly for its mamma: our bait, delicious to both rabid coyote and chupacabra. Mickey Free closed up the file, and the shavetail didn't seem to notice the flour sack hanging from his saddle horn, or the way it gave out the occasional squirm . . .

All that day we rode that trail, over wash and hill, through sand and cactus brambles, over rocks and gravel, following sign that only Al could see because it wasn't really there at all. Soon enough we might be riding this same trail for true, looking forward to hunger, thirst, and glory, but right now it was all in fun, and we were enjoying ourselves, though trying to keep sober scared faces whenever the shavetail might glance our way.

Every now and a while, Al would call a halt, and he and Mickey would go off on foot, cutting make-believe sign, while the rest of the company waited. They'd return with reports of chupacabra tracks, and bits of bloody fur, spit-up bones. Once they displayed the discarded skin of a rabbit, the interior of Mr. Hare sucked out like pulp from a fruit, a nice detail that I was glad I had not been asked to provide. The shavetail squirmed at each discovery, and when Al offered him the rabbit skin, saying it would make a nice little hat trimming, he declined with a shudder. The boys could barely contain their mirth.

Still believe it's a rapid coyote, Lieutenant? Al asked, and the shavetail shook his head.

At dusk, Al said he'd lost the trail, and the shavetail ordered us into bivouac for the night. He put the camp square in the middle of a wash, and though it weren't the time of year for a storm, this bit of foolishness only increased our lack of faith in him and made us more resolute. The shavetail wanted to bait the trap right there and then, but Al shook his head, saying it were too dark, that we should wait until tomorrow when the moon had more light, otherwise we risked shooting each other. The real reason, of course, was the shavetail wasn't quite soft enough yet. We didn't want to pluck him until he was truly ripe.

We picketed the horses and made camp. After a dinner of salt pork and hard crackers, Al poured us all drinks of the clear liquid in his canteen that was not water, and which the shavetail did not notice, bless him. We sat around our fire, hot and high, and the fun really began.

I first heard of the chupacabra, said Al, *when I were down scouting with Nantan Lupan around the San Bernadino spread. We were after Cochise then, and we'd been up and down the Sulphur Spring Valley for weeks, and not seen a jot of him or any of his crew. We stopped off at the San Bernadino Ranch to freshen our horses, and of course Texas John invited us to dinner, like the gentleman he is. He sets a fair table, and after weeks of hard beans and bread, we were glad to eat like kings for a change.*

After, we were sitting over brandies, feeling mighty homey, when a hysterical woman bust in. She was screaming that a chupacabra had crept into her house while she was fetching water and stolen her child. Well, of course, probably she'd just let it wander off, careless, like, but she was truly hysterical, like women often are, and she was waving one tiny bloody shoe that she said she had found on the baby's bed. Texas John sent out some boys, and we added a few boys of our own, and eventually we found that child, or what was left of it, that is. That baby looked like an empty sack, its skin all loose and floppy, nothing inside at all. I've seen some things in my time and even done a few of them myself, but I hope never to see aught like that again.

Al took a sip of mescal and grinned at the shavetail. The shavetail tossed his head and laughed. He had a habit of doing that when he was edgy, laughing nervously, and tossing his head while he giggled, like a schoolgirl. This action always made my heart nigh on melt, it was so dear.

Poor baby, the shavetail said. *And poor mamma—*

Something rustled beyond the light of our fire, and we all froze, stiff as statues, and didn't hardly dare to turn our heads. Only the shavetail moved, fair near to twitching out of his blouse, looking over his shoulder into the deep darkness that surrounded us. I knew it was only Mickey, hiding in the bushes and cracking his knuckles, but I had to admit that when there ain't nothing between you and the Arizona night but a thin little fire, it's hard not to be nervy.

Do you really believe in this chupacabra, Sergeant? the shavetail asked later. I was checking the picket line, and he was standing by, smoking a cigarillo. We didn't let him check the line himself ever since he had left it too slack and his idiot horse knocked into the idiot horse next to her, dissolving the line into a mess of kicking and biting, and almost stomping Jackson flat.

Oh yes, I answered. *Arizona's a hard place, full of mysteries. It's the devil's own land, but they say even himself would rather live in Hell and rent out Arizona.*

The shavetail answered: *Think of that poor mother, with her empty baby. I had a sister once who died, and how it would have tormented my mother had she thought some monster, rather than the good Lord, had taken her.*

He showed me a tintype then, of a little baby that looked more like an withered crone than a mother's child, a dead infant with an elderly wizened face. I had a little tiny twinge then, because for all that he was a jonah, he was a good fellow and perhaps our trick was a bit harsh. But I remembered the mail rider Geronimo's crew had killed last year: his entrails fat ropes piled on the ground and his balls sitting where his eyes used to be. Sometimes, like Will Shakespeare said, you got to be cruel to be kind. During the Great Rebellion, more of our boys died of foolish officers than of Corn-fed shot or the flux. Colonel Shaw weren't no fool, but there were plenty more that were. Having escaped before, I didn't wager to succumb now.

As the boys were bedding down, I noticed the shavetail placed his blanket so close to the fire that he would be lucky not to burn during the night, and he went to sleep clutching his fancy pants officer's Springfield carbine to his breast. Our plan was fruiting nicely.

I lay down in my bedroll, the little goat tucked up next under my blanket, knobby knees pressing into my side. Our white man's fire had burned down to a good Indian fire, and the boys were little lumps scattered around it, sleeping. The horses on the picket-line snuffled peacefully. All was quiet and still.

I lay there, waiting, and the night drew on, a bit of a wind slipping through the mesquite, the high sky washed white with moonlight. Damn that Mickey, why was he taking so long, I wondered, and then my wonder began to slip into sleep. Despite myself my eyelids drooped. A noise snapped me to—the soft rasp of feet on dirt—and as I turned my head, my eyes caught movement, a stealthy sort of creep across the silver ground in between the mesquite. I couldn't help it then, laughter began to swell up inside of me, and I had to put my fist against my mouth to keep it down. Mickey, about to put the chupacabra scare into the shavetail.

And then something black came hurtling out of the sky. It landed on my chest and my lungs emptied out. I gasped for air, sucking in an acrid stench. I flailed about, trying to find my carbine.

The baby goat screeched and hollered. Then the horrible stench overwhelmed me, and I knew nothing more.

Voices brung me to, yapping like dogs. Al shouting for a lantern, the boys hollering this and that, and the shavetail bending over me, asking in a quaver-y voice: *Are you all right, sergeant?*

Yes, sir. I wheezed. My chest felt as though Forrest's cavalry had just ridden over it, and my head throbbed.

I was answering nature's call, and I saw you struggling with something, the shavetail said. *But by the time I could run over, it jumped off and was gone—*

He gave me a hand, and pulled me up, thrust a canteen at me, but my throat was so burned I could barely swallow. My limbs felt like jelly; I had to lean on him to stand. Thought I knew the chupacabra was harmless to me, I could not help but be rattled. The horses were fussing, pulling and yanking at the picket line, eyes rolling, and the boys were trying to calm them. My head swum with a kind of sea-sickness, and when the shavetail ordered me to lie back down, I was glad to do so. As I did, I saw that my bedroll was empty.

The kid, I wheezed.

We shall find it, Mickey Free said, coming up behind the shavetail, and he winked.

And we did, the next morning. Or rather the shavetail did, when he went to saddle up. Its skin was draped over the seat of the shavetail's saddle, sucked and as empty as a cast-off sock. At the awful sight the shavetail's face went ashen, and his eyes grew as large and round as joe frogger's. Even the boys looked somewhat discomfited. My head still throbbed from the night's antics. Damn that Mickey, how did he mistake me for the shavetail and sic the chupacabra on me wrongly?

Mickey said: *The kid was small. It will want more. We must catch it before it does worse.*

The shavetail was biting his lip, and he had a look about him I've seen before, in men waiting for the order to advance, a nervous wild look that means they will bolt when they get the chance. We were getting close, and at this thought my headache began to lift.

Your orders, sir? I asked the shavetail maliciously.

He had no choice but to call boots and saddles and order us after the thing, although I could tell he wanted to do nothing of the kind. But he was dutiful. He called his orders with forced bravado. As we finished breaking camp, Mickey took me aside and whispered unwelcome news.

The chupacabra had escaped.

Of course, I was not happy with this turn of events, but Mickey assured me that the chupacabra would not go far, and we could follow it, this time for real. Then when we bivouacked for the night, Mickey said he would sponge some of the goat blood he carried in a vial on the shavetail's boots as he slept. This lure would be irresistible to the ravenous creature, and the shavetail would wake to a nightmare. With this plan I had to be satisfied, for there was no other.

So off we went, cutting real sign this time. The boys were still lively and pleased, though trying to hide their slyness behind grim faces. The shavetail rode loosely in his saddle, long knees hiked in short stirrups, the way they tack up at the Point, but he was whistling nervously: "Garry Owen," an unlucky tune, but we had to bear it, for he was the boss.

Now the sign—real—was easy to cut: hoof prints left in the dust, a tuft of singed hair hanging on a cactus twig, and the noisome whiff of hell in the air. All morning we followed the chupacabra's trail, and I could see the shavetail was winding up tighter and tighter. When we broke for water at Alamo Spring, he confided in me that he hoped we would find the creature before night fell, for he did not want to confront it in darkness, and I was hard pressed to suppress my joy. He was almost done.

But in the late afternoon we came upon different sign, sign that made my blood run cold and which drove all thoughts of chupacabras from my mind. A mess of unshod ponies had come from the northwest and were riding hard south. Unshod ponies meant only one thing: Apaches. And there was no good reason for a mess of Apaches to be riding pell-mell south, unless they were making for the Line.

Well now, the shavetail said, looking thoughtful.

We should return to the post and raise the alarm, Mickey said. *There are many of them. More than us.*

How far ahead of us are they? the shavetail asked, instead of giving that very order.

I'm not a profane man, but I cursed then, silently to myself. To come so close, and now to be in the exact situation of which I was trying so hard to avoid. I recognized the look on the shavetail's face. Men think they see glittering glory ahead, but it's only the gleam of Death's scythe.

Mickey's right, sir, I said. *Our mounts are tired, and we'll never catch up with them. Best get back to the post. The major can send message by the heliogram to Bowie, and they can ride out from there.*

But the shavetail weren't having that, of course. All thoughts of the chupacabra were gone from his pretty blond head, too, to be replaced with visions of medals and his picture in *Leslie's Illustrated.* If Al hadn't been insensate with drink, he might have been able to counter the shavetail's idiocy, but he'd slid right off his horse some miles back and was now tied to his saddle, barely able to sit upright. His spare canteen hadn't been filled with water, either.

We'll catch up with them, the shavetail said. *And bring them back.*

They will ride until their horses drop and then go on by foot, I answered.

And then we shall catch for sure, he said.

Mickey and I exchanged glances. No man on horseback had ever caught an Apache on foot and, anyway, our horses wouldn't last much longer than theirs. I thought, then, about just shooting him, but I wouldn't save myself from an Apache knife only to give myself over to a noose. So when the shavetail gave the order to ride on, I echoed it, and on we rode, this time hard.

We caught up with the Apaches at the Black Badger water-hole. They'd stopped to water, but they were on guard and saw us coming. There were about twice as many of them as us, and even at a distance I recognized the big bay horse that Geronimo favored. Only a fool would urge the boys forward, with no cover and the Apaches already raising their rifles. Before Mickey could argue otherwise, the shavetail gave the order to charge.

Well, it was a rout, of course. Our horses were lathered, and Geronimo and his comrades were determined not to be caught. And anyway, it don't do to try to shoot off your horse anyway, except in magazines. Two horses were downed almost immediately—one of them shot by its own rider. The rest of us were just hitting dust.

Ride for the rocks! the shavetail hollered, which was his fancy way of retreat. We wasted no time in following his first ever sensible order. We wheeled about, all thoughts of formation gone, and rode for cover, bullets zipping overhead like overeager bees. I was almost there when my mount stumbled and began to tumble. I tried to pull him up, but a heavy blow to my shoulder spun me down. I tasted dirt in my mouth, the sharp burn of rocks on my side. I rolled like a wheel, and my horse hit the dirt with a wallop of dust, shrieked, and subsided into a death quiver. The dust parted and I saw a horse bearing down upon me; saw the dull gleam of a rifle raised to a shoulder, saw the red head-band, the flying black hair. My carbine still hung from its sling from my shoulder. I tried to pull it around, but my fingers were nerveless and numb,. But the shot never came. Instead, the Apache himself flew off the pony, hit the ground and did not get up.

Let us advance in the opposite direction, the shavetail hollered to me. He let his pistol fall to the end of its lanyard and, slinging me over his shoulder like a bale of hay, ran. Somehow we reached the rocks despite the uncharming whiz of bullets over our heads. The shavetail laid me gently down on the dirt. His face was a-streak with dust and sweat, but he was grinning. The pain I had not felt when I was shot awoke and began to burn, but I slung my carbine around and joined the shavetail in returning fire. The Apaches wheeled about on their ponies, shooting and shouting, but we were nicely dug in and they could not dislodge us. Nor we were hitting them, either, for none of the boys was much of a shot and firing blindly for the most part anyway, afraid to give up their cover.

The shavetail hollered encouragement to the boys and slurs to the Apaches, and seemed in the spirit of the thing, while I only wished it to be over, with ourselves the victors, before our cartridges ran out. It's funny the things a man can think of when he's in a tight spot. When I was lying in the mud at Fort Wagner, listen to my friends die around me, all I could think of was how I wished I'd finished that long book about the whale and the mad sea captain. Now the words of *Drink Puppy Drink* were rolling through my head, over and over again.

Then the gunfire suddenly ceased, although its echo still rang in my now almost deaf ears.

They are scattering, the shavetail said, his gleeful voice barely piercing my deafness. He had poked his head up over the edge of the rock, and waved at me to do the same. I did so, and saw he was right: some of the Apaches were scattering. But two horses stood firm—one of them Geronimo's—and it seemed as though their riders were watching something, their attention focused above us. I looked up and saw quick movement, a scuttle on the rocks.

The shavetail was still looking out. He said: *What are they—*

And then something small and smelly dropped on his shoulders and knocked the rest of his words out of his mouth. The shavetail flailed, but I knew from my own experience how tight the chupacabra's grip was. Mickey said it was harmless to men, but it didn't look harmless now, as it ripped and tore at the shavetail, who kicked and hit back. Then the shavetail gave out a thin yelp and went slack, and I saw the chupacabra clearly for the first time.

The thing was the size of a small child, a small burned child; its blackened skin cracked and charred looking. It had childlike arms and spindly little legs, covered in ashy fur, but these legs ended in hooves, not feet. There was nothing childlike about its head, though. Goaty ears sprang from a narrow skull from which two red slitty eyes glittered like rubies. It had no mouth, just a jutting insectile snout, already tinged with red from where it had bitten the shavetail. Judging from the shavetail's slackness, this bite was venomous.

The chupacabra crouched on the shavetail's chest, tearing at the neck of his blouse with its childlike hands, and when the shavetail's white throat was exposed, the creature leaned over him and placed its snout against the shavetail's skin. I heard the sickening sound of flesh being punctured, and then the chupacabra began to suck. The noise of its sucking was delicate, almost dainty, and so too was the almost tender way the creature held the shavetail's head steady in those small hairless hands. The shavetail shuddered and quivered, but he did not struggle. His eyes fluttered open and he stared at me in horror.

My knees were suddenly as wiggly as noodles. As my carbine began to slide out of my grip, I remembered it and somehow managed to raise it to my shoulder, though so shakily I was in danger of shooting myself. Then I recalled why I had lured the chupacabra in the first place and why I was lying in the dust, feeling the blood trickle down my back. But if the shavetail hadn't carried me to the rocks, I would be dead now, and perhaps that cancelled the other out. I fired and the hammer clicked uselessly. I was out of ammunition.

And then another shadow fell across us, and I looked up to see a stocky man in a calico shirt, red head-band holding back black hair. I knew him well, and indeed, once won a dollar off him in an ant race, back up on Turkey Creek.

Geronimo.

He bent down and took a hold of the chupacabra, pulled on it slightly. It did not detach from the shavetail, nor halt its sucking. I thought Geronimo would wrench the chupacabra off the shavetail, but he did not. He merely rubbed its back in a circular motion, while chanting something in the Apache palaver. After about ten seconds of this, the chupacabra let go of the shavetail, and only then did Geronimo wrench it away. The chupacabra dangled limply in his grip, its muzzle stained red, its belly now fat and swollen. Geronimo dashed the chupacabra against the rocks, barking more Apache as he did so. In a flash of green light, the chupacabra flamed briefly, and then was nothing more than a settling of ashes.

I didn't even bother to lift my rifle. But Geronimo did not raise a hand against me. He just glanced at the shavetail, lying limp and deflated, and shook his head as though he was puzzled.

He said in Mexican: *I have never seen one eat a man before. But there is much I have not seen. The poor lieutenant. It is not a good way to die.*

Geronimo turned then, and left us. And though I might be chided for it later, I called for the boys to hold their fire, and so he returned to his horse unmolested and rode away. We wrapped the shavetail in his bedroll, tied up each end with a rope, and then lashed the package over the back of one of the remaining horses. By the time we got back to the post, Geromino and his comrades had crossed the Line into Mexico, where our troops could not easily follow. Colonel Grierson wrote a beautiful report of the shavetail's heroic death in a scrape with the Apaches, and his tribute was so well done that Mrs. Colonel sent it to the *Army and Navy Journal,* where it was printed on page two. Later, the shavetail's parents paid to have the shavetail's body removed from the post cemetery. It was wrapped in oil cloth dipped in wax, and shipped Back East in a wooden coffee where Uncle Billy was the guest of honor at the internment in the national cemetery across from Washington City. The boys and I took up a collection and sent a wreath.

But before that happened, it was a hot time along the Line, with Apaches running this way and that, and the boys chasing after, before Lieutenant Gatewood persuaded Geromino to surrender, and he and all his pals were shipped off to Florida. We rode behind the captain, who was a seasoned campaigner and as sober as they come, but I couldn't help but think that perhaps the shavetail wouldn't have done us such a bad turn after all. In the end, he showed sand, and I regretted the joke we had played upon him. A joke that hadn't really been funny after all.

But I couldn't figure it either and neither could Mickey Free, couldn't figure why the chupacabra had killed him. Like Geronimo, Mickey'd never before heard of a chupacabra hurting man, woman, or child. The creature was hideous but steadfast in its habits, and it tastes ran to goat only. It was only much later, when my army days were long behind me, and I had naught to do but think on the auld lang syne, that I realized the joke had been on me and the boys all along, with the poor shavetail the punch-line. For what do they call the cadet who graduates last in his class at the Point, as did poor Lieutenant Cameron?

The goat.

Afterword

The character of the incompetent junior lieutenant is a staple in messhalls and barracks throughout the world; here it has been transplanted to a fantastic desert world which is clearly based upon Arivaipa, once a territory of the Republic of Califa, now its own sovereign nation. Seeing as it is doubtful that an enlisted soldier would be capable of writing with such skill, this historian believes it is safe to postulate that this yarn was written by an officer, incognito.

While the depiction of military life was obviously written from experience, the events and characters referred clearly spring from the overgrown imagination of the author.[24] Similar tales were published as a series Beedle's Half Diva novel, perhaps by the same novelist.[25]

This historian can personally attest to the existence of the chupacabra, having had a close encounter with one of these appalling but mostly harmless creatures, during an expedition to excavate the ghost-town of Calo Res.[26]

---

24   Yagathai, P.T.J. *Rowels, Chap-Guards and Jingo Bob: An Illustrated History of the Spur in Arivaipa.* Pumpkinville, Arivaipa: Fly Trap Publications, 8-Tochtli-156-17.

25   *The Colonel's Daughter or Winning her Spurs.* Bexar: Beedle's Half Diva Novels, n.d. *Trials of a Staff Officer.* Bexar: Beedle's Half Diva Novels, n.d. *A Garrison Tangle or Love Among the Guidons.* Bexar: Beedle's Half Diva Novels, n.d

26   For more information on chupacabras see Vespa Nyx's *Morphologies of Arivaipan Desert Creatures, including the Chupacabra, Hila Monster, Rollaway Skink & Jackalope.* New London: Museum of Unnatural History Press, 1312.

Publication History

"The Biography of a Bouncing Boy Terror!" *Asimov's*, 2004

"Quartermaster Returns," *Eclipse One: New Science Fiction and Fantasy*, 2007

"Metal More Attractive," *Fantasy & Science Fiction*, 2004

"The Lineaments of Gratified Desire," *Fantasy & Science Fiction*, 2006

"Lovelocks" appears here for the first time.

"Hand in Glove," *Steampunk! An Anthology of Strange and Fascinating Stories*, 2011

"Scaring the Shavetail" appears here for the first time.

About the Author

Ysabeau S. Wilce was born in California and has followed the drum throughout Alaska, Spain, Mexico, Arizona, and Elsewhere. A lapsed historian, she turned to fiction when facts no longer compared favorably with the shining lies of her imagination. Prior to this capitulation, she researched various arcane military subjects and presented educational programs on how to boil laundry at several nineteenth century army forts. She is a graduate of Clarion West and has been nominated for the World Fantasy Award, the James Tiptree Award, and won the Andre Norton Award. She lives in the San Francisco Bay Area.